Yorkshire Rose

Yorkshire Rose

Ann Cliff

ROBERT HALE · LONDON

© Ann Cliff 2007
First published in Great Britain 2007

ISBN 978-0-7090-8470-9

Robert Hale Limited
Clerkenwell House
Clerkenwell Green
London EC1R 0HT

www.halebooks.com

2 4 6 8 10 9 7 5 3 1

Typeset in 11/15.5pt Galliard
Printed and bound in Great Britain by
Biddles Limited, King's Lynn

For Neville, with love

CHAPTER ONE

1890

'My word, that's a big bag for a little lass! D'you want a ride?' Susan stopped dragging the bag along the ground and peered up through her fringe to where, far above her, a large man sat in a cart. Oh goodness, she'd been noticed. It was impossible to hide, but she'd been hoping he would clop on down the road with a wave of the hand.

The voice sounded jovial enough, deep and pleasant, but she wasn't taking any chances. 'Thank you – I can manage.' She gave the bag an extra tug and fell over, into the snow. How embarrassing. Struggling to her feet, the girl felt icy cold and deathly tired. She clutched the precious bag, wishing she were big enough to fight for it. Maybe if she bit him like a terrier, he'd let her be.

'I won't take it off you, don't worry. What is it – potatoes? Look, little lass, I'll give you a ride home. Where do you come from?' And the man jumped down and heaved the bag on to the cart, out of reach. He could easily steal it now. She'd have to take the offered ride, to stay with the spuds.

Brushing the snow off her patched and mended skirt, Susan tried to be evasive. 'Well, you could drop me at the Larton Road end,' she quavered. Few people knew where she lived for sure, and it was desperately important to keep it quiet. Larton was the next village, big enough to be anonymous. She'd have to look normal; how did normal villagers look? Susan dropped her mouth open a little and then stifled a giggle, tired as she was. Larton folks weren't stupid, she'd have to look more alert.

'Nay, I'll do more than that.' He handed her politely up into the cart, settled her on top of the load of turnips and jumped back up.

The horse set off again with a jingle of the harness and the driver looked quizzically at his small passenger. 'I'd better introduce myself … I'm Martin Gill. Ellen and I have just come to live at Holly Bank yonder – we've taken over the farm this month.'

Susan nodded, looking straight ahead, wondering how to get out of this pickle. The winter dusk deepened as the sun went down behind the moor, leaving a blue twilight, lightened by the snow.

'And who might you be, love? Your pa should be moving those spuds, not leaving it to a slip of a lass.' The deep voice was quiet, but it held concern. Susan felt a sudden alarm. This Mr Gill's blue eyes looked kind, she thought, but you could trust nobody.

'I'm Susan. Did a bit of work and got paid with potatoes. Didn't steal them.' That much was true, and gave nothing away.

The man shook his head. 'I'm sure you didn't. But you look too young to be out on your own. What are you – a young miss of ten or twelve?'

Much of her face was hidden beneath the fair fringe, but Susan couldn't help sitting up straight and saying with dignity, 'I am fourteen and quite strong.' Under the dress she flexed her muscles, convincing herself. She knew she was small for her age, but fairly strong and sometimes quite prickly. Just now she was nearly exhausted. Dragging a bag too heavy to lift from Umpleby's farm had been too much, even though the snow had helped a little by smoothing the track.

Mr Gill laughed, but she felt his sympathy. 'Good lass. Well, Susan, how old d'ye think I am?'

Susan looked sideways at the weather-beaten face, firm in

profile, with a determined chin. The farmer wore a collar and tie under his good tweed jacket; he looked respectable, but quite old and tired, she thought. 'About thirty?' she ventured.

'That old? It shows what worries do for a man! I'm nearly twenty-four. I suppose that's very old, to you. A working lad with a rundown farm to tend.' He laughed and his face changed, so that you could see there was humour underneath. 'Where did you say you live?'

No good falling for that one. 'I didn't. We keep ourselves to ourselves … please put me down here. It's not far, now. I can manage quite well,' she ended stiffly.

Mr Gill peered around. 'I can't see any houses near here, little Susan, and you're not to go dragging that bag any further. Now, I'm your new neighbour – and you've nothing to fear from Ellen and me. So be a good lass and tell me the road. It'll soon be dark.'

Beaten, Susan pointed to a narrow track, half hidden by dead bracken and snowdrifts. 'Down there … but don't tell anybody.' She thought quickly. Don't give him time for questions, keep talking. 'And what will you do at Holly Bank? Do you keep sheep?' She leaned back as the horse clopped down the steep lane.

'Aye, we've got a few sheep, beef cattle too. And Ellen wants a dairy, when she's well enough. My father farms over at Pateley, I've been working with him until now.'

'Has your wife been ailing, then? What's wrong with her?' Susan felt a pang of sympathy. Mama had been ailing, and she hadn't recovered. It was cruel when people died.

'Aye, she has, poor mite.' The reply was bitter. 'Her breathing's bad, after last winter. We had bad hay with a lot of mould in it, the dust gets into your lungs.' He shook his head. 'We're hoping she'll get better when spring comes.'

'I hope so, too.' Susan stole another look at the driver. He was very tired, almost as tired as she was. His head was bowed, the broad shoulders hunched over the reins.

'It's hard for her, and hard for me without any help, but we must make the best of it,' Mr Gill said quietly, as if talking to himself, and he straightened up with an effort. 'We were lucky to get a farm of our own ... with my dad's help, of course.'

The track took a turn and they could see the cottage below a bank, nearly hidden by the snow. The roof was thatched with heather, making it invisible from the road.

'Thank you, Mr Gill, that was kind. Must hurry.' Susan found herself babbling as she jumped down from the cart and grabbed her precious bag. 'You can drive right round the apple tree to turn round. Goodnight!' And she lugged the bag into the house and locked the door.

Two young faces turned expectantly to Susan from under the table, like small birds in a nest. 'We're not supposed to let anyone come here. You came home on a cart – we heard it!'

'Couldn't help it, Ben. That's the new neighbour, he lives at Holly Bank now. You can come out, he's gone. Now, pull the fire together, John set the table, we'll have potatoes for supper, won't that be good?' Tired as she was, it was important to sound cheerful. Hunger gnawed in Susan's belly, she'd felt it for days, and she knew the boys must feel the same.

The younger boy came out slowly from under the table. 'We hid when we heard the horse, just in case. He won't tell, will he?' The pale face was anxious.

'Shouldn't think so, Johnny. I told him nothing,' the girl said proudly. 'I nearly bit him at first, but he seemed decent.'

They stood quiet for a moment, but there was no sound of the cart departing. Then the door rattled alarmingly, and the three children froze. He was coming to get them.

'Here's a couple of turnips!' They heard a thud as something heavy hit the door, then a creak as the cart moved off.

After a few minutes Ben looked cautiously outside. 'Nice big turnips, Susie. Can we have 'em mashed with potato?'

Susan nodded. 'And an onion, and maybe an egg. That's a good dinner. It was kind, but we don't want to owe him anything. I suppose, though, we'll have to get used to having neighbours. It's a pity.' She took the turnips into the scullery. 'Holly Bank's been empty for years, ever since our family bought the cottage. I never thought anyone would live there.'

'If we just keep quiet and act normal, they'll soon take us for granted.' That was Ben, always looking on the bright side. 'Why should they worry about us?'

People living in Holly Bank was a problem, but maybe there could be a good side to it. Mr Gill looked as though he'd be able to afford a worker, and he'd said something about it being hard for him with no help. What if they gave her a job? A regular job would be heaven, with money to bring home, as long as the new people didn't interfere, or tell anybody else about them. Ashtree Cottage, their little home, and its few acres, was hidden in a coppice of trees on the edge of the moorland. It was a perfect place for keeping really quiet, keeping your head down.

'I could go over tomorrow, ask if they want a maid, or a farm girl. It'd be nice and close to home.' Best get on with scrubbing the potatoes, she thought, before she fell over with sheer tiredness. 'Mrs Umpleby would give me a character, where I cleaned today. But those Gills might wonder what we're up to. That's the danger of getting to know them.'

'Well, they shan't find out!' John said defiantly, then he paused, standing on one leg. 'Can I come with you?'

'You can come, if you promise to keep to the story. Put these plates down by the fire to warm, Ben.'

'John always get the trips out! I want to go too. I haven't been anywhere for ages.' Ben put down the plates with a clang.

'You'll be working on the rug, remember? But you can come to Kirkby with me when we sell it, and help me to choose what to buy with the money.'

Ben brightened immediately at the thought of spending money, and got out the knives and forks. While the potatoes and turnips were boiling, Susan took off her wet boots and held her skirt to the fire. Looking round the kitchen with satisfaction, she noted that all was in order. The boys had swept and dusted, their books were put away and the room was cosy in the firelight. A pile of peat for the fire stood in one corner, and some dry wood in another. Their one candle was in the scullery and she moved it to the kitchen.

'If people came in here, they wouldn't see anything strange.' Ben must have been thinking about the new neighbour still. 'Would they?'

Susan loved the room, larger than many a cottage kitchen because it was two rooms made into one. She'd kept the walls neatly whitewashed, and her dried herbs hung from the beamed ceiling. Maybe Papa's bright paintings would give them away? Toby Wood was quite well known on the moorland. Too many books, maybe? Most cottages didn't have them.

The big gap on one wall where the piano used to stand reminded Susan all too often of their loss: her mother's piano, sold to pay that old trout to look after them – a sad waste of money that had been. Now there was no music in the house and Susan missed it, more than she missed anything else in their old life.

Most of the back of the room was taken up by rug-making. Nobody could find that strange; a lot of cottagers made rugs from old scraps of material, either for themselves or for sale, to make a bob or two. Rag rugs were warm and cosy and helped to cover up the old stone floors. You could see they had all worked hard, cutting up old clothes into lengths and rolling the strips into balls. There were hessian bags with patterns on them, foundations for new rugs, and against the wall stood a big frame with a half-finished rug stretched on it. Susan let her eyes rest on a rocking chair by the table, draped with a shawl: Aunt Jane's chair.

'I did a square yard today!' John pointed proudly to his work on the new rug.

'Well done, John. What can we take for Mrs Gill if we visit Holly Bank?' It was good manners to welcome a new neighbour with a small gift. She looked into the pantry, but there were no eggs to spare. There was very little in the pantry for that matter. The potatoes had come just in time. But it would soon be spring, wouldn't it? And there might be a rabbit in the snare tomorrow. Anxiously Susan prodded the vegetables in the pan, but they needed more cooking. She carefully put another piece of dry wood on the fire.

On a sunny, frosty morning, it felt good to be alive – once you'd got out of bed and into your clothes. There was no need to give orders, they all knew the routine: Ben milked the goat, John fed the hens and Susan made porridge on the fire. Porridge was good and filling, with a little sugar and warm milk from the goat, but there should have been more of it.

'If Ben can finish the big rug this week, we'll have a shilling or two to buy some flour,' Susan promised. 'Mrs Brown at Kirkby said that she wants it, and I think we can carry it between us, if there's no more snow.'

'Are we still going to Holly Bank?' John demanded. 'There's a few snowdrops under the apple tree, we could take them if you like.'

The problem was solved, then. It was strange how something always came along when you needed it, like Mr Gill last night, when she was too tired to walk much further. Susan shuddered to think what would have happened if she'd not been able to bring the bag of potatoes home.

'Yes, we'll go this morning, and then come back and work on a new rug later. It's going to be a bit hard until the garden starts to grow again; we need money at the moment.' Steady, girl, she

13

thought, you'll frighten the lads if you go on like that. 'Here, let me wash your face, Johnny. Brush your hair ...' There was to be no suggestion of neglect.

Susan's boots were stiff after being soaked in yesterday's snow, but a clean dress would nearly cover them. It was important to make a good impression when asking for a job; she'd better not look too vacant. It was a pity she wasn't bigger and older, and a shame she'd already admitted her age to Mr Gill, but it couldn't be helped. Maybe a dignified manner would impress them ... it was worth a try. In any case, most of the local girls left school at fourteen to go into service. It was the age of maturity in Kirkby, if you could only look mature enough.

They puffed up the steep track to the road and then dipped again at the other side down to Holly Bank. Mrs Gill was ironing when they arrived, and there was a warm, tantalizing smell of baking. Sit down politely when asked, hands on knees, prepare to tell the story, Susan reminded herself.

'It's very nice of you to come to see me, and to bring the snow-drops!' Ellen Gill took them gently from John and put them in a small vase. 'We're neighbours, Martin tells me. What are your names?'

So this was the potential threat, the new neighbour. She had a beautiful face, Susan thought, but pale; the woman's dark hair was tied back and she looked like one of those Pre-Raphaelite paintings in Papa's art books. Mrs Gill looked tired and you could see she wasn't well, from the effort it took her to move.

'Susan and John – Wood. We would like to welcome you to the High Side and hope you will be happy here.' That sounded as if she were at least sixteen, spoken in a prim little voice and with her best Harrogate diction.

The woman smiled. 'Thank you. Are you related to the Woods at Kirkby? I knew the old lady ...' Mrs Gill coughed, and turned away.

They were; Papa had been born in Kirkby. Old Mrs Wood had been their grandmother, Papa's mother, well known for being on every local committee during her lifetime, and evidently still remembered. John shook his head and Susan said quickly, 'It's quite a common name, I believe.' Her back ached already from sitting up so straight, trying to look older.

'Will I be able to visit your mother and father?' A tricky question, and the woman looked puzzled. Maybe she'd expected a visit from Mama instead.

Susan decided to tell some of the truth. 'Mama died last year.' It was still a difficult thing to say. It brought back to her memory the terrible days after the funeral, when they'd all sat on the floor by the fire, huddling together for comfort. Then Papa had moved them to the cottage, into the quiet of the country. There eventually they had made up the story, for family survival.

Mrs Gill looked sympathetic. 'I'm so sorry. That would be hard for you. So your father ...?'

Susan looked at John; it was his turn. 'Father is away on business. But we have Aunt Jane to look after us and teach us our letters and keep the house and things.' His eyes were wide and innocent – a good piece of acting. Nobody knew, even Papa didn't know that they were alone and that she, Susan was head of the family. She was glad he didn't have to worry about them.

As soon as he knew that he had to go away, Papa had found a retired housekeeper, Mrs Lawson, to care for them all, and had paid her in advance. But she was a Harrogate woman and hated the country. She'd moaned and groaned, and was frightened of night sounds like foxes barking and the hoot of owls. She believed in ghosts, and witches and wizards and all the other peasant superstitions, as her father called them. One day, she'd announced that the money was all gone. 'You'd better find an auntie to look after you,' was her advice. She'd been a bad manager, or perhaps she'd been dishonest; Susan couldn't tell.

In the end, they had all been relieved when the widow had taken her bags on the carrier's cart down to Ripon, to catch a train back to her own home. That was when the deception had started, because at the last minute she seemed to feel guilty about leaving them alone. 'Don't worry, Mrs Lawson, I've had a letter from my aunt. She's coming over to look after us, we'll be well taken care of.' Susan had even written the letter, in what she thought was an old-fashioned, copperplate hand, just in case Mrs Lawson wanted to see it.

'Yes, we have Aunt Jane,' Susan murmured again, now they had to stick to the story: they were being looked after by a loving old lady, who sat in the rocking chair in the kitchen and who wore the shawl. Aunt Jane was careful with money, Susan saw to that. She only lit a candle when it was needed and she never wasted a scrap of food. They told everybody that Aunt Jane was their guardian and made them mind their manners. People were pleased to know that the 'motherless bairns' were being cared for, somewhere – they were vague about where they lived – on the edge of the moor.

Susan hardly admitted even to herself that Aunt Jane was imaginary. They'd all had a hand in inventing her, because she was needed. John was talking away about her now. 'Her favourite colour's lavender, she likes to grow herbs and she knits a lot, woolly caps and socks for us all. She likes living at the cottage.'

She was softly spoken, never raised her voice, but all the same Aunt Jane was quite strict, being a Quaker and keen on morals. July the tenth was her birthday, but nobody knew exactly how old she was and nobody dared to ask her.

It was good to be able to tell nosy people that they had a guardian. In case a visitor called, they kept pillows in the spare bed and said that Aunt Jane was asleep. The aunt was almost real by now. It worked if they kept away from local people, didn't get involved. Thank goodness they'd only lived here for holidays before, and nobody knew them well.

'Yes, Mrs Gill, this is a very pleasant place in summer and the moorland air is said to be good for the health,' Susan put in. 'Of course in winter, we tend to get more snow than they do in Ripon ... do you shop in Ripon, yourself? The carrier goes down each Thursday from Kirkby with a covered cart, to take people to market. It's very convenient.' It sounded quite like one adult speaking to another; she was doing well, so long as she didn't laugh.

'We're more used to shopping in Pateley,' Mrs Gill explained, smiling slightly. Perhaps the adult conversation amused her. 'We used to go to Harrogate for important things ... do you know Harrogate?' The beautiful face turned slowly in her direction.

'Yes, Mrs Gill. We used to live in Harrogate, and came here for the summer.'

The house in Harrogate where the Woods had lived before Mama died seemed like a dream now; big windows overlooking the Stray, Papa painting in his studio and the sound of Mama giving a piano lesson, drifting down the stairs. Then poor Mama had a growth, and got thinner and thinner ...

The worry of the workhouse had been there for a long time, ever since that day in the Kirkby shop. A woman said she'd heard about a new law that came in last year. Children deserted by their parents could be held in the workhouse until they were at least sixteen – eighteen for girls, she said. It had been a terrible threat, hanging over their heads ever since.

Everybody up to now had been told the story, and had gone away satisfied. It should work with the Gills, shouldn't it? thought Susan. If the parish finds out, we'll be split up and sent off to the workhouse school. The parish mustn't find us, or the policeman, or anyone in charge. But if they could imagine Aunt Jane, Susan was sure that she could also invent an older, very competent

Susan Wood to cope with their situation. It was quite funny when you thought of it; Susan was a young lady now, having just promoted herself.

CHAPTER TWO

'We grow our own vegetables and keep hens to lay eggs for us,' John confided, bringing another smile to Mrs Gill's pale face. Susan sat straight on her chair. We have to stay together, and to keep the home together, she thought, because one day, Papa will come home. This was the happy end to the story, but it was getting harder to feed the family, as winter dragged on. There was no work. Perhaps I'm too skinny, she wondered. Maybe the farmers are suffering from the hard weather too, and have nothing to spare for wages. It had been two days' hard work for the potatoes, cleaning a big house for Mrs Umpleby.

'And how old are you, John?' Mrs Gill was placidly smoothing the iron over the sheets.

'I'm six, and I can read quite well. Listen ...' And he read the headlines from the newspaper on the table.

'Are there any more of you at home?' The woman put down the iron and moved to the oven by the side of the fire. John's eyes widened as she took out a tray of perfect, pale brown currant scones, the Fat Rascals of the district.

'My big brother Ben, and Aunt Jane,' said John, his eyes still on the scones. Susan too felt that the porridge breakfast had been a long time ago, but she tried to look away.

'I'm sure you could both eat a Fat Rascal.' She gave them one each, swimming with fresh butter, on a pretty china plate, and with a cup of milk.

Forget the story for a moment, Susan told herself. Just enjoy the food.

'You could ask your Aunt Jane if she'd like to step over for a cup of tea.' Mrs Gill sounded rather sad. 'We don't see many folks, since we moved from Pateley.' Mrs Gill was trying to be friendly, but it could be dangerous ground.

'Well, Aunt Jane doesn't go out much, she's lame, you see – and very shy, too.' Was that convincing enough? 'But maybe, in spring … when the snow's all gone.'

By spring, Mrs Gill might have forgotten about Aunt Jane. She'd write her off as one of those moorland women who were so very shy that they were never seen. Mama once talked about them, after a long walk over the moor. She'd met a woman who hadn't been off her farm for thirty years; life on the lonely moor had made her timid and afraid to go beyond the farm gate.

'And how long before your pa comes back?' The face was kind, but the woman asked a lot of questions.

'Er …' Thank goodness, she was saved from that one. Mr Gill came in with a blast of cold air, and nodded to them kindly. He sat down at the table and his wife poured his tea. These people had the luxury of tea and scones in the middle of the morning, between breakfast and dinner.

'Thank you for the delicious turnips, Mr Gill.' It was as well to remember their manners, a part of the myth that they were being well brought up. It's a good job I can remember a lot of Mama's sayings, Susan thought, and make up the rest, telling the boys how Mama would have liked them to behave: sit up straight at all times, keep elbows at your sides at table, and never speak with your mouth full. Pay attention when your elders speak and always say 'please' and 'thank you' with a smile.

It was important to make sure that the boys didn't grow up as little savages; important for its own sake of course, but also as part of the story. Folks had to be able to see at once that Aunt Jane was imposing standards, and that she was a stickler for good manners.

Mr Gill's blue eyes were trained on her, with a thoughtful expression, over the rim of the cup as he sipped his tea. 'Delicious? You've eaten the turnips already, have you? That wouldn't be because you were hungry, would it?'

Susan felt her face go red. 'No, of course not, Mr Gill. We had potatoes ... and Aunt Jane likes turnip and potato mixed together, so we did that.'

'I just thought that the two of you look a bit thin. That's nothing to be ashamed of, nothing at all. We've had a hard winter. Would you like another Fat Rascal?' The blue eyes were quite kind, but now Mrs Gill was peering at them too, in a concerned sort of way. This was just the sort of attention that they should avoid.

'Their mama has passed away and their pa isn't here. Just an auntie to look after them ...' The rest of Mrs Gill's sentence was lost in a cough, which she tried to smother. Her husband shook his head.

'No, thank you, nothing more to eat,' Susan managed, but John wriggled and looked sideways at his sister. After hesitating a moment, he couldn't resist another scone.

'Yes, please. They're so good!' And his clean and shiny face lit up.

'We've never seen you at church?' It was a question from Ellen Gill as she buttered the scone lavishly.

The story had that one covered, too. 'Well, you see, Aunt Jane is a Quaker, and there's no meeting house near here. But she reads the Bible to us and hears our catechism, every Sunday, 'cos Papa's Church of England, of course ...' No good pretending they were Quakers: she didn't know much about them, except that they were said to be very quiet, decent folk who kept their hats on.

'So she explains all the different – er – demominations, she calls them,' John chimed in between mouthfuls of scone. That was a good touch. They could all see Aunt Jane in their mind's eye, Bible in hand, the children at her feet.

'Denominations,' corrected Susan gently. 'And we celebrate at Easter and Christmas, we have an almanac, we know the dates, and even some of the saints' days as well, like Michaelmas.'

'When is Michaelmas?' Mr Gill asked casually.

'Twenty-ninth of September!' Everybody knows that one.

'Well, I think I'll walk over and see your aunt …' Mr Gill broke off as they heard a sharp rap on the door. A coarse voice called out.

'Open up! Police! We know you're in there!'

The next second John dived under the table, still clutching his scone. There was a loud and indignant mew and a grey cat flew out, displaced by the little boy. The Gills looked at each other as Mr Gill went to the door and opened it. Were they going to be found out so soon?

'That's a strange way to talk to honest citizens in their own kitchen!' The deep voice was as quiet as ever, but it was stern.

Keep still, Susan, don't let them know your heart's hammering, she admonished herself. Surely Mr Gill won't let them take her away? As the eldest she might be held responsible for the crime of hiding the children.

A rough-looking, red-bearded man stood on the doorstep, and he took off his cap when he saw Ellen Gill. 'Sorry, ma'am. I thought this place was empty. We've lost sheep, and we're looking for a couple of villains …' His voice trailed off. Not the police, thank goodness.

'Obviously you're not police, far from it. We have taken over, bought this place. My name's Gill, from Pateley, and I'll thank you to leave us in peace. Who might you be, anyway?' Martin Gill looked down at the visitor. Wouldn't it be marvellous to impress people with your size, as Mr Gill was doing, thought Susan. It must solve a lot of problems for big people.

The man shuffled uneasily. 'Sorry, Mr Gill. I work for Hedley, over the moor at Bramley ... and we keep losing good ewes, they just disappear. And Boss, he said there might be a gang hiding out in one of these empty farms. Sheep-stealers, like. I didn't know you'd moved in, honest I didn't.' He glanced behind him to the farmyard, where three other men were wandering about, cudgels in their hands and evidently ready for trouble. 'Leave it be, lads. Mr Gill here's farming the place now.'

Breathe out slowly, wait for the man to go. But as he turned in the doorway, his eye fell on her. 'Hey, lass, where have I seen thee before?'

Martin Gill moved so that he stood between Susan and the stranger. 'We're from Pateley. Now, take your men and be off.'

There was a silence in the kitchen after the door was shut. Mr Gill put more wood on the fire and slowly, John emerged from under the table.

'Thank you,' said Susan faintly. He'd implied she was one of his family, just to protect her. 'Come, John, we'd better go home.'

'Aunt Jane will be wondering where we are,' John added with his innocent look.

'You're a nervous pair ... might the police be looking for you? I hope not. You don't look like hardened criminals to me.' Mr Gill laughed and took down a large ham from a hook in the ceiling. 'I'll cut you a couple of slices to take with you.'

She'd nearly forgotten the real reason for the visit. 'Do you need any help at all? A maid in the house, or a farm girl? I've done a lot of cleaning, I would be able to help with that ... I wasn't brought up on a farm, but I can learn very quickly.' Wait now, give them time, she told herself. Remember not to talk too much like Harrogate folks, you're on the moor now. Stand tall and think old, think sixteen.

It didn't look very hopeful. The Gills looked at each other doubtfully and Martin shook his head. 'Money's tight, lass, especially just now. We can't pay a worker, not until we get some sales … lambs and bullocks, later on. Maybe even a corn crop, but that's not certain. We've just bought the farm, you see.'

'Shouldn't you be at school anyway?' Mrs Gill must think she was too young.

'I'm fourteen, village girls go into service at fourteen. I'm very strong.' Stand up as tall as you can, fluff out the dress to look bigger.

'I'll ask at market, somebody might be looking for a maid.' That was the only hope he could offer. She felt her heart sink right down, but then, maybe it was for the best. They did seem to want to know too much.

For the next few days, the scene at Holly Bank kept coming back as Susan went about her work. Maybe they shouldn't have visited the farm. The Gills were kind and decent; it was somehow a comfort to think of them living so near, but they might talk in Kirkby without meaning any harm, and set the parish on to them.

'They'll forget about us now, likely enough,' suggested Ben.

The ham had made a huge feast, with potatoes and dried peas, the best meal for weeks. The rug was finished and delivered, getting heavier all the way to the village shop.

'My, that's a grand rug! Very neat! Would you like to make me one?' The shopkeeper had beamed at them as she handed over the money.

'Aunt Jane might be able to make you one soon.' There were at least three other customers behind her, ready to digest this information and pass it round. It was a good idea to mention Aunt Jane often in the Kirkby shop.

The precious money had been soon spent. Most important was as big a bag of flour as they could carry and a little yeast twisted in a paper cone, and Ben had a can of paraffin, so that they would be able to light the lamp. There'd been enough for a big piece of Wensleydale cheese, pale and crumbly. It made your mouth water to smell it when it was cut.

Bread-making seemed to take a long time, the dough slow to start rising on such a cold day. But there it was by evening; fresh bread and cheese, with a little treacle for supper. It was wonderful to sit by the fire, comfortably full.

The paraffin lamp was dazzling in its brightness; there'd been no paraffin for a long time. By its light they needed to do all that they wanted, quickly. Ben drew geometric shapes on sacking for a new rug, while John tried to make a plan for the vegetable garden on a big piece of paper. And now it was time for another chapter of *Treasure Island*.

'It's funny, but when we lived in Harrogate I never thought about food,' said Ben thoughtfully.

'I can't 'member much about Harrogate,' John admitted.

'Remember, remember … can you say it? Well, it was very different …' Susan said. Papa had been a popular member of the community. He'd painted portraits of important citizens; mayors and presidents of societies. He worked with an engraver to produce book illustrations. His landscapes of windswept moorland hung in London galleries, and every summer they had lived at this cottage for a month or two, while Papa – the famous Toby Wood – drew and painted. Mama, poor Mama had a rest in summer from teaching music. If they'd only known how fragile her health was …

In those days, the cottage had been a change from the busy Harrogate life. It was always good to come back to the sheltered little valley, the garden and the woodland with a stream running through it. Mama had loved her garden, and Susan had inherited her mother's interest in plants, especially herbs and country remedies. But in those days, there had been plenty of money for everything. Now, it was hand to mouth. Mama was dead and Papa was … away.

For a few days after they sold the rug there was no worry about food, but it didn't last long. The bag of potatoes was finished too and then there was nothing left in the pantry, and no rabbits caught. It wasn't easy to catch a rabbit.

The boys were looking very thin. After this winter, she'd see that they were never hungry again. By the end of the week there was a little oatmeal left, enough for half a bowl of porridge each for supper.

'I'll go to Kirkby tomorrow, find some work to do,' Susan promised, guiltily. It was hard to be a good provider. Thank goodness there was plenty of firewood and peat, to keep the place warm.

'Don't worry, Susie! It'll soon be spring, and we'll have garden vegetables and things we can gather ... watercress, nettles for soup, the lot!' Ben was trying to cheer her up as he raked the fire together. Poor Ben, with no bright side to look on.

There was a rap at the door. Her heart beat fast ... The boys just had time to dive under the table before the door opened and a deep voice said, 'Don't worry, bairns. It's your friendly neighbour!' And Martin Gill stepped into the room.

Mr Gill looked round as he took off his cap. 'My word, it's a snug little place, and warm too!' He winked at Susan and said without turning round, 'You can come out now, lads.'

The boys came out looking sheepish and Ben was introduced. Mr Gill shook hands with him gravely. 'And now, I'd like to meet this aunt of yours, if you please.'

Susan's hand went to her mouth before she could stop it. 'Oh ... but Aunt Jane is asleep, she's very tired!'

That determined chin turned in her direction. 'Then I'll just take a peek. Where's her room?'

There was nothing left to say. She had to take him to the room that used to be Papa's studio. It was now Aunt Jane's room, quite suitable; there was a brass bed, covered with a vivid patchwork quilt. And under the quilt was the long shape of the bolster that was Aunt Jane. She hoped he wouldn't look too hard, that he would stop at the door. Gentleman didn't go into ladies' bedrooms. 'Don't wake her, please, Mr Gill. She won't like it, she'll be embarrassed to see a stranger in her bedroom.'

He didn't let that put him off. Cap in hand, Mr Gill tiptoed to the bed and gently turned back the cover to reveal the snow-white bolster. 'Good evening, ma'am!' There was silence for a while, and then the farmer turned the cover back again. 'She's very pale, I must say!' He smiled grimly, then went back into the kitchen. Was he going to go along with the deception? The three Woods all looked at him fearfully.

'Just one more thing, lass. Ellen says I must ask to see your pantry. Now it's very rude, I know, but ...' He strode over to the pantry door and flung it wide. His face was bleak as he looked over the empty shelves. 'Worse than we thought. Just as well I brought some emergency rations, isn't it?'

The farmer went back outside and brought in a sack, which he gently tipped out on the table. It was full of packages, neatly wrapped parcels. There was half a cheese, slices of ham, two crusty loaves of bread and a pat of butter. Best of all, from his pockets he brought out some eggs. Their hens had stopped laying, because it was winter. By now, there was no meal left and the poultry had to live on what they could find in the way of worms.

'Can we eat now?' asked John wistfully.

'No, you've had your supper ...' Don't tell him how hungry we are, she pleaded silent. Let's get rid of him as soon as we can and hope not to see him again. But he knows, now, that there is no Aunt Jane. That puts us in his power.

The farmer seemed to have other ideas. 'Now lass, get out your frying pan and we'll have a fry-up. Fried ham and eggs and fried bread, there's nothing like it!'

The fire was bright and it didn't take long to get the ham

sizzling and its fragrance filling the kitchen. Susan cut slices from the newly baked loaf and added the eggs to the pan, her mouth watering. Ben got out plates and cutlery and John, barely able to wait for the food, went to the back of the room and pretended to get on with his rug-making. When the meal was ready, Martin joined them, taking only a slice of fried bread and a cup of tea. It was hard to eat slowly and politely and keep your elbows in.

'Thank you very much, Mr Gill. That was delicious, we really appreciate it.' There was no possibility of pretence, now. She got up to clear the table.

Mr Gill motioned at Susan to sit down again. 'I want to talk to you all. Now you're feeling better after a good meal.'

Oh dear, he wasn't going to forget about the myth of Aunt Jane after all. 'You won't tell anyone?' John asked, before Susan could say anything.

'I know why you've been talking about Aunt Jane. It's because you don't want to go to the workhouse school, and I don't blame you, it's a grim enough hole. But you shouldn't be living on your own, you know. Why is no one here to look after you?' Mr Gill meant to be kind, but he sounded very stern.

Gripping the table nervously, Susan silenced the boys with a look. 'We had Mrs Lawson … but she went home. She didn't like living here, so far out of town.' Better not say that she ran out of money to keep them, that she was the wrong person to leave in charge, or that they had not been particularly kind to her. There was no bond between Mrs Lawson and the Wood children, and the fault was not all on her side, Susan had begun to realize.

'And now, you've no food left and it's not very comfortable.' The blue eyes seemed sympathetic as he looked round the group at the table. 'Ellen and I would like to help you, we've guessed that you might need some help. But it will be on certain conditions.' His mouth set in a straight line.

Why would the Gills want to help them? They seemed to have

quite enough problems of their own. It must be the old-fashioned moorland way, Susan decided. Papa had often told them his view of the characters who lived on the moor, the farmers and poachers he liked to paint as a change from sleek city councillors. Papa had said that there was a definite moorland personality; proud, hard and often quite mean with money – careful, they called it, but also quick to help other folks. They seemed to see themselves as a group, with a duty to support each other. 'If you're in trouble, a neighbour will be sure to help. That's because they know that they themselves might need help one day,' Papa had said. They often worked together with seasonal work like shearing and harvesting.

Susan stole another look at Mr Gill. How could such a pleasant face be so severe? 'What sort of conditions, Mr Gill?'

'You can all come over to Holly Bank for dinner tomorrow, and we'll talk about it then. When I've had a chance to talk it through with Ellen. We didn't know how bad things were ... we hoped you were comfortable. This is a shock.' The farmer looked at Susan. 'But one condition I am quite certain about; you must all stop lying, at once.'

CHAPTER THREE

There was silence for a while after Mr Gill had spoken. 'But we don't lie. We just ... invent things,' said Ben reluctantly, piling up the dirty plates.

'You don't tell the truth. And it's very bad for you, you know. I don't want to sound like a parson, but any sort of lying is bad for the liar.' Mr Gill's blue eyes were very clear and direct. Susan felt a guilty blush rising to cover her face.

The strong voice went on relentlessly. 'It's bad for you because you know, deep down, that it's wrong. If you say one thing and believe another, the two don't agree, and you're all mixed up inside.'

'Yes, and it's hard to remember.' Ben looked thoughtful. He wasn't as good an actor as John.

'And then,' Mr Gill was still stern, 'your good name is blemished. Just to take one example, if you want a job, as you do, Susan, liars get found out, and then nobody trusts them any more.'

She did want a job, very much, but it didn't sound as though they would trust her in their house after this. Susan felt impelled to say what she thought, even though it might sound rather prickly. 'Excuse me, Mr Gill, but it's all very well to talk. In our situation, what else were we to do? It worked well until the snow came ...' He couldn't know what it was like to have the workhouse hanging over you. She'd held on so long, and now the

30

world was crumbling. It was all over. He was going to report them to the parish. 'I wish you'd just ...'

Mr Gill hadn't quite finished. 'Are you going to tell me about your father?' he asked quietly, ominously, it seemed.

Anger welled up as Susan looked up at the tall man. 'Leave us alone, we'll manage! It's our affair, we'll deal with it. Just go away.' She shook with agitation. Nobody should know about Papa.

Susan felt a gentle hand on her shoulder. 'Now, bairn, don't be so defensive. We'll try to help you, Ellen and me. We won't report you, that's for sure. There's some bad folk in those workhouses.' Mr Gill was just as calm as ever; there was a tiny ray of hope. Maybe they could trust him. 'But we'll have to be honest with each other, from the start.'

Susan sat down suddenly. The *Darlington and Stockton Times* was read over all the North Riding. Anybody with a good memory would know what had happened to Toby Wood last year; no wonder Mr Gill was worried about their good name. They didn't have one.

Martin turned to the boys. 'And another thing; Ellen thinks you should all come to church with us on Sunday, before dinner.'

When Mr Gill had gone, the Woods looked at each other. 'He might know about Papa.' Ben looked worried.

'But he won't tell.' After thinking for a while, Susan was beginning to feel that they might survive. In one way, it would be a relief if the Gills knew the whole story, but she couldn't bring herself to tell them yet.

'Why don't we ever go to church?' John wanted to know, snuggling down on the rug in front of the fire.

'Because ... oh well, you were too young to know about it. Papa fell out with the parson one summer when we were staying here.' She'd only dimly understood the quarrel. 'You see, Papa read Charles Darwin, all about the theory of evolution.

Everybody was talking about it. One day he tried to tell the parson that the world had been formed over millions of years, and all the different animals had gradually developed. But Mr Grimshaw wouldn't have it. He said the world was made in seven days, it says so in the Bible.'

John was digesting this information. 'We've read the story,' he began.

'Well, yes, Papa had read the story too, but he said it was a myth to explain difficult ideas.'

'Like the myth of Aunt Jane?' asked Ben hopefully.

That was a good argument, Susan thought. 'Maybe we should tell Mr Gill that Aunt Susan was a myth to explain our difficult situation!' They all laughed. It was surprising how much better you felt after a good meal.

'I'm going to miss Aunt Jane,' said John dreamily, as Susan tucked him up in bed later.

'I'm looking forward to breakfast,' said practical Ben from the adjacent bed. 'Eggs on toast!'

Susan blew out the candle and went down the twisting staircase. She too would miss the fun of inventing sayings and doings for Aunt Jane. Perhaps one day she should try to write stories? It was hard to imagine a world where she would have enough time.

The dinner at the Gills the next day was vast and satisfying: leg of lamb with sprouts and potatoes, luscious gravy and mint in vinegar, followed by suet treacle pudding – the best meal for months. Susan found that she couldn't eat a second helping of pudding and wondered whether her stomach had shrunk these last few months. Martin Gill waited until they could eat no more, and then put his hands on the table.

'Ellen and me have thought about what we should do.' He turned to his wife. 'Once we knew for sure what the problem was.'

Mrs Gill's pale face turned to Susan and she said quietly, 'Martin thinks you could help me quite a lot, lass. Washing day is hard for me with this cough, the steam makes it worse ... and brushing carpets is the same. You might like to come over here, two or three days a week.' She didn't sound quite convinced.

Martin Gill's deep voice broke in. 'We can't pay you in cash, love, not at the minute. That's what we told you the other day. But we've always got plenty of grub. If you'll help Ellen you can earn decent food for the three of you ... we've vegetables in store, plenty of flour and we'll be killing a pig again soon.'

Plenty of food ... Susan watched the boys' faces change from suspicion to relief. Food was the priority, just now.

'The boys are too young to do much now, but they'll grow, and it'll help them to learn how to work.' Ben and John looked interested. Martin continued, looking at them. 'There's always wood to chop – you can do that? And at busy times, hay time and the like, an extra pair of hands is always useful, even if they're small hands.'

Ellen Gill still looked serious. 'It's a big responsibility for us, as I said to Martin. Three children, out of the blue!' Mrs Gill started to clear the table. 'But then, we've no bairns of our own, and I'll be glad of a bit of company. You seem to have looked after your-selves until now.'

'We'll be no trouble, Mrs Gill, I promise you. Will we, boys? I would like to help you, as much as I can.' But what about our family history? Susan wondered. Can they trust me not to steal the silver?

Martin sat back with satisfaction. 'So that's settled, then. Now ... we think that the little lads should go to school at Kirkby. They can help a bit at harvest time, but school's the number one priority. I can tell that you're very keen to go.'

There was consternation at this statement; Susan felt the boys move restlessly, felt her heart go down to her leaky boots. 'But ...

they've never been to school in Kirkby, and the parish might catch them, the teacher might report them.' Her hands twisted themselves together. 'They went to school in Harrogate, last year. Nobody knows we're here.' Ben and John nodded vigorously.

'Some folks know … I knew the Woods owned this cottage, for a start. You've had it for years. Everybody knows your business, on the High Side. And when I bought Holly Bank, the owner told me who the neighbours were. He thought you only came here for summer holidays, though. So you may be right, not many will know you're here over the winter.'

John began to cry. 'I don't want to go to school. I want to stay at home.'

Susan reached out to comfort him, feeling nearly as bad as he did. 'Don't cry, Johnny boy. Thank you, Mr Gill, but we'll go home now. Perhaps you didn't know, but the boys do their schoolwork at home, we have plenty of books.' She stood up to her full height, but Martin towered above her.

'I should ha' put it differently. No call for alarm!' And his deep voice sounded suddenly reassuring. 'I will tell the schoolmaster that we're looking after you all. There'll be no thought of deserted children or vagrants or any labels of that sort. You're nearly old enough to run a household, lass, with a bit of help from us. Now, Ben and John, you'll get to know a few other lads, it's not all bad, surely?'

Ben looked down at his ragged suit, with comically short sleeves. Susan shuddered; they all needed clothes, but what could she do? 'We haven't any decent clothes, not any more. The folks at Kirkby'll laugh at us.' He was matter of fact; it was the plain truth.

Ellen Gill tutted impatiently. 'But we've thought of that, didn't we say? I'm good with a needle and there's rolls of cloth I brought from Pateley. I can make clothes for you all, if I measure you first. And there's some pretty stuff for a summer dress or two for you, Susan. Don't say no, because I love sewing and it's one job that doesn't tire me too much.'

'Think it over, and let us know on Sunday what you decide, bairns. But I hope you'll decide to join us. It will be a great help to us, as well as to you. Not one-sided at all, if that's what you're thinking.' Mr Gill wasn't going to back down; it was obviously school or nothing. Blackmail, with good dinners as the carrot, dinners they desperately needed.

'One last word,' said Mr Gill as they left. 'I was lucky enough to get a good education, and I've always been grateful. My father put me through the Ripon grammar school. So I can tell you from experience, school is what you need, lads.'

Susan realized that her boys might have a hard time at the Kirkby school, even in new clothes. They all tried to talk like the locals, but years of living in Harrogate had given them a more refined accent. Papa and Mama had taught them a lot of big words, and they loved to read and to learn new ones, which often sounded odd. They had no real idea of how to talk to other children, having not met many since they came to Kirkby. But that wasn't all. They had to consider what would happen if anyone they met knew their father.

'If I help you, Mrs Gill, will you teach me to cook – Yorkshire puddings and such? I'd like to be able to make suet puddings too, like that one.' Susan noticed that the boys nodded energetically. They hoped she'd make steamed puddings.

Mrs Gill smiled as she said, 'Of course I will, lass. It's easy enough. You can write down the recipes as I tell you, they're all in my head. Now, if you don't mind I will just run a tape measure over you all, so I can cut out some clothes tonight.'

As they walked home in the late afternoon, Susan talked about the benefits of schooling and how a spell at the little school at Kirkby might lead to a good career. 'Now Ben, we'll have to bind you as apprentice. You'll need to know how to talk to folk. What would you really like to be?' Ben's aspirations changed weekly as he thought of new paths for the future.

'A doctor … but we can't afford that. I wouldn't mind working for a printer, though, to learn the trade. Not a butcher or a baker, if you don't mind, nothing too sticky. But it's years off, isn't it? Three or four years of school, what a thought.'

John looked disappointed. 'If you worked for a baker we'd get lots of buns.'

No more snow fell during the week, so there was no excuse; the Woods had to wash their faces and walk demurely down to church at Kirkby with the Gills. It was only two miles but it seemed a long way to Susan, conscious of their worn and mended clothes and wondering what their reception might be.

The sermon was long. John shuffled his feet in the pew and Mrs Gill passed peppermints to them all. The vicar preached about the virtues of poverty and humility and yet he could hardly ever have gone hungry or cold. That was what poverty really meant and if you were poor, humility came easily. It was hard to imagine being anything other than humble; small and weak people knew their place in the scheme of things. Why did the vicar think it was a virtue? Susan frowned up at the pulpit.

The Gills stopped briefly in the churchyard to speak with neighbours after the service, but they didn't yet know many people. A few of the farmers and their wives spoke as they passed and the vicar asked how they were settling in, while the Woods tried to look as though they were not there.

'We must get home to make the Yorkshire puddings!' Ellen Gill said, taking her husband's arm purposefully.

Little notice was taken of the Woods, although the woman from the shop smiled at them kindly. Just as they were passing through the churchyard gate, a podgy child came up to them, resplendent in a shiny Sunday suit. He looked them up and down. 'Hey, you lot! You're the Woods, you are! Is your father still in jail?'

The children drew back in horror, but Mr Gill pushed them gently forward. 'Come on, we'll be late for dinner!' He turned to the lad in the shiny suit. 'That's not a very Christian way to behave!' A woman who looked like his mother dragged him away.

Devastated with shock, Susan walked silently back along the lane, holding John's hand, Ben tagging on close behind. The worst had happened; the truth had come out. She dared not look at Mr Gill.

Ellen Gill insisted she had dinner ready for them all. 'Twice in one week? That's too much!' Susan protested, but Martin Gill laughed.

'By the look of you three, you've got some catching up to do.'

Susan looked at Ben and John, thin and white faced, and down at her own skinny frame, thankfully hidden by winter clothes. It would soon be spring, but there were a few weeks of winter to get over first.

Sitting round the table with plates of roast beef, Susan could tell the boys were hoping that the mention of prison might have been forgotten. But Martin Gill shook his head sadly when Ellen asked how soon they would be ready to go to school. 'I fear there'll be more of the sort of taunts you got today, in the church-yard, if what the lad said was true. Is your pa in prison?'

Susan nodded, unable to speak.

'It's not going to be easy for you, lads, when you go to school. But it has to be faced … you can't hide away for ever. We thought there must be a problem of that sort, although we didn't know your pa. We were waiting for you to tell us about it, in your own good time.'

'He's innocent! He didn't do it!' They all cried in chorus. This was terrible; first they'd lost Aunt Jane, and now Mr Gill was stripping away their last secret.

Martin Gill laid down his knife and fork. 'Well now, that's not for me to say. I won't presume to judge anybody. But maybe I should remind you of that sermon I gave you three the other night, about lying ... you will all have to be even more careful to be honest and truthful, with a father in jail. It stands to reason; folks'll be slow to trust you. That is something you will have to remember, even if he's innocent, and even though it was nothing to do with you.' He turned back to his dinner.

It was hard to eat, although she'd been hungry a few minutes ago. Susan gulped and looked at Mrs Gill. 'Well, you won't want me to help you in the house now, will you? But we really believe he didn't do it.'

'It must be hard for you, I see now why you're alone, keeping to yourselves. No, it makes no difference, Susan. I'll be glad of your help and I believe you're honest. As Martin says, we won't judge. Now, eat up your meat like a good girl!' Ellen's pale face was smiling. 'And let's talk of something else. What do you grow in your garden?'

They tried, but the memory of Toby Wood still hung over the little group. 'I don't even know what Papa's s'posed to have done,' John confided as he spooned up his rice pudding.

'It was something to do with an engraver.' Did Mr Gill think he was guilty? Susan had to defend Papa. 'And it was for his work, I remember they did illustrations for magazines ... Papa did the drawings and the engraver etched them on to metal plates. He is a very *good* artist, and then one day, he was accused of forgery. So he and the engraver were found guilty and sent to prison for – seven years, I think, less for the engraver. So he'll have six to go,' Susan calculated.

Ellen Gill looked puzzled. 'But didn't your father make some arrangement for you children, to be looked after while he was gone?'

Susan wriggled uncomfortably. 'Mama had died just before. Everything at Harrogate had to be sold, it all happened in a hurry. I don't think he expected to go to jail, because he hadn't done it. As I told Mr Gill, Papa gave some money to a woman to look after us … we didn't like her much, and she didn't like the country. I suppose we made it hard for her. We were glad when she went back to town.' She paused, rather ashamed of the story. 'Papa believes she's still with us. It's better if he doesn't worry.'

'Another little invention?' Martin asked with a lift of the eyebrows.

'Well, yes.' Susan looked at her plate. 'When I write to him, I don't mention that she's gone, you see.'

The new life started straight away; Susan felt breathless, swept along by the speed of change. The family was split up during the day, only getting back to the cottage at night. It was wonderful to have enough to eat. They still knew how important it was never to waste anything and any scraps from their plates were saved for the hens.

Most of the time, Ben and John did as Susan asked them, but there were a few rebellions along the way, and a few fights. 'Don't want to wash the dishes, I'm tired!' John sometimes came home from school in the wrong frame of mind, although he usually revived once supper was over. They had to learn to help with the housework. Susan was tired herself after a day at Holly Bank and she also believed that even though they were boys, there was no law that said they should be waited upon. They were getting to be more independent as a result of going to school.

'It's only normal to fall out sometimes,' Mrs Gill told her. 'It's part of growing up and learning to think for yourself.' That made her feel much better, less of a failure.

School was not easy at first, of course. But both Ben and John had to face up to the fact of having a father in jail. They both admitted it at once and then got on with other things, such as practising cricket and football. The other children soon tired of trying to tease them about it.

It was good for Susan to work at Holly Bank, and not just because she took home food at night. Susan knew the basics of housekeeping, she'd kept the cottage in good order, but now she learned a great deal that Aunt Jane had never told her. For the first few weeks Susan was set to cleaning and the old house was scrubbed from top to bottom, and the furniture polished until it gleamed, with beeswax from Mr Gill's two hives. Washing day was hectic, but Susan managed to cope with heaving the sheets and towels from one tub to another, although the possing stick was taller than she was and the mangle was rather high for her to reach. It helped to be able to laugh sometimes at the struggles she went through to learn the knack of mangling, but it was much easier to laugh when you'd had a good breakfast.

'It's good that Mrs Gill doesn't see me do the washing,' Susan admitted to Ben one Monday evening. 'I must look silly.'

'As long as you keep your fingers out of the mangle, Susie. We don't want a sister with fat fingers. And don't fall into the washing tub.'

The next week Susan found a wooden box by the mangle, at just the right height for her to stand on and she saw Mr Gill looking in as he wheeled a barrow past the wash-house door. 'Thank you, Mr Gill,' she called. Being higher up made the job much easier. She hadn't realized that Mr Gill knew of her difficulty, but it was nice of him to solve the problem for her.

Whereas in Harrogate, in the old life, Mama had bought what she needed from the shops, a woman like Ellen Gill seemed to be able to make most things for herself. The shops were far away in Ripon, but there were plenty of raw materials to hand. One wet day Ellen decided that they could make some new cushions. She brought out a bag full of feathers. 'I've been saving these, for when I felt up to the job. We plucked a few ducks and geese for sale at Christmas … but we've got to get the grease out of these feathers first.'

Susan was set to stirring lime into a bucket of water and then she had to stir the feathers into the water. 'They must soak for three days,' Ellen told her. 'Please keep stirring them, every hour or so.'

After three days the horrible soggy mess was lifted out and washed under the pump, not once but several times. How could they ever make cushions from this? Susan shuddered as she lifted them out of the sink. 'I must have done something wrong.'

Ellen laughed at her. 'Nay, lass, we haven't finished yet. Get some newspaper and we'll lay them flat, and then dry them in the oven.' The coal oven at the side of the hearth was warm, but not hot except on baking days, when the fire was stoked up.

The next day, soft and fluffy, the feathers were stuffed into cotton bags and then into the velvet cushion covers that Mrs Gill had sewn, the material coming from some old curtains. 'So now you know how to make a cushion, Susan,' said Ellen. 'Or a pillow, or even a feather bed, if you've enough poultry.' It seemed that you didn't need a lot of money to be comfortable, after all. You just had to use what you had.

CHAPTER FOUR

Deep winter had always looked to Susan like a time for rest on farms, with the land sleeping and waiting for the spring. But at Holly Bank there was a great deal of work to get through before the spring. Fences were being repaired and walls rebuilt; the cattle and sheep were on winter rations and needed to be fed with hay every day. Mr Gill had no time for anything except work and more work.

'It wouldn't be so bad if a proper farmer had lived here and done some of the maintenance,' Martin explained one day as he rebuilt a stone wall. 'But Mr Brown was old and had the rheumatics, and didn't get out here much. He lived in Kirkby of course, and let off the land for sheep grazing. And the house was practically ruined, needed a new roof, we had to do a lot of work before we moved in.' So that was why they had a bright new wood stove in the kitchen and new plaster on the walls.

The Gills were not typical moorland farmers, Susan soon decided. Maybe it was because of his education, but Mr Gill was keen on reading scientific journals and he often told her of some new idea for improving stock or crops. 'Not that we can afford to experiment much, but you never know when something useful might turn up, if you keep your mind open.'

There were so many new experiences for a girl who'd been brought up in Harrogate. 'Martin's got the pig sticker coming tonight. That means work for you and me,' Ellen told Susan, a month or so after the start of her employment.

Not sure what this meant, Susan waited for more information. She soon understood that they were going to kill a pig before the warmer weather; there would be sausages and black puddings, meat to share with Martin's family at Pateley and two hams to cure in salt.

'You can only kill a pig when there's an "r" in the month,' Susan was told. The months without an "r" were too warm and the hams might go bad before they were cured.

The thought of ham and bacon was good, but Susan's stomach turned at the idea of the killing. She might faint or otherwise disgrace herself. Blood-curdling screams, flickering lamplight … her vivid imagination could picture the scene. The professional 'sticker' went from farm to farm where pigs were to be killed. How could anyone be induced to carry out such a dreadful job?

Thank goodness that the worst of the horrible business was over before she went to work the next morning. By the time Susan saw it, the pig had been cut in two and the bristles scraped off the skin; it looked amazingly clean and clinical. 'That's men's work,' explained Ellen Gill.

There followed several days of hard women's work, with the big farm scullery looking like a butcher's shop. The most urgent job was the black puddings, made from the blood that had been carefully collected in a bowl. 'Waste not, want not. The only thing we don't use is the grunt.' Martin quoted the old joke.

Oatmeal was added to the blood to make black puddings; it tasted very bitter, fried with bacon, but Ellen said they must eat it up. 'It's specially good for us women.'

Susan operated a mincer that chopped up odd bits of meat, then Ellen mixed it with breadcrumbs, onions and dried herbs, sage and thyme. The casing for the sausages was part of the pig's intestine. Susan had never before thought about how sausages were made and her interest overcame the shock of handling such things.

The hams and a side of bacon were put into a shallow trough, and for hours Susan rubbed salt into them with her hands, with a little brown sugar. It became her job to turn them in the salt and rub them again every day for three weeks, until Ellen decided that they had cured enough and could be wrapped in muslin and suspended from the big hooks in the kitchen ceiling.

'Some folks put the ham up the chimney and smoke it – they use oak wood for that. Maybe we should try it one day,' Martin suggested, but Ellen didn't think it was a good idea, they would lose sight of good food if it went wrong.

While the work went on, Ellen talked more than usual and Susan began to think she had something on her mind. The older woman spoke about her own childhood at Pateley and of working with her mother in the big farmhouse kitchen there. 'I never knew how things would turn out … I always thought in those days that you could get what you want, if you worked hard enough.'

Susan looked at her. 'But you can, can't you? Mr Gill says that if the boys work hard at school, they can get a good job. And you've got a farm of your own.'

'Aye, Susan, in some ways that's true. But there's things in life that don't go right, however much you try. There's such a thing as luck, after all.' Mrs Gill washed her hands under the pump and, drying them, looked out over the fields to where Martin was working in the distance. 'Me and Martin didn't have much luck, you might say, although I was lucky to get a good husband. He's a grand lad.' She was speaking quietly, almost talking to herself.

'What went wrong, Mrs Gill? You mean your cough?' It must have been hard not to be able to run after the sheep, or even do the laundry, and to be kept awake by coughing at night. Sometimes it was sad to think of how other people's lives might be.

'That of course, my lungs are that bad, it stops me helping

Martin as I'd like. But there's another sorrow that we must bear, as best we may.' She stopped and looked at Susan. 'But I don't want to burden a young lass like you with our troubles.'

'Please tell me what makes you so sad, Mrs Gill.' Perhaps it would help her to talk about it, even to a young lass. They were getting to know each other, working together in the kitchen and that must be good for both of them.

'We wanted bairns, you see. We always said we'd have a family, but it's never happened, even after three years. We were married at twenty-one, both of us, younger than many a couple on the High Side. But ... likely it's too late for me, now. The lungs are getting worse, and Dr Bishop can do nowt. I wouldn't like to leave a bairn to fend for itself.'

What could anyone say? Mrs Gill knew she'd never have children – what would that feel like? It was hard to imagine the future, to think of a time when Susan Wood, adult, wiser – and much taller, of course – might marry a good man, as Mrs Gill had done. Of course she would want to have babies and watch them grow up. It would be rather like looking after Ben and John, but with a husband to help her. But, as Ellen had pointed out, it was a matter of luck and it might not happen.

Susan looked up from her work. 'But then, you've got us, Mrs Gill. You're like a mother to us.' It was true, and it might be some comfort to her.

'That I have, and you and the boys have made a difference. You're a good help to us ... and somebody for Martin to take an interest in. That was why, I suppose, he wanted to help you, without knowing what you could do to help us. I wasn't sure, but I'm right glad we did. It's grand to have young folks about the place ... lightens it up a bit. And I'd find it hard to manage without you now, lass.' The poor woman actually laughed, but it made you feel like crying to hear her cough straight afterwards. A laugh was risky for Ellen Gill.

After this, Susan appreciated even more the feeling of being involved with the family at Holly Bank. She and the boys were wanted, they filled the place of the children the Gills would never have. It felt good, too to produce their own food, to turn the hams and make the sausages.

At home the Woods kept a few fowls and collected their eggs and that was satisfying, now that they had some grain to feed them on. They were trying to turn Ashtree Cottage into a little model of independence; it was good to feel that they were independent because they earned their living at Holly Bank, and they had their own place to retreat to, once the work was done.

Ellen and Martin seemed to take their teaching role very seriously, especially where Susan was concerned. Sometimes she was challenged. One evening Martin came into the kitchen holding his arm. 'Burned it on the stable lamp,' he said briefly and sat down in his usual chair, grimacing.

'Come to the sink, Martin, I'll pour cold water over it. Now, you'd better treat it, Susan, so you learn what to do.' Ellen was looking over at her. It was important not to panic, but there poor Mr Gill was, in pain.

'I can't! I might hurt him,' Susan gasped, appalled. Why hadn't Mrs Gill told her what to do before such a thing happened? She couldn't do it, she didn't know enough.

Ellen was calm. 'Grated raw potato is good for burns and it keeps out the air. Now, fetch a potato, peel it and shred it up. I'll find a clean bandage.' She went to a cupboard where they kept strips of old sheets, rolled up into bandages.

The sooner she conquered her fear and did something, the better for Mr Gill. Quickly, biting her lip, Susan shredded the potato and applied it to the bandage, and then wrapped it gently round Martin's arm. Close to him, she breathed in the smell of horses and the open air, a comfortable scent of security; it made her feel more confident. When it was done she looked down into his face. 'Did it hurt too much?' It would be terrible to hurt him.

Martin shifted slightly in the chair. 'Nay, lass, you did well. Thank you.' He gave her his rare, heart-warming smile and that was a reward in itself. Mr Gill was sometimes quite funny and made jokes, but he didn't often smile.

The lesson was not quite finished yet. 'If there's no potato handy, cold tea leaves are quite good,' Ellen told her. 'So is honey, it keeps out the air and dirt.'

Martin looked up. 'I remember Billy Watson from Pateley, I went to school with him. He tried honey for a cure. He had boils all over his hands and the doctor couldn't cure them, so Billy's mother wrapped them up with honey and they were right in no time. I always thought to remember that.'

This was another item for the notebook and Ellen agreed that honey was a useful treatment, even for ulcers. 'But the main thing with burns is to keep out the air, keep everything clean, and not to panic so much that you're no use at all. That's what some folks do.'

After that lesson, Ellen kept thinking of things that Susan should learn about emergencies. It seemed that farms were places where emergencies often happened.

'If they're not getting kicked by a cow, they cut themselves on the scythes in the hay field,' Ellen told Susan. 'They bleed and you have to stop the bleeding, as quick as you can. Shepherd's Purse is good for that – you remember seeing it in the summer? And then there are the winter ailments that can turn nasty if you don't look after them. Everybody on the High Side is frightened of pneumonia, even the doctors. So you need to know a few home remedies, for if Ben or John catch a chill.'

The 'home remedies' must have been handed down over hundreds of years by people who couldn't afford a doctor, or lived too far away from a village, isolated on the moor. The thought of losing either of the boys to pneumonia was so dreadful that it was best to write down all Ellen's advice, in case any of it was forgotten. She called the notebook 'Mrs Gill's Remedies', and she would keep it for the rest of her life.

There were several entries under the 'colds' heading and Susan was glad that she didn't have to encounter the crisis before she learned the remedy. Treacle Posset was a favourite with the Gills and sometimes Ellen made it for herself when her cough was bad, or for Martin when he'd been out all night with the lambing.

Treacle Posset was made by boiling milk and adding treacle and the juice of a lemon, not always obtainable on the High Side, but you could get them in Ripon on market day. The juice curdled the milk and the posset consisted of the strained liquid, drunk hot. Just why it was so good for you was hard to understand, but it was a great favourite.

Eventually the long, dark winter came to an end and a slow spring began to touch the moorland with a tinge of green. You knew it was spring when the curlews came back, swooping and crying, even though the moor wind was still cold enough to freeze you through. Ahead were the warm summer days and that was something to look forward to. Maybe Mrs Gill's cough would get better when the summer came.

In April Susan turned fifteen and the Gills invited them all to a birthday tea with jelly and cake. 'You're not very big for fifteen, Susie,' John said critically, as they sat round the long kitchen table. Hetty, the blacksmith's daughter at Kirkby, was the same age as Susan, but twice as tall and built like her burly father. She even had a bosom. The comparison was annoying and the boys made it often, but it was going to get worse; Ben was taller than his sister already and John only needed a few more years before he'd be able to look down on her. The only possible response was a withering look, and that made John laugh.

Ellen came to the rescue. 'Good things come in small packages. Now don't go teasing your sister, John.'

April was the time to plant the garden and also time for a series of spring lessons. Martin planted his seed potatoes in long rows on Good Friday, the traditional time for putting in the spuds, he said, and gave Susan some for their little plot. 'The old folks thought that you should plant with the waxing moon,' he said mysteriously.

What did he mean? 'Moons keep changing every month, but what's that got to do with gardening, Mr Gill?' Susan asked. She'd heard that women's monthly cycles were linked to the moon, but she couldn't mention that.

'Well, at Easter the moon is full, of course, that's how they fix the date every year. So, on Good Friday it's still waxing – coming up to the full moon. Waning means the opposite, when it's getting smaller. They used to think that the moon and tides affected the sap, the juices in the plants and maybe it's so, for all I know. Then there's the opposite, when you gather them in. You should harvest your crops when the moon is waning, they said, and the sap is falling.'

Did that mean you should go out and cut your cabbages only at night, when the moon was shining? 'But we harvest our garden vegetables when we want them. Is this wrong?' Susan frowned. It sounded suspiciously like an old folk tale.

Martin grinned. 'I suppose they meant the ones you take up all at once, like turnips, for the winter. There's nothing wrong with picking a lettuce now and then. No, it doesn't mean harvest at night, love, just do it on the right date.'

The cottage in spring, once the snow had melted, was a lovely place. Daffodils danced down the garden path, primroses peeped shyly out from the edges of the little stream, and their world seemed altogether changed. On the days when she was not at the farm, Susan worked in her garden; the cottage had a big garden and the plot of land was capable of producing all their summer vegetables, with some fruit.

49

The herbs had lived through the winter under the snow and now they were putting out their spring leaves. Sage and rosemary, mint and thyme were scattered through Susan's flower garden, with due attention to their needs, the mint nearest to the stream. Then there was fennel and horehound, marjoram and the big coarse leaves of comfrey that Mama had said you could still see growing by the walls of Fountains Abbey, a legacy from the monks.

One Saturday, Mr Gill came over with some cabbage plants for Susan's vegetable plot. He looked round and he was impressed. 'I like a tidy garden ... you've done well, lass. Now, I wonder if my Ellen could have a few cuttings of herbs? We've still to set up properly at Holly Bank.'

That was a nice idea. 'I'll grow some cuttings for her, to plant out.' It was not often that she had something that the Gills lacked. She'd better look up some of the uses of the plants; she remembered the obvious ones, but Ellen could probably tell her more.

There was a need for fresh vegetables and fruit in spring. By the end of winter, all the apples had gone and at Holly Bank they could only have bottled gooseberries as a special treat. It was strange how you longed for fruit, for something acid, or for fresh lettuce. There would be nothing to eat from the garden until nearly June; spring came late to the High Side.

Ben and John took out the weeds from their patch of garden and turned the soil, digging in the old poultry manure that Mr Gill said would make the plants grow bigger. Impatient for summer salads, Ben revived the idea of eating wild greens. 'Let's try nettles, I used to like them last year.' He brought in a basket of fresh green shoots and tipped them into the sink.

'Stinging nettles – they sting, and it hurts!' John complained theatrically.

'The sting goes when you boil them up, let's try.' And when

Susan had boiled them in a little water, chopped them and added butter, the resulting greens were quite good.

'We'd have been living on these, if it wasn't for the Gills,' Ben reminded them.

Susan said nothing, but she knew how close they'd been to disaster when Martin Gill had found her in the snow. She sometimes wondered whether the worry and the lack of food had affected her reason … but the alternative, the workhouse, had been impossible.

When they told Ellen about eating nettles she offered a spring recipe of her own and suggested that Susan make them a sour dock pudding. 'Folks go short of green food in winter. My mother always gave us watercress in spring, and this sour dock pudding. We used to like it when we were bairns.'

Ben was sent out to gather a basket of sorrel, a small acid dock leaf, and more nettles. The leaves soaked overnight in a muslin bag, with pearl barley added— 'Three handfuls, no more and no less.' The next day the bag was boiled until everything was cooked, then turned into a dish and beaten up with eggs and butter. It didn't taste of much, but it probably did you some good.

'Thank goodness the Gills haven't tried to dose us with sulphur and treacle,' John said after the pudding was eaten. 'I think Mrs Lawson enjoyed seeing us suffer.'

'*Get it down you, children, you must take it, to clear the blood*!' Ben pitched his voice high, to sound just like Mrs Lawson. 'How can you tell whether your blood needs to be cleared every week?'

CHAPTER FIVE

1894

'You're a handy little lass, Susan, in spite of your size. You can do just about everything I can do.' Ellen Gill still looked down at the helper from her greater height and it was a pity she had to mention it, but what she said was true. Ben and John had grown quite quickly thanks to a better diet, but Susan's growth seemed to have halted during the time when they had little food to eat. At nineteen, sad to say, she was small and young looking, in spite of all the work. Maybe she'd have grown by the time she was twenty-one?

Looking back from the grand old age of eighteen, it was hard to remember the fourteen-year-old Susan and how little she'd known. But now she could milk a cow without being kicked and then strain the milk, set the cream to rise and even make butter. All the Woods knew how to turn the hay until it was dry enough to cart into the barn and they were experts at catching sheep. Extremes of weather made things hard of course, and breaking the ice in winter on the cattle troughs was not easy to enjoy.

The Woods had worked hard at the farm, but over the last four years they'd all had plenty to eat and good clothes to wear. The boys had helped during the school holidays, raking the hay and stacking sheaves in the corn harvest. Their reward was a new pair of boots each, bought by Mr Gill.

It was good to work in the harvest: the long days out in the fresh air, the feeling of urgency and the satisfaction when the job was done. Every day was different with Mr Gill, who knew so much. Not just about farming. He knew about the wild creatures that lived round them, stoats and badgers and foxes, and the little bats fluttering past in the evening light. He knew the call of many different birds, and the names of the wild flowers in the hay meadow: milkmaids and ladies' bedstraw and the herb, self-heal. Susan's favourite was the lovely, delicate harebell, sheltering at the bottom of hedges and stone walls.

Adapting to country life, they'd felt like a normal family. The boys had done well at school thanks to Mr Gill's encouragement, and the best of all, they'd kept together and avoided the dreaded workhouse.

Life was good during those years, apart from the worry of Ellen Gill's health. As time went by you could see that Ellen was deteriorating, but she fought the illness and tried to live a normal life. Quite often she teased Susan about her prickly side, the way she gave quick answers, especially to defend the boys. One day she gave her helper a rose bush to plant in her garden. 'This is a white rose, love – the white rose of York, it's the emblem of Yorkshire. Small and white, pretty but with plenty of thorns! It reminds me of you, Susan … and it might remind you of me, when I'm gone.'

What could she say? 'I'll try not to be too prickly in future, Mrs Gill.'

Martin repeated the joke one day when Susan was irritated after failing to catch a straying lamb in the pasture. The lamb evaded her and ran away, but was brought back by Martin and the sheepdog. 'Stupid animal! He did it on purpose to annoy me.'

'Nay, lass, patience with stock is everything. You're a little Yorkshire rose, as Ellen says – with the prickles and all!' After this, Susan tried to be a little less quick to fire up. After all, there was nothing to worry about now that she worked for the Gills.

The time flew by, the work changing with the seasons. Every

season brought new lessons and every year there was something new to learn. In the summer, you had to daub your face with buttermilk before going out into the sun. 'Your fair skin will burn if you don't, you little white rose,' warned Ellen. It was hard at first to turn the hay with a long fork, but once Mr Gill had demonstrated how to do it with a flick of the wrist, it was just a case of developing the right muscles.

The autumn was just as busy in the kitchen; there was so much preserving to get through before the winter. Surplus eggs were put down in a solution of waterglass, in which they would keep for months to tide them over the period when the hens didn't lay. Apples were carefully wrapped in newspaper and stored in boxes under the beds. In the hazy autumn sunshine they picked as many blackberries as time would allow, to make into jam. It was satisfying to look along the pantry shelves at the rows of bottled plums and pears, jams and jellies. Even the tiny, sour crab apples were made into a clear red jelly. Ellen could do some of the work on good days, but she relied on Susan to stand at the stove, stirring the jam or the pickles for hours.

Martin organized an apprenticeship for Ben, as a printer in Ripon. He boarded with the printer's family and seemed to settle down quite well. John studied hard and managed to win a scholarship to the Ripon grammar school as a boarder, coached and encouraged by his teacher at the Kirkby school, as well as by Mr Gill. So the boys were provided for, for the present at least. But the cottage was quiet without them except in the school holidays, when John came home.

Walking over to Holly Bank one spring morning, Susan heard a plaintive cry and realized that the curlews were back on the moor above them once again. The sun sparkled on dewdrops in the hedges in the farm lane and the pastures were tinged with green. On the lower slopes of the High Side near Kirkby, moorland merged into farmland. Some of the Holly Bank land was ringed by stone walls, where the curlews nested and sheep grazed. The land sloped down to the east towards the gentle valley of the Ure and the lower fields had hawthorn hedges, now bright with new green leaves. There on the better land the Gills could grow corn and make hay, and watch their cattle grow sleek and fat over the summer.

It would have been so good to settle there, to know that they had a place in this quiet farming world. Susan felt it would be dreadful to live in a town again, even a pleasant town like Harrogate, after the experience of Holly Bank. But it might be difficult to stay in the country. Time was going by, and the worry always at the back of her mind crept forward again; she knew that she should be earning a proper living by now, to keep herself and John, until he was able to earn his own living.

The Gills needed Susan more and more as Ellen grew weaker, and she had learned a great deal from them both. She had grown to love Ellen and wouldn't leave her now. But they'd rarely been able to pay her except in kind, with food and clothing. There had been a farming depression, starting about the time when the Gills came to Holly Bank. Livestock and wool prices had not been high enough for the farm to earn much of a surplus, and any money earned had gone back into farm improvements. Martin was not mean, far from it, but the farm wouldn't support a paid worker. The Woods were just as poor now as they had been when they first went to Holly Bank.

If your only skills were farm and domestic ones, what can you do? When Susan was little, she had talked to Mama about training to be a teacher, but that was out of reach now. What would happen to her? She couldn't stay here for ever. Who would want a small farm worker who was not strong enough for heavy work? She had made a little butter and cheese from their house cow's milk, but the Gills had decided not to set up a dairy. You needed at least eight cows to produce two cheeses a day for sale, and Ellen wasn't up to the work. So Susan couldn't call herself a dairymaid. She wasn't anything, really, that you could give a name to. It would be good to learn more about herbs and be a herbalist, but Kirkby already had one of those.

Pushing the thoughts away, Susan laughed as she watched some of Martin's lambs skipping around their stately mothers, until one tumbled down a bank, head over heels. It was good to look forward to the summer, and to spending days in the open air.

At the big kitchen door, Susan called, 'I'm here!' But today there was an odd silence. No doubt Mr Gill would be going round the sheep on his morning routine, but Ellen should have been there in the kitchen.

There was a sound from upstairs. Mrs Gill must have been too ill to get out of bed. Better go upstairs and find her, thought Susan. The bedroom on the right was Mrs Gill's room. She'd slept on her own since the cough worsened, not wanting to keep Martin awake at night. Ellen was in bed, tossing restlessly, her fragile beauty now gone. She was gaunt, ashen, with sunken cheeks and heavy eyes. 'Could you fetch me a drink of water, Susan?' She sounded very faint and far away.

This was an emergency, of course, the one they had all dreaded. 'Can I get Mr Gill?' Susan asked when she brought the water with a hand that trembled slightly.

'Nay love, Martin's gone to fetch doctor,' the woman gasped. 'But you can get eggs ready for market, can't you, lass? And feed fowls, you know how to do that. There's a sight of work waiting, but I can't get up ...' She struggled for breath.

'I can do it all, you've taught me,' the girl said reassuringly. 'You've got to rest, Mrs Gill, to get better.'

Ellen shook her dark head. 'My time's nearly over,' she said sadly. 'Doctor can't do much now.' She looked up earnestly and Susan somehow felt that the older woman was envying her.

Susan found herself saying soothingly, 'Of course I'll do what I can, Mrs Gill.' It was like poor dear Mama all over again.

Ellen suffered for two more weeks, and then it was all over. Why did God allow a good woman to suffer? Why did He leave a good man like Mr Gill alone without his other half? It was hard to hide the bitter rage, to tend to the sick woman with a cheerful face and to report to her all the small events on the farm.

One morning, Ellen said weakly to Susan, 'I've been selfish, keeping you here, lass. I should have found you a place by now, but I didn't want to part with you.'

Susan shook her head. 'No, Mrs Gill, you're not selfish. I owe you so much! All my life I'll remember the things you taught me, and how you saved me and the boys when we were starving. We'd have been in the workhouse without you.'

Moorlanders didn't often express emotion. Ellen reached out and grasped Susan's hand with her thin, blue-veined one. Gasping for breath, she wheezed, 'You're a grand lass, Susan. I hope you'll find a good husband like I did … and you'll have little children just like my … adopted ones.' She fell back, exhausted, her eyes closed. 'Take some of my rosemary, lass, and plant it in your garden. It's a special one Martin found for me, with bright blue flowers … rosemary's for remembrance. Plant it next to your white rose.'

That was the last time Susan spoke to Ellen Gill; the farmer's wife died that evening, as the rooks were going home, black against the evening sky.

Martin was grim, silent, stoical in the moorlanders' tradition. He went through all the duties, the formalities, the rituals of death, mechanically playing his part. Susan felt that he had retreated to a great distance. She longed to put her arms round him and comfort him, but Mr Gill was too remote; he seemed not to notice Susan's anguish, he scarcely looked at her. What could the maid do but keep on cleaning the house, doing the chores as she had been taught, with her heart aching for Ellen? The life had gone out of the house, and out of the master too.

Only once, on the day after the funeral, Susan said, 'I'm so sorry, Mr Gill.' She saw the farmer's chest heave.

'Her suffering's over, that's a blessing. Mine's just starting ... I blame myself, in a way. I should have known what mouldy hay can do, the mould gets into your lungs and it grows there ... horrible.' He looked up. 'But it's not going to happen to you, lass. Ever since then, I've burned any bad hay, never let you or the boys near it. But I learned too late for Ellen, the poor lass.'

The work increased as summer drew on, and there was no time to think about the future. It was a struggle to do everything Mrs Gill would have wanted her to do, and to help with the farm work as well. Susan found a little comfort in working side by side with Martin; they understood and respected each other. But it was not so easy as in the old days. Martin avoided her eye and they spoke only of work, never about feelings. He was pleasant and courteous as ever, but impersonal and subdued by grief.

In early July the moorland sheep were gathered, the farmers who grazed the moor combining to sweep the vast moorland with their dogs and bring the sheep down for clipping, sorting them into batches from the different farms. The lambs were given their flock mark and the sheep farmers had the chance to hear the local gossip and lament about the poor price for wool.

Susan had helped before at the gathering with Ellen, mainly to serve the food, although she'd been pleased to carry a couple of tired lambs and reunite them with their mothers. This year she was to go again, but nothing was the same. Martin was grave and quiet and Susan trotted along at his side, wondering whether to talk or to keep silent.

It was a cool and rather windy day, but the operation went smoothly and the small groups of sheep gradually joined up into a broad river of woolly backs, pouring down off the heights into the sheep pens. Susan held the pen gate as Martin deftly dived in and selected his own sheep from the rest. There would be a short break for food and then the shearing would begin.

The Holly Bank moor flock was not large, so Martin went to help his neighbour, once his own sheep were penned. Susan watched the busy scene, wondering where she would be when the next gathering took place. An old shepherd worked with Martin, and Susan was standing near enough to hear what they said.

'Now lad, frame yourself and we've nearly finished.' The older man evidently thought he was in charge. 'And what's this young lass you've gotten yourself? Didn't waste much time, did you? But then, there's nothing like a bonny young lass to keep you warm in bed!' He winked at Susan.

Martin's face was a bright red as he looked over to see whether Susan had heard the man's remarks, and she turned hastily away. 'I'll thank you to be civil, Joe,' he snapped. 'Don't speak like that.'

Joe looked surprised. 'Nay, lad, I was nobbut thinking she looked right handy ... even though she's a little 'un.'

'Shut up, won't you?' His tone was savage.

The old man chuckled. 'What's come over you, Martin Gill? You used to be able to take a joke ... not in love, are yer?'

A skylark spiralled into a patch of blue sky, seeming to rise effortlessly on a silver thread of song. How embarrassing for Mr Gill, to be teased about his servant girl ... but surely it wouldn't upset him too much? These old moorland folk loved to make outrageous remarks, but nobody took them seriously. It was their form of entertainment, and Susan usually managed to find a witty answer when it was her turn.

It did upset him. For some reason Mr Gill seemed to be devastated, angry and embarrassed. He stalked off to the pens at the other side and Susan didn't see him again for some time. To make herself useful, she went to help a farmer's wife to spread a trestle table, bringing out some of the food she'd brought as the Holly Bank contribution.

'What's up with young Martin?' the woman looked curiously at Susan. 'But of course, he's just lost Ellen, he'll be feeling it still. Pass that apple pie over, will you, love?'

Eventually the sheep were sheared and turned back up the hill. Most of the shepherds lingered to talk, but Martin nodded to Susan and they made their way quickly back to the track for home, Susan almost running to keep up with Martin's pace, carrying her empty wicker basket.

After about five minutes, Martin seemed to realize she was there. Looking down at Susan he said gently, 'Here, let me carry that basket, lass. Now ... I'm sorry you were insulted today, right sorry. By golly, I could have killed that Joe.'

'Don't worry, Mr Gill, it was nothing really. Just his idea of a joke, most of the men do it. Everybody really knows that I'm just a servant, don't they?' Bobbing along, Susan tried to sound cheerful and normal.

Mr Gill stopped dead on the track, staring down into Susan's eyes. 'Just a servant? You are more than that, Susan.' He passed a hand over his face wearily. 'Oh dear, I'm that tired ... you are a perfect little white rose, as Ellen called you.' The deep voice was very soft. He sighed deeply. 'You children are almost my family, and I hate to see you belittled.' He went on in a different tone. 'I shouldn't have brought you here today.'

One sunny day later in July, after they had been working in the hayfield with a couple of hired labourers, Martin broke the news. 'I'm not stopping here, lass. My father's ailing and I'm off back to Pateley to live at the old home, as soon as haytime's over. I'll maybe keep Holly Bank, run a few sheep here. But that means you'll have no job.'

Susan handed him a mug of tea, trying to keep her hands from shaking. She'd known that there would have to be changes in her life; it was three months since Ellen died, she'd wondered what to do, but Mr Gill had still needed help. So she'd said nothing. 'I'll find a job, Mr Gill. I can do most jobs in a house, the proper way, too. Mrs Gill taught me.' She knew the correct way to make a sauce, to iron a frill, to keep the washing snowy white. She knew how to make jam and how to bottle gooseberries, how to make a bed and whitewash the scullery. She could even cure ham.

'She was a grand lass, my Ellen.' Martin rubbed his eyes. 'Yes, I'll speak on your behalf, of course, give you a character. So will the vicar, you've been a regular at church.'

Good, there might be some reward for all those boring sermons. She'd never gone to church willingly, but only out of respect for the Gills, because it was important to them. As Martin had foreseen, their demure presence at church had helped folks to forget about Papa.

Martin's voice was calm, but now had an infinite sadness. 'Another thing ...' He looked at her now, the blue eyes clear as ever. She felt her heart melt. Poor Mr Gill.

Martin started again. 'It's worried me ... you're a young woman now, although I still think of you as a child. Time goes by.' He gave a tired smile. 'And folks will talk, if you stay here working alone with me, now that Ellen's gone. They like to gossip about single men and women spending time alone together, you see. Look at that Joe, at the gathering. That's not fair to you, of course, we have to think of your reputation, Susan.' He sighed and stood up. 'I'll be going back to Pateley next month, soon as I've sold the cattle. Some of the furniture can stay, I'll probably sleep here at lambing time.'

Susan washed the dishes after that with more ferocity than usual, angry at the world for having such misery in it. Underneath the anger, though, were other emotions. One of them felt very much like fear. The tears splashed into the bowl.

Mr Gill tried all the larger farms in the area and some of the big houses, but nobody wanted a maid just at that time. 'I'd rather stay in the country,' said Susan firmly. She wanted to live at the cottage and tend her garden, but it wasn't likely that there would be work close enough to home.

'Aye, lass, but you can always move if you're not suited. I'd take the first place that turns up if I were you. Then you can look around.' Martin obviously wanted her to get settled quickly, before he left.

In one way Susan welcomed the change, which had loomed over her for years. She'd always known that the safe haven of Holly Bank wouldn't last for ever. But it was agonizing, now that it came to the point. She would miss Mr Gill so much; his quiet presence had seen her through the worst, and she felt she was a better person for trying to live up to his standards.

'Martin's a good man, really good,' Ellen had said to her once. 'Me, I'm an ordinary mortal … but I'm better for knowing him. And so will you bairns be.' It was true. The worst thing for Susan now was watching him suffer, and being able to do nothing to help him.

One evening Martin came home from Ripon, where he'd been selling cattle at the market. Susan was preparing his evening meal before going home to her cottage, and looked up as he came into the kitchen. 'Soup and dumplings tonight, Mr Gill!' It was important to sound cheerful.

'Very good, Susan, but never mind that now. Come and sit down at the table, I've got some news for you.' His voice held a sort of excitement, the first sign of emotion for a long time.

Looking across the table, her employer smiled at Susan and she thought again how much she would miss him when they came to part. His face was thin with sorrow, but his eyes were as steady as ever in the brown face. 'Listen to this. I've found you a place! To work there and live in. You start next week, I'll take you there with your things … I know it's very sudden, but we've got to get on with it.' He paused. 'I don't like it either, you know.' It was said so quietly that she hardly heard him.

Susan's head was spinning. This was far too soon, the cottage would have to be locked up and left. 'Where is this place, Mr Gill?'

If only it could be a country house, with a garden and chickens, and perhaps little children to care for. She'd missed the boys so much since they'd grown up a little and moved away, even though John still came home for the school holidays. Would she be able to keep in touch with her brothers when she had a place? Maids got very little time to themselves, they were often on call for seven days a week.

Martin hesitated. 'Well, it's maybe not ideal, you might say, it could be a mite rough at times ... but it's a start.'

Susan's heart sank. It would be in Ripon, that's where he'd been.

'It's at the Mermaid, on the square in Ripon. Quite a respectable inn, they want a chambermaid, and to help in the bar when they're busy. And in the kitchen too, most likely. It's a busy place, they've got livery stables at the back and they see a lot of travellers passing through on the way north.'

There was nothing she could think of to say. Susan looked mutely at Martin.

'You'll be working at the Mermaid, Susan.'

CHAPTER SIX

The sun was parting the soft morning mist and dewdrops sparkled in the hedgerows; the lanes were bathed in a froth of white summer flowers. But there was a feeling of doom even on such a beautiful summer morning as the Holly Bank trap plodded down to Ripon, carrying Susan away from home. She watched the cathedral towers grow slowly nearer, wondering when she would see the cottage again. Even the grey, stone village of Kirkby seemed friendly, familiar, now that she was leaving.

The trees cast their heavy summer shade and the sound of bees filled the air as they passed the cottage gardens. It had been so hard to say goodbye to Ashtree Cottage and the little garden by the stream. Ellen's white roses were in full bloom, but they would scatter their petals on the grass unheeded this year. A few sprigs of rosemary to put among her clothes were Susan's only memento, the scent of home.

It had been sad to part with the goat and the chickens, but Susan had given them to the schoolteacher who had helped John, so they'd gone to a good home. The house had been locked up and left, with many a backward glance.

The man at her side seemed to be just as gloomy as Susan. Something more than grief at the death of his wife seemed to be troubling Martin. 'I hope I've done the right thing for you, lass,' he said as they reached the outskirts of the old town. He must be feeling just as bad as she was: in the depths of misery, fully aware that life was never going to be the same.

'I'm sure you've done the right thing, Mr Gill. It will be a new start for me, and the boys are both here in Ripon. I'll maybe be able to see them sometimes.' Keep smiling, keep smiling, she urged herself.

Far too soon, it was time to say goodbye. Goodbye to childhood, goodbye to the country and to the dear man handing her down from the trap in the inn yard.

It was time to be brave. 'I'll miss you, Mr Gill. Thank you for looking after us all so well. You know we'll never forget you. Don't know how we'll manage without you ...' The fringe was getting in her eyes.

Martin put his hands on her shoulders, something he hadn't done for a long time. 'And I'll miss you, my little lass, my word I will.' He paused, as if wondering what to say next. 'Look after yourself, love. You're a bonny lass now, you'll have to keep the lads at arm's length!' He kissed her lightly on the cheek. 'I'll not forget you, honey, and the way you helped me and Ellen through her last months ... I'll call to see you in a few weeks, to see how you're getting on.'

Four years of working together, laughing together and caring for Ellen were gone. Susan's arms went out of their own accord, Martin moved towards her and for a moment they clung together. It was the last time she'd breathe in Martin's country scent of horses and tweed, with a hint of soap. He'd dressed carefully in his good jacket to bring her to Ripon. He hugged her tightly, his cheek against her hair and then, abruptly, he swung her bag down and climbed aboard without another word. But he was looking at Susan as he drove slowly away.

'So that's how the land lies! Cuddling and kissing with the men? We'll have to watch you, my lass!' A rough voice spoke behind her, laughing. Somebody was looking at her, a dark man leaning on a stable door, a man with a smile that did not reach his eyes.

'Mind your own business!' she said furiously. Who was this lout, to watch them saying goodbye?

'That's no way to speak to your new boss! Come here, you daft bitch.' The man didn't move from his lounging position, but the leering smile vanished.

Nerves already stretched by stresses of the morning seemed to snap and a tide of rage swamped the sadness as Susan walked unwillingly towards the stable door. 'Don't speak to me like that! I'm supposed to see Mr Sanderson ...' Oh goodness, it might be him. New boss, he'd said. 'Are are you Mr Sanderson?'

The man was dressed in rough riding clothes, but he had an air of authority. 'That I am, lass, although most people call me George. Impudent young hussy, aren't you? You're from the High Side, I've no doubt. They're a bit backward up there on the moor. I suppose we'll have to polish you up, starting right now.' The laugh was not pleasant.

'They are not! I'll thank you to be civil! Never mind who you are, I'm not going to put up with this sort of treatment.' She would go and find work somewhere else.

George Sanderson seemed quite unruffled; he was amused by his own wit. 'Rule number one: never be rude to folks if you don't know who they are. Now, you'd better come with me to the missus.' He looked down at Susan critically. 'Bit small for a chambermaid, aren't you? Need developing, like. But if you like the men, the bar might be the place for you, if you lean forward enough.'

'I don't answer personal remarks.' Seething, Susan picked up her bag and followed George into the inn. How did he know who she was? But of course, he'd have recognized Martin, who had arranged the job for her. She was starting at the bottom as a chambermaid, with no rights and no defences; and making a bad start, at her most thorny. But she wouldn't put up with insults. Surely there was somewhere else she could work? But with nowhere to stay in Ripon, she'd have to put up with the Mermaid until she found something better. Bite her tongue, and not answer back. It was going to be difficult.

There were empty barrels at the back door and a smell of stale beer. Down narrow dark passages they went, until they reached a small room full of ledgers and papers. A woman sat behind a desk and Susan thought she had never seen such a thin person. Her black dress and scraped-back hair starkly contrasted with a gaunt white face.

'Here she is, Maud. New lass.'

'And not before time!' sniffed the woman. 'Are you sure you're nineteen? You don't look it. Oh well, we've said we'll take her, so we might as well give her a try.' She moved her skeletal frame across the room to a row of keys hanging on the wall and took one down. 'This is your room key, keep it locked at night. You're up in the attic, next to the cook. And don't let anyone in, do you hear? This is a respectable house. And we mean to keep it that way.' She glared at George.

Who did they think she was? How long could she put up with this kind of thing? There was nothing polite to say; Susan seethed.

'And another thing.' The woman pursed her lips. 'You're not in the family way, are you? That farmer seemed very keen to get rid of you, said you were a wonderful worker. It all sounded a bit suspicious to me, too much of a hurry.'

Susan stood up straight, as tall as possible. 'I am not sure that I want to work for you, if this is your opinion of me.' She'd go away, as quickly as she could.

'Aye, well, she was hugging and kissing him just now,' said George laconically. 'But we can't do with a bastard here! It's a respectable house, this is,' he echoed.

Mrs Sanderson looked grim. 'Your morals are your own affair,

I'm sure. But don't go kissing in broad daylight. You never know who's watching. If you encourage the men they'll be all for it, especially the young bucks round here. A little bit of flirting is good for trade, but be discreet, woman, and keep yourself out of trouble, or you'll be out of a place.'

'Rule number two: keep yer legs together.' George grinned and surveyed her from head to foot, his eyes travelling slowly over her. Susan shook with pure rage. 'She might go well in the bar, with her hair up, and a low neckline to show a bit of bosom. She's got a bit of shape to her. Sometimes the lads like a baby face, and they nearly allus like a blonde.' George considered Susan, head on one side.

'I'm afraid it will not be possible for me to take up your offer.' Susan swung round and went to the door. She'd go and look for Ben … nobody would treat her like a piece of meat.

Mrs Sanderson looked surprised. 'Now then, woman, don't be so hasty.' She glanced at her husband. 'Now you just leave her alone, George. Keep your hands off her, or there'll be trouble.' She smiled sourly. 'I know what happened to young Betty last year, although you think I don't. Go and check the cellars, will you? That Jim doesn't know what he's doing down there.' George leered at Susan and departed. Turning to Susan, the woman said, 'Don't take any notice of George. You'd better stay, we'll give you a trial. There's nowhere else for you to go, is there?'

'No, not at the moment.' But just give me a week or two, she said silently. I certainly won't be staying here. 'I expected to be treated with respect, and to be given a chance to learn the work. I did not think that anyone would start off by accusing me of – immorality.' And I won't put up with it, she added to herself.

The thin woman was not listening. 'Now, about wages. You won't get any for the first two weeks, while you learn the ropes. After that, we'll see what you're worth. What can you do?'

Anger was still raging, making it hard to think. What could she do? Anything that they asked of her, given time to learn. 'I can cure a ham and trim sheep's feet ...' That just slipped out; it was the wrong thing to say in the Mermaid Inn.

Mrs Sanderson sneered. 'Very useful, I'm sure. Not much call for that here. I can see we'll have a sight of teaching to do.'

Over the next few hours as she met at least a dozen new people, Susan wondered how she would survive. Looking after their little cottage and the work at Holly Bank had filled up most of her time, with church on Sundays and the occasional visit to the shop at Kirkby, or the Ripon market with the Gills. But she'd loved the life. Even when the Gills had made them respectable, they'd still tried to avoid attention. With Papa still in prison it was better to keep quiet.

School at Kirkby had been good for the boys, giving them a change of company, and eventually the confidence to talk to strangers. But working at the Gills and meeting very few people had made Susan rather shy by contrast. She didn't feel very grown-up, deep inside. Although she had vague hopes of marrying one day and having children, she had never thought much about how she appeared to men. The coarse remarks of the Sandersons had taken her completely by surprise.

In the little attic room that first night, Susan sat by her candle and faced the loss of her world, gone for ever. She remembered her fourteen-year-old self, meeting Martin that snowy evening on the road, and how she had looked up to him like a favourite uncle as she was growing up. Martin and Ellen had been almost like parents. They'd never shown her much outward affection, but she'd felt secure with them, and appreciated, all the same. Now Martin was gone, she had lost him too, after four years of being constantly in his company. That in itself was a terrible shock and added to the reception at the Mermaid, she felt numb.

Susan put her clothes away and sniffed the sprigs of rosemary.

Rosemary for remembrance ... She blew out the candle and climbed into the little narrow bed. Perhaps after a few months she'd get out of here, find another job. Downstairs, she could hear the laughter and talk from the bar and the sound of an accordion. The sounds were friendly enough, but the unknown customers filled her with fear.

About midnight, someone tapped softly on her door. Susan pretended to be asleep. For hours she lay in the dark, wondering what had happened to young Betty, whom Mrs Sanderson had mentioned. Had Betty been foolish enough to open the door?

The next few days were so busy that there was scarcely time to think. First came a sort of uniform, a little cap and a print dress with a tight-fitting bodice and full sleeves that all the maids wore, some with more grace than others. It made Susan look less conspicuous in one way, just one of the maids, although it revealed her figure more than anything she'd worn before. The clothes Ellen made had never fitted very tightly, partly because they were optimistically designed to allow Susan to grow.

She was put with the two other chambermaids, cheerful, chattering girls not much older than Susan, who enjoyed airing their superior knowledge. Patty and Sara were quick and neat workers and it was easy to pick up the routine of changing sheets, making up beds, sweeping and dusting, carrying hot water for the wash stands. There was nothing about the work that she had not done many times at Holly Bank.

'It's worse in winter, we have coals to carry as well,' laughed Patty. 'But you seem quite strong for your size, don't you?'

The girls told her to knock on every door and listen before going in, because 'you never know'. They warned her that many of the guests were travelling gentlemen, most quite sober, but some inclined to drink too much. 'And then we keep out of their way.'

Sara said that she thought Mrs Sanderson was an old hag, but she was reasonably fair to work for. 'And she doesn't expect us to, you know, do anything we shouldn't. Some houses have lasses that get hired out to men for a fee.' The girl's eyes were startled. 'Although … because of the mermaid on the inn sign out in the street, some folks think we might be for sale.'

'And what about Mr Sanderson?' It was important to know how they dealt with him.

The girls both giggled. 'Well, yes, that painting of the mermaid was his idea. I reckon she should have worn more seaweed. But … have you had any trouble? You're from the High Side, you might not be able to look after yourself yet.' Sara looked at her keenly.

'No trouble. But I wondered.' Susan picked up her broom and dustpan and moved to the door.

Patty stopped her and closed the door quietly. 'Just a word in your ear, lass. Watch old George, he's frisky. He's got a few girls into trouble in the past and as we all know, it's the woman that gets the blame. Don't go near the stables, and if he finds you on your own, go and do a job somewhere else.'

Sara smiled. 'Or you could tell his missus, but you might not last long here, if you did that.'

The bedroom door opened suddenly. 'How much longer are you girls going to take with that room?' Mrs Sanderson's clawlike hand shot out and grasped Sara by the hair. 'The guest's waiting for his room, hurry up now.'

The chambermaids looked at each other as they scuttled down the passage and Susan suddenly felt that it was good to have the company of other girls, even worth being patronized a little. It might be best to stay at the Mermaid for a little while, before looking for another job; it would take time to get used to being with so many people.

The next week, Mrs Sanderson decided that Susan should work in the bar. 'We need all you girls to be able to do everything, you have to learn the ropes. We need three in the bar when it's busy.'

The bar was frightening, but no doubt the work could be learned, given time. The main bar was the noisy heart of the inn, a place that seemed to attract the lonely commercial travellers in the evenings. Sometimes there were raised voices but there never seemed to be any trouble. It was a new experience; there had been nothing at all like it at Kirkby, where the two pubs were small family affairs, patronized by people who knew each other and who went to bed early. Women were never seen there and Mr Gill had only called in occasionally on market day.

The only nagging doubt was George, who often entertained his friends in the bar. It would be hard to avoid him if you were on duty there for the evening.

Bar work was new to Susan; it was different from anything she'd ever done. It was difficult to draw beer from the big brass pumps and almost impossible to carry a tray of jugs and glasses across a crowded space, where people were talking and laughing and jostling at every step.

Susan found two people behind the bar: Sam, a youngish man with oiled hair, and Violet, a middle-aged woman who seemed to be clinging to the last vestiges of her youth. Both were looking quite critical.

'I want Susan to learn the routine, so we've got a spare hand when we need one,' Mrs Sanderson explained as she took Susan in. 'That is, if she has any aptitude at all,' she added with a sour look at her new chambermaid.

It was difficult to learn anything at all when the bar so was full. Of course, it was market day and all the farmers except the Methodists came in, some for dinner and others just for a glass of beer or gin. There was a pervading smell of sheep, overlaid by beer. It was easy to feel lost, everything was happening so fast and the noise was such that you could hear little of what you were told.

'You deaf, or what?' demanded Violet, when she had to ask

Susan twice to bring clean glasses. 'Or is just that you're a dumb country lass?'

Another voice spoke in her ear and turning, she found Sam at her side. 'Never mind her, love, she's just jealous. She'll settle down.' And the barman winked as he passed her the required tray of glasses.

'Whatever do you mean? Nobody could be jealous of me.'

'Course she is. You're young and bonny, and she's – er, old. The young men'll go for you, mark my words.'

'I do hope not!' wailed Susan, but Sam had vanished into the crowd.

During the next few days Sam patiently trained Susan, since Violet declined to help. Choosing times when the bar was quiet, he showed her how to pour drinks properly, wash glasses and give the correct change. 'And don't forget to put all the money straight in the till, never in your pocket, however busy we are. You've got to be seen to be honest.'

Violet's heavily rouged, sulky face haunted Susan for the next few days. Wherever the girl turned Violet seemed to be watching her, waiting to pounce when she made a mistake. One day Susan escaped from the bar for a few minutes to take some cloths from the washing line in the yard. She looked up at the blue summer sky and realized that it was a week since she'd had any fresh air. Martin would be thinking of harvesting the corn by now, over in Pateley. She couldn't picture him there ... it was a bigger farm than Holly Bank, more prosperous. How she missed the country life!

Violet flung out petulantly into the yard behind her. 'Are you going to take all day with them cloths? We need one now, a bloke's just spilled his beer ... go and mop it up, look sharp!'

Susan sighed and went back into the stuffy, smoke-filled atmosphere of the inn. She found the beer and mopped it up and while she was bending down, a customer pinched her on the bottom.

Quietly, she took her revenge and stood heavily on his foot as she passed him. She was learning the tricks of bar work quite fast.

George undertook to teach the new barmaid how to draw a jug of beer. 'There's the right way and the wrong way, and the Mermaid's reputation depends on you getting it right. We're proud of the head on our beer.' Sam the barman was hanging about nearby, busy polishing glasses; maybe he knew that it wasn't wise for a female to be alone with the boss.

It took quite an effort to pull down the brass pump handles, especially for a short person. George stood behind her, far too close, barking instructions. 'It's good for developing the bosom,' he smirked. 'Did you know that's why barmaids have a big bust? But remember to use your left arm as much as the right, or you'll end up lopsided. That would be a pity, now. We'd have to sack yer, ha ha.' His eyes raked over her body, as if calculating how much development she needed.

'Mr Sanderson, that's ridiculous.' It seemed best to laugh, and not to take him too seriously. That was another thing to learn about bar work: take the comments lightly and laugh at the jokes.

There was much to learn about drink for a girl who had worked at Holly Bank. The Gills were not total abstainers like the Methodists, but they hardly drank alcohol at all. Susan dimly remembered that Papa had served wine to his guests at Harrogate, a long time ago. Now, at the Mermaid she had to find out quickly what people drank, which sort of glass to use and how much was required.

The first time behind the bar, the new barmaid filled a beer glass with whisky. The patrons, always looking for a diversion, went into hysterics, while Susan stood there turning red and wondering what she'd done. She provided so much entertainment that George forgave her. 'Have you never seen drink before, lass? Where've you been?' he said indulgently. He was keen to teach her all about alcohol in its various forms, and suggested a tasting session later that night. 'I'll let you try anything on the shelf, how about that? And then you might relax a bit.' George grinned and squeezed her arm.

Susan made sure she was not available after the bar had closed, so the lesson had to wait. It was Sam who quietly explained the next day that gin, whisky and brandy were spirits, distilled from grain, much stronger than beer and served in small glasses. Many people drank them diluted with water. There were various types of beer, some stronger than others. Wine was sometimes served in the dining-room, and Sam was usually there to open the bottles and advise on the wines.

'I don't like the smell of drink,' Susan admitted as she helped Sam to wash the glasses. 'Especially second hand, on peoples' breath.'

Sam laughed. 'That's just as well, Susan. A young lass working here last year got herself into trouble through taking a drink with a man.'

'You mean she got drunk? It must be very bad for you.'

'Well, yes, but the real problem is the effects of drink – it makes you sleepy, or perhaps silly. Drink makes it easier for a man to take advantage of a lass, you see.' The barman looked at her. 'You seem very young – you do know what I'm talking about?'

'I can imagine what you mean.'

'So she ended up with a little baby and nowhere to go. And of course the father had disappeared, he was just a traveller, passing through. Her mistake was to go up to his room with him for a glass of gin. He made her tipsy and then seduced her. It's something to watch out for, young Susan.'

Gin had a strange smell and Sam said it was flavoured with juniper berries; how could anyone want to drink it? How could anyone want to go upstairs with a stranger, to drink the horrible stuff? 'I don't think I'm in much danger from that temptation, Sam.'

In spite of everything, her new life wasn't so bad, if only Mr Gill would come to see her. But the days stretched into weeks and he didn't appear. Perhaps, being at Pateley with his father, he went to the Pateley market and never got to Ripon. Where are you, Mr Gill, and how are you getting on? For the first time, a cold feeling of rejection crept over Susan. Mr Gill had not wasted much time in getting rid of her. He'd maybe forgotten all about the Woods by now. Perhaps, too, he really believed that their father was a criminal; a horrible thought.

CHAPTER SEVEN

'Where's Susan? I want her immediately!' Maud Sanderson stormed up the stairs, obviously in one of her bad moods. Susan dropped her duster and went forward while Sara stood behind a door to listen. 'That dratted kitchen girl's gone sick again, you're needed in the kitchen. Right now! Go down to Cook.'

'Yes, Mrs Sanderson. I'll just get my—'

'Right away! Did you hear, girl? And you may be there for a while. That Margery's not up to the work.' Maud swept away and the girls rolled their eyes at each other.

'Rather you than me! That Cook's a tartar, you'll see. Poor Margery could do nowt right for Cook.' Sara was obviously relieved that she hadn't been chosen.

At first sight, Mrs Thomson the Mermaid cook was a comfortable woman with a round face and a round figure, her hair screwed up into a round bun. She'd been strict, but reasonable on the occasions when Susan had carried out meals from the kitchen. Mentally rolling up her sleeves for peeling potatoes, the new scullery maid went in quietly and found Mrs Thomson waiting for her with a grim expression on her round face. What have they sent me this time? she seemed to be thinking.

'Sit down at the table – Susan, isn't it?' They sat opposite each other at the big scrubbed table in the middle of the kitchen. 'Now, we may as well get it straight from the start. I'll take no lip and no answering back. And I certainly won't be told how to do my job. But if you do as you're told and try to learn the routine, you and me'll get on fine.'

'Yes, Mrs Thomson.'

'It looks as though you'll be stuck here for a while. Can you stand the heat of the kitchen? I don't want no fainting females in here and I must say you look a bit young for the work.'

What was the right answer? 'I like cooking, Mrs Thomson, I'd like to learn more. I have worked in a kitchen, on a farm.'

That seemed to be acceptable; the cook nodded. 'Very well, lass, but you've got to start at the bottom, washing dishes like everybody else. Now get going.'

The kitchen was hot with the coal stove roaring and the immense pans were heavy to lift. The scale of operations was so big, so unlike the Gills' farmhouse kitchen. Catering for up to fifty people every day called for vast quantities of food and there was a huge pantry to store the hams and cheeses, the bags of carrots, potatoes, flour and dried peas. There were rows of bottled fruit, jams and pickles, more than Susan had ever seen before. And everything was scrupulously clean and neat.

Washing up went on all day and seemed endless, but there was one great advantage of working in the kitchen: no George. Whether Mrs Thomson had scared him off or Maud had told him to keep out, was a mystery, but in the kitchen she was safe from those roving eyes and searching hands. It was a great relief. As she got used to the routine Susan was quicker and then she had time to learn some of the other work.

'What's your day off?' the cook asked Susan suddenly after she'd been in the kitchen for a week or two.

'Er, I haven't been given a day off.' It was somehow difficult to ask for time off, but without it, Susan wasn't able to see her brothers. One day she'd called at the printers where Ben was apprenticed to let him know where she was working, and he'd said that he and John met at Trinity church on Sunday mornings, mainly because John could get out of school for a few hours if he went to church.

'I know you'll come if you can,' he said. 'We both miss you, Susie!'

'That Maud Sanderson – she's downright mean. I'll have a word with her.' Mrs Thomson wore her grim look. Soon after that, Susan was given Sundays off until the evening. That was when the commercial travellers came in to stay overnight, ready for an early start on Monday morning, riding out on one of George's horses.

'Back by six to serve the evening meal, and don't be late!' Maud warned her.

It was wonderful to see Ben and John again and to go for a walk with them after church. Mrs Thomson had given her some bread and cheese to share with them and they all walked along the river, where the autumn wind was whipping the leaves off the trees. It was good to see, but also a little sad, that the boys were making their way quite well without their sister. John was to stay at the school during the holidays since Susan had moved to the Mermaid, and he said it would give him an advantage. He could see the local boys quite often and catch up on his studies.

Gradually Susan was introduced to other jobs in the kitchen. She waited at table, took the orders and carried them out to the diners. She mixed puddings and cakes, peeled potatoes and scraped carrots, becoming quicker and neater with practice.

One day Mrs Sanderson spent some time with the cook in her office, planning ahead, as she called it. 'We're going to change the menus,' Mrs Thomson announced the next day. 'Try to get more folks in … we'll need to look for new recipes and such, but my poor eyes'll never stand the strain. Can you read, lass?'

'Yes, I can read – would it help if I read the recipes out loud? Mrs Beeton, you mean?'

'Her and others, yes.' Cook lowered her voice. 'The fact is there's a new cook, it's a man and they call him chef, at the Black Bull, yon end of the market square. We've noticed the difference here, especially on market day. Maud thinks they need a bit of competition, so it's up to you and me.'

It was flattering but also alarming to be included in the cooking team. The kitchen soon became busier, as news of the changed menus got out. Mrs Thomson had a wonderful memory and once she had made a new dish she could remember it. But she had great trouble reading – perhaps she'd never learned to read well. Susan decided to record the dishes they tried in a note-book of her own, for interest.

A new scullery maid called Ruby was hired, which left Susan more time for helping to cook and serve the meals. Waiting in the dining-room was an ordeal at first, hoping she wouldn't drop a tray or spill the peas down some farmer's neck. Walking right across the big dining-room by herself was frightening; she felt that everybody in the room was watching. But gradually it became just another job because on the whole, waitresses were invisible and the customers were too interested in the food, or their companions, to notice who waited at table.

One Thursday when the dining-room was crowded with market goers for the midday meal, a tall figure walked in and took a table by himself. Martin Gill had appeared at last, coming to the Mermaid for the first time since Susan left Holly Bank. Walking towards his table Susan found his eyes fixed on her intently, leaving her feelings in shock. They stared at each other.

Demure and calm in the black dress, white apron and cap, Susan felt inward turmoil. It was so good to see him, but why had it taken so long? She'd felt abandoned. 'Good day, Mr Gill, what can I get you?' You look sad and tired, she wanted to say.

'Susan, lass, it's good to see you. Er, you can call me Martin by now, surely?' He smiled wryly. 'Are – are they treating you right?'

He looked round, but the other customers were talking loudly about the shocking price of wool. 'I'll have the soup, please, and a glass of water.'

When she brought the soup they had a few more precious words together; Susan told him that the boys were doing well and that they met most Sundays. 'I'm working in the kitchen and learning a lot,' Susan told him.

'Could you fetch me a bread roll, please?' So she had to go back. And then Mr Gill ordered a meat pie, followed by a pudding. He told her, as she was serving and clearing the plates as slowly as possible, that he might be going back to Holly Bank. 'My brother's back from Lincolnshire, so he can help my father instead of me. But as you'll know, prices are poor ... you're much better off here, lass, than working for me.'

This was too much to bear and the emotion boiled up underneath. Oh, Martin, I would far rather be working with you! I miss you. This would never do, Susan swallowed the pain and straightened her apron. He'd obviously wanted to get rid of them, after all. 'May I fetch you a cup of tea ... Martin?' It came out in a shaky little voice; he could see she was upset.

'Yes, tea, please ... I miss you, lass, believe me. I'd have been here before, but – but I can't come to see you, it's not right. I've told you before how people talk.' Martin looked bleak.

Well, that was true; George had made much of their parting in the inn yard. But who cared if people talked? Mr Gill evidently did. 'But ... can't we be friends?' she asked.

The steady blue eyes were troubled, sad. 'Nay, Susan. I was your guardian, you know, and you're a woman now. It's not proper, as I said.' He stood up to go and looked down at her. 'I hope things go right for you, little lass.' It was said quietly – did he really regret casting her off? 'Here's a small parcel I brought for you ... goodbye.' Martin strode out of the dining-room and Susan pushed her parcel into the foliage of an aspidistra plant, where it would be safe until she'd finished work. She might never see Martin Gill again; there was such finality in that goodbye. But then, never was a long way off.

Thursdays were always busy and it was late when Susan tiptoed into the now deserted dining-room to retrieve her parcel. It consisted of many layers of paper, inside which was a ball of damp moss. In the centre of the moss, smelling of home, were a few herb cuttings: thyme, sage and rosemary. Rosemary for remembrance. Martin knew that, Ellen had said it often enough. Perhaps he was saying he wouldn't forget her? She would grow them in a pot on her bedroom windowsill, and the scent of growing herbs would be a reminder of the country. Holly Bank was only about eight or nine miles from Ripon, but it was a world away from the Mermaid Inn.

The next day Susan went up to the office with the menus, which Maud liked to approve for the week ahead. Instead of Maud, there was George sitting in the big chair with his feet on the desk, smoking a cigar and looking dangerous. His eyes narrowed as he looked at her in a calculating way.

'I brought the menus,' Susan gabbled, and made for the door as fast as she could.

George beat her to it and stood with his back to the door, grinning at her. 'Not so fast, young woman. I want a word with you. Now I've got you cornered at last … what do you say to me now? Bit of fun, isn't it?' He was savouring the moment; Susan had been dodging him for a long time and she suddenly realized that he thought of her resistance as a challenge. He thought that she was enjoying the game. It seemed best to stand perfectly still, not to say or do anything to encourage the man.

'What have you been up to, down by the river on Sunday? Hugging and kissing a young man? It won't do, you know. I've told you before about kissing in public.' He smiled and moved nearer, blowing cigar smoke in her face. 'Puts the reputation of the Mermaid at risk.' He moved suddenly and pinned her against the wall. 'What have you to say for yourself? Hot little thing, under that quiet look, aren't yer?'

She'd sworn never to let George grab her and now it had happened. Keep calm, Susan said to herself. Look him in the eye. 'I go to church with my brothers on Sundays and then we go for a walk. That's all, Mr Sanderson. Just my brothers, Ben and John. Please can I go now? Mrs Thomson is waiting, she'll be here looking for me in a minute.' Susan moved and George held her tighter, crushing her to his chest.

'Bugger Mrs Thomson, it's not her I want. That tale is rubbish. Brother, my eye! You was with a big strapping chap, hugging him. It's immoral – and on a Sunday, too.' He was fondling her, but his fingers were cruel, digging into her, handling her familiarly. He was not a big man, but George was bigger and much stronger than Susan. 'Now, if you was to give me a kiss and a cuddle, it might be forgiven ... I'll lock the door if it makes you feel better.' George had opened the front of her dress. 'Come on, don't be shy. You know me well enough by now, don't yer?'

'Please don't, Mr Sanderson ...' Desperate, Susan tried with all her strength to get away, but it seemed to make George more excited. He still believed she enjoyed this kind of thing and he was not going to listen to anything she said. It was time for action, but her arms were pinned. She brought up her knee and jabbed him with it, and that had immediate effect. George let her go and bent over, moaning. Wrenching open the door, she heard him swearing and she banged it shut again before running down the stairs. She didn't stop until she got to the kitchen.

'Seen George, have you?' Mrs Thomson carried on beating eggs with a steady hand. 'Do your buttons up, lass, you look untidy. And then we'll have a nice cup of tea.'

'I thought it would be Maud in the office ... where is she?' A cup of tea was very soothing, especially the Inn's best Earl Grey, and Susan began to feel more normal. Working in the kitchen had relaxed her vigilance a little; she'd nearly been caught this time.

'Gone to see her sister in Leeds. I never thought he'd be in the office when I sent you, lass. I just thought you could leave them on the table, for when she gets back.'

Susan took extreme care until she saw Mrs Sanderson stalking the corridors again, but George had disappeared to the stables. 'I'll have to find another job, he's dangerous,' she said to Mrs Thomson, who looked shocked.

'Nay, lass, don't leave. You're quite safe in this kitchen. We'll mebbe make a cook of you one day.'

As it turned out, she was not safe in the kitchen for long. 'Did you once say you can play the piano, Susan? Right. You can play in the bar tonight, there's a bit of a meeting, with refreshments afterwards.' Maud threw her a bag. 'Wear this, it might brighten you up a bit.'

'This' turned out to be a beautiful, clinging, silky red dress. When she tried it on, another person looked back from the mirror: an older, more assured woman. Perhaps the colour would give her courage; she would certainly need it. Play in the bar! She wouldn't dare to do it, right among all the drinkers. The last time Susan had touched a piano was at Holly Bank, where she had sometimes played to Ellen. Beethoven was very different from music hall songs ... they gave her half an hour to try out the music on the rather tinny piano, that was all.

There was a moment of panic when the guests began to arrive, but the evening was not too difficult, after all. It was a fairly staid gathering of local workmen, a sort of friendly society calling themselves the Ancient Order of Foresters. They were honest folk who looked after other members when they were ill or fallen on hard times, and they liked old-fashioned songs. Susan played 'The Last Rose of Summer' so poignantly that even she felt like crying for her lost youth. Folk songs went down well and some of the men liked to sing, but they were all polite and respectful. Thank goodness George was not a member. These were not his sort of folk; he preferred the more raffish of the race-going public.

'Why Foresters?' Susan asked one of the members, and he laughed.

'We help each other through the forests of life. But you may as well enjoy a bit of music on the way, lass.'

Playing the piano in the red dress, Susan left the kitchen behind for a few hours; she felt less like a domestic servant, more like herself. Music of any kind was such a pleasure, after so many years without it.

One young man with plastered-down hair seemed to be there every time the piano was opened. He volunteered to turn the pages for her and gradually, Susan and William Darley started to talk to each other. He told her that he came to the regular gatherings of the Foresters because his grandfather had been a member, years ago.

'I'm a blacksmith, work with my father,' he said. 'We shoe all George's horses, of course, and that's a lot of work. The Mermaid stables always have at least twenty and they're ridden hard.' You could see from his burly chest and solid arms that he worked hard physically.

William confided to Susan that he wanted to save up and open a business of his own one day. 'Shouldn't you like to work in the country?' Susan asked wistfully. Spring was on the way out in the country, but the rooms at the Mermaid were stuffier than ever. Here the seasons scarcely mattered except for changes to the kitchen menus.

'Well, I probably wouldn't set up in Ripon against my Pa, that wouldn't be right. But business is bound to be better in a town, there are more folks and more horses, and plenty of wrought iron work.'

'I come from Kirkby ... I like the moors, myself,' Susan admitted.

William gave her a pitying look. 'Nothing but a few old sheep! Not much opportunity there to make money and nobody to talk to. Now, Miss Susan, you look very nice tonight. Can I get you a glass of lemonade?'

As the days lengthened, Susan felt more restless. She was pining for fresh air and so when William Darley invited her the next week to go for a walk on Sunday afternoon, she accepted. 'We'll go down by the Alma Weir, if it's fine, that is. I'll meet you on the square.'

William had only seen Susan in the red dress and she thought he looked rather surprised when she walked up to him in her quiet grey Sunday dress and coat. It was a blustery spring day, with white clouds scudding across a cold blue sky. 'You don't look like the girl at the piano,' he said, taking her arm as they crossed the road.

Coming towards them was a tidy-looking trap with two occupants, an elderly woman and a fair-haired man. They were looking at her and Susan suddenly realized with a sinking heart who it was: Martin Gill, evidently taking his mother for a drive. He acknowledged them gravely and passed on. Martin Gill, in Ripon on a Sunday afternoon; who would have thought it?

William looked after him. 'That's Mr Gill from Pateley, we've done work for him.'

Mr Gill from Pateley, so near and yet so far away, in another world. He'd looked shocked, she thought, to see Susan arm in arm with William. If only she hadn't agreed to go for a walk with him … but it was too late, now.

'I didn't tell my mother who you are,' William confided. 'She might not have liked to hear I was out walking with a girl from the pub. But in that dress, I'm sure she'd approve of you!' He grinned down at her.

The path by the river was quite pleasant, but William seemed to walk very close to Susan and he held on to her as though he thought she'd fall into the river. Once they had passed the thundering weir they could talk again. But under the shadow of the trees, William didn't want to talk. He wanted a kiss, and this was quite pleasant, too. It was the first time that any man had kissed Susan on the lips. Except that ... it was the wrong man. Susan realized that William was not the right man. She had finally grown up, she could imagine loving a man ... but not this one.

And yet, why not? William was young, he was wholesome and well mannered. When he kissed her again, Susan allowed herself to relax a little in his arms. Then she suggested that they walk back, and steered him firmly towards a family walking by the river.

As they went, William talked about his work and future hopes and he hinted that he was looking for a decent young woman to share his life – and his prosperity. He liked children, he wanted a family. Susan thought about the possibility of marrying a young blacksmith, of having a little house of her own and a couple of sturdy babies. Although this was the first time that William had asked her out, it seemed that his intentions were already heading in that direction.

One advantage of William's interest was that other young men left Susan alone. There were several young Foresters in the group and quite a few Ripon lads who visited the bar and seemed to take an interest in the music, but William discouraged them from Susan's vicinity. Had she encouraged William too much? It was hard to know how a modest young girl should behave in a case like this.

CHAPTER EIGHT

1896

'Two cups of coffee and a pot of tea ... three mutton chops with gravy ... Yorkshire pud with roast beef and can he have it quick, he's catching a train ...' the orders drifted through your dreams when you worked in a busy kitchen.

Seasons came and went across the patch of sky in the attic bedroom window. The pots of sage and rosemary grew into bushes of a respectable size, a constant reminder of how long Susan been at the Mermaid. The time was well spent because she learned a great deal in a kitchen like this, but ... what next? To be a good assistant cook, was that all? After two years, the autumn was declining into winter once again and the work was relentless. But it wasn't the work; the problem was that Ripon was far from the moorland and the future was dark.

Martin had gone; better not to think of him, to get on with life. Before she went to sleep, Susan told herself stories, tales with happy endings about seeing Papa again, about getting back to the country. Sometimes she imagined that Martin asked her to be his housekeeper, and they went back to the old easy relationship. But there was no going back, there was only the future. Martin would need a wife, if he was to have a life of his own and the children he had hoped for. He may have already found a lass to suit him.

But how could Susan improve her own situation? A suggestion of sorts came eventually from Mrs Thomson, who seemed to approve of Susan, although she was severe with everyone else. One day when they were drinking tea in a rare moment of calm between dinner courses, the older woman looked across at Susan thoughtfully. 'I've got a proposal for you, my girl,' she began. 'How you and me can help each other.'

Susan put down her cup and stared at the cook. 'How can I help you?' It didn't seem likely. 'You've already helped me, taught me a lot.'

A slight smile flitted across Mrs Thomson's face. 'We've done well with the new menus, Maud's pleased, although you'd never think it. If you like, Susan, I could teach you a few more sauces and such ... and there's a lot to learn about ordering, choosing meat, all that. But in time I could make you into a cook.'

'Make me into a cook?' Susan had never considered this.

'Aye, and you could better yourself. Apply for a job in a big house, get away from the inn. You're not cut out to work here, that's for sure. Too refined, you are, for the Mermaid, and that's nowt to be ashamed of.' Mrs Thomson poured herself another cup of tea. 'And even in an inn, you're safer in the kitchen.'

That was true. There was a feeling of safety with Mrs Thomson; Susan didn't need to watch out for George until she went out of the kitchen. 'But I've never been a cook. How could I say I'm a cook?' And how could I look old enough? she wondered. Most cooks were solid, middle-aged women who commanded respect. They had a lot of bulk, as a rule.

'I'd give you a character and say you were my assistant. You're far more than a scullery maid already, lass. A year or two, an apprenticeship like, and you could qualify as a cook. I'll let you do more on your own and keep watching you of course, it wouldn't do to make a mistake. Maud doesn't like us to waste food.'

It seemed that the cook didn't want anyone else to know of her reading difficulty and Susan guessed that it was more than poor eyesight. Mrs Thomson had probably never been to school. She'd once told the girl that as the eldest of a large family of children, she had helped to bring up the younger ones.

Susan went on collecting recipes; she made a scrapbook of information from the home pages of newspapers. She found an old book about herbs, to add to the herbal recipes they already used. And she wrote down all the traditional recipes Mrs Thomson used, to add to the ones from Ellen Gill. Yorkshire Parkin, a solid affair of oatmeal and dark treacle, was one of the winter favourites at Holly Bank and Mrs Thomson had her own version.

After a while, Mrs Thomson suggested that Susan should make two copies of the recipes, one to keep for herself. ''Twill come in handy when you get a job in a big house.' Susan's career was being carefully planned.

'You'd need to cook game in season, in a gentleman's residence,' said the cook one day. 'I'll try to get Maud to put game on the menu.' A group of solicitors met once a month to dine together at the Mermaid and Maud Sanderson agreed that the butcher could deliver a saddle of venison that week. It was more expensive than beef, but it would please the lawyers.

Looking at the dark meat, she wondered how they could make it palatable. Susan had never eaten venison and didn't know where to begin. The meal turned out to be a sort of test for an apprentice cook. 'Right,' said her mentor. 'What do you notice about this meat?'

'It's very dark ... and there's no fat on it. And it smells quite strong. It's deer meat, isn't it?' Would the clients like it?

'It's local, from the deer park at Studley. But of course, with game, you hardly ever know how old it is. It could be an old stag. So what does all that tell you about cooking it?'

Susan had to think fast. 'Well ... we'll need to keep basting it, or bake it in a covered dish – or the meat will dry out. And I should think some mixed herbs would help ... we could soak it in something for a while, to make it more tender – marinate, did you call it?' She'd seen the cook use marinades before.

Mrs Thomson nodded her approval. 'Well done. We'll let you plan the whole dinner. Folks often serve braised red cabbage with game, but I think you know that one.'

Susan waited on the solicitors in the dining-room, butterflies in her stomach; the venison had better be tender, or she'd be in trouble if they complained to Maud. The first course was mulligatawny soup, which she had made several times before. Turbot formed the fish course, simmered slowly in the turbot kettle and served with lemon, parsley and melted butter. Mrs Beeton's book had told them it should be served with shrimp sauce, but shrimps were hard to find in Ripon.

The venison roast turned out to be a great success. It was followed by syllabub, an ancient recipe of sherry and cream that added to the medieval atmosphere of the evening, Susan thought. She smiled to think of the difference between the dinners at the Mermaid such as this one, and the suppers she and the boys had enjoyed at the cottage, where potatoes and eggs were their staple diet.

The solicitors were so pleased with their dinner that they asked to see the cook and Susan was pushed forward. 'My, it's the little waitress! Well done, my dear! An excellent meal, we all agree. But you don't look old enough to be a cook!' The chairman of the group smiled kindly over his spectacles. 'Now,' he said fussily, 'may I trouble you for the bill?'

Susan blushed. 'Thank you, Mr Jordan.' She knew the man slightly, because she'd often seen him at church in Kirkby, before she came to Ripon. At the Mermaid, he usually paid the bill and gave her a tip. But she wished he hadn't mentioned how young she looked.

After that night Susan saw Mr Jordan quite often; he lived out of town and rode in to his office each day, and seemed to take most of his midday meals at the Mermaid. Susan thought he must be a typical solicitor, looking over his spectacles at her and asking for minute details of every dish. 'Is the fish really fresh, my dear? I must be sure it is fresh before I order. And perhaps you could explain to me just what ingredients make up the hollandaise sauce? I must be careful what I eat, you know.'

Susan's education continued, with Mrs Thomson trying to emulate 'big house' cookery with the more modest resources of the Mermaid and without Mrs Sanderson becoming alarmed at the expense. It was interesting, it was something to focus on, and time spent in the kitchen was time safe from the attentions of George, who seemed to have forgotten their last encounter and had started to leer at her again.

'I'll not be able to show you pheasant or grouse unless we get lucky, but I'll ask the butcher – he might be able to lay his hands on a guinea fowl or two. They're tame birds, but quite like game. And that's another thing,' continued the cook, 'always remember to keep well in with the butcher. A butcher can make or break a cook.' Mermaid rule number three, thought Susan grimly.

One result of Susan's lessons was that diners began to notice the more varied menu and demand increased again, which pleased Mrs Sanderson, though you'd never think it from her face. 'That and better'll do,' she said sourly to Susan one evening in spring, after several guests had complimented the chef. From Maud, this was high praise. 'And you'd better stay in the kitchen, you're too slow in the bar, and not chirpy enough. No sense of humour, Violet says.'

Susan kept her eyes down. The jokes Violet told were not very funny, but the customers seemed to think they were hilarious, just because they were often rude.

Mrs Sanderson was still looking at her. 'So – we'll make you assistant cook.'

Thank goodness! Susan rushed off to tell Mrs Thomson, and they celebrated with a cup of the best coffee, from a pot sent back from the dining-room. Mr Jordan had decided it was too bitter, but they found it perfectly good. 'I think we must be beating the Black Bull,' Mrs Thomson said gleefully.

The spring and summer went slowly by, with just once a few days free so that the Woods could all visit the cottage. Together they whitewashed the walls, tidied the garden and chopped up fallen branches for firewood. 'It seems a long time since we lived here.' John looked round on the first evening and screwed up his face. 'I can hardly remember it!'

Susan looked at him. 'It's maybe a good job you don't remember ... it was hard, at times.'

'Do you remember Aunt Jane?' asked Ben mischievously.

'Course I do. I remember we had to mind our manners and do our schoolwork for her. And I remember Mrs Gill's lovely Fat Rascals, and Mr Gill, too – but he was a bit stern. He still is, you know. He comes to school sometimes and talks to the teachers about me,' replied John.

Ben disagreed. 'Never ... Mr Gill's straight, that's all. You wait till you're a bound apprentice. Then you'll find out what stern means!' He laughed. 'Mr Gill comes to see me too, and he tells me that I'm doing right well. But I'll be out of my time before too long and a printer in my own right.'

So Martin still kept an eye on the boys, that was nice for them, but for some reason it 'wasn't right' to keep in contact with Susan. Forget him ... 'Will you lose your job?' Susan asked. The boys' future was still a worry.

'Give over, Susie. You're like a broody hen, always clucking about our clothes and worrying about the future. The Lord will provide, as the vicar says.' Ben smiled reassuringly. 'Well, I'll lose the apprentice place, of course, they'll get a new one. But Mr

Smithson thinks there may be enough work to keep me on. In a few years, though, I'd like to start a business for myself.' He added lightly, 'But you need money for that.'

'What about you, Johnny?' It was easy to worry about John. He spoke the rather genteel English of the grammar school, whereas Ben had developed a Ripon accent. But after school, what then? People might think he sounded too refined for an ordinary job. But he was taller now and carried himself well; the fair hair was neatly cut and always well brushed. John should be able to make his way in the world. This must be just how a mother feels.

John grinned as he said, 'Well, I'll be finished with school before very long, and I wouldn't mind printing – I can spell quite well. Although I'd have loved to go to university, of course. To study architecture.' They were quiet for a while and then John said, 'I wonder whether Ben's master would take me on.' He turned to Ben. 'In your place, as apprentice?'

'I could ask him. You're right, Johnny, a trade is about the best any of us can hope for, with no money. Susie here, she's nearly a qualified cook, now – and that's a good job for a woman.'

It was late August, and the brief moorland summer would soon be over. From their garden, Susan caught the scent of heather flowers on the breeze. Suddenly she said, 'Well, I want to come back to live here, or somewhere near. I've had enough of the town.'

Ben shook his head. 'But folks with no brass have to live in the town, to find work.' He gestured towards the moorland. 'Who up here could employ us, except as farm servants? And that's heavy, rough work. We're doing better than that. It's not ideal, Susie, but Ripon's the place for the Woods, as far as I can see. There's nothing for us on the moor. P'raps we should sell the cottage, and try to buy a little house in town.' He was talking like William Darley.

'No! We can't sell the cottage. Because Father will come back here, it's all he has left. It is important to keep it at least until he comes out.' Toby Wood was not the only reason for wanting to keep the cottage, but it was the rational one. It was their one link with the old life, and with the country. And it wouldn't be worth much, anyway, not out here, miles from the village.

'All right, we'll see what Father says.' The Woods sat in silence in the garden for a while on the old stone bench. The peace was beautiful after the bustle of Ripon's streets. The last rays of the evening sun dropped down over the rim of the moor, leaving them in a greenish twilight. From the valley below they heard the hoot of an owl.

The other attachment to the cottage, to be honest, was the link with Martin Gill. He farmed Holly Bank nearby and even though he might not always be there, his presence was about the hillside.

'It's a grand place in the summer.' Ben spoke quietly. 'But in the frost and snow, it is different. You've got to remember that.'

Martin Gill was gathering in his corn harvest at the end of August, helped by a neighbouring farmer. As a young man he'd loved the long days of hard work and the satisfaction of seeing the neatly thatched stack of oats in the farmyard at the end. But Martin felt little enthusiasm now and although he went about his work as usual, it was no longer a joy. Perhaps this was middle age, then, when the shine seemed to go out of things.

David Slater, from the next farm over towards Dallagill, was in his twenties, strong, cheerful and ready to talk. 'What's up with you these days, lad?' he asked Martin one afternoon, when they had loaded a cart with sheaves of oats in silence for half an hour. 'You used to like a joke as well as anyone ... but you're that quiet, I thought that dog had died.' Martin's two sheep-dogs looked up and wagged their tails, as though to disprove the theory.

Martin laughed. 'When you get to my age, David, you'll see, as my father says. To be honest, I lost quite a few sheep in the snow last winter, it sets you back a bit. There's always something, bad weather or bad prices ... folks say that farmers are a dour lot, and I can feel it coming on.'

'Nay, Martin, it's over soon for you to be talking like an old man! Brighten yourself up a bit, get out more, that's what I would do.' David looked at him with real concern. 'My Alice says there's more to life than work and bed, although for most of the time that's about it for us as well. But I'll tell you what you need, lad, if you'll take my advice.'

Martin said nothing, but threw up the last sheaf, which the young farmer placed precisely and stuck his fork into the middle. 'That shouldn't move, load's safe. What you need is a good woman, a wife and a few bairns running round to keep you young. We were having a rare struggle with our first, until we found he thrived on goat's milk. But Alice and me have that much more interest in the farm, now that there's a young lad coming on.' Remembering that Martin's wife had died, he said quietly, 'You've got to get on with life, you know.'

The two men walked across the stubble beside the plodding carthorse, followed by a cloud of flies. Martin sighed rather wearily. 'I'm not sure that this is the place to bring a wife ... all hard work and no brass, you might say. And then, I'm getting older, over thirty now, it wouldn't be fair to shackle a young lass.'

As Martin backed the cart up to the half-formed stack in the yard, David looked on. 'A well set up farmer like you might get killed in the rush, if folks knew you were after a wife,' he said lightly. 'Young or old, there's plenty of women without a husband in the parish, if you know where to look for them. Unless you've your heart set on one that's out of reach, o' course. That's always a bad move.'

'Whoa, Prince, that's enough.' The horse stopped obediently

at Martin's command. 'Aye, well. Let's get on and unload.' That last comment was a little too near home.

Once she was back at the Mermaid, the visit to the cottage seemed to Susan like a beautiful dream. This was reality, in the hot kitchen with younger girls rushing in with orders. 'Two mutton chops, potatoes and peas and the gentleman's in a hurry!' Planned dinners for a group were fairly easy, but Susan and Mrs Thomson offered variety in the daily menu and they had to be ready to cook at very short notice. Market day on Thursday was especially busy.

William Darley had asked Susan out a few more times and once she had gone to drink tea and eat a cake in the little café across the square. William talked mainly about himself and his work and he laughed at Susan's preference for a country life. It was plain they would never be suited, quite apart from the fact that she didn't love him. When William invited her to meet his mother, Susan said very politely, 'I don't think so, William. I am too much of a country bumpkin for your family, and I really don't want to waste your time. You should be looking for someone more suitable.'

William looked rather surprised, but not much hurt. 'If you really think so ... that's a pity, I thought we were getting on quite well.' He laughed. 'Apart from the fact that you don't like me to kiss you too often, but that's just modesty, I think. You're a good girl, Susan.'

'You are a nice person, William. I hope you find a better girl than me.' William was calm and rational and Susan knew he was not in love. Perhaps that was the best way to choose a wife. You must be better off without the sadness of love, the ache that wouldn't go away.

One day towards the end of winter, the local paper was lying on the scrubbed kitchen table. During their tea break, Susan was turning the pages idly when Mrs Thomson looked at her sadly.

'Are you looking for a job in the paper? Aye well, I always said you should.'

Of course – why hadn't she thought of it before? People advertised for servants in the *Clarion* and she might find an advertisement for a cook. For weeks after that, she took the paper up to her room and searched the 'Situations Vacant' columns. There were a few cooks wanted every week, but always in Ripon or Harrogate. No country houses were advertising for servants.

Was it disloyal to Mrs Thomson, who had taught her so much? Susan would feel guilty if she let Cook down. Time went by, and then one day the cook brought up the subject again. 'I wouldn't blame you, lass, if you want to better yourself. Young Ruby is improving, she's never going to be as good as you, but if you go, we can manage.'

A scream made them both jump up and Ruby came in crying. 'It's Sam, in the bar ... he was mending the fire and the coals fell out and his hand is all burned.' The maid's freckled face was screwed up with anxiety.

Mrs Thomson threw her apron over her head and went into mild hysterics on the spot. Followed by Ruby, Susan went into the bar and made Sam put his hand under the water tap. Violet was nowhere to be seen. 'Peel a potato and grate it, quick!' Ruby scuttled off back to the kitchen. Soon the grateful Sam was much more comfortable, with grated raw potato and a clean towel wrapped round his hand.

'Now, you can go to the doctor,' Susan said firmly. 'It's quite a bad burn and I don't want to be responsible if it gets worse.'

'Thank you, Susan, I will. You're a grand lass, it feels better already.' And Sam went off to ask Mrs Sanderson if he could have an hour off to see the doctor.

When she got back to the kitchen, the chambermaids were there and all eyes were turned on Susan, the heroine. 'How did you know what to do? I never told you owt of that.' Mrs

Thomson was as impressed as any of them, admitting she panicked when there was an accident.

'Well, on a farm you have to be ready for emergencies,' Susan explained, feeling embarrassed.

It wasn't until the next day that Mrs Thomson remembered what she was going to say to Susan. 'I heard tell that Mr Jordan wants a cook ... that gent who pays the bill when the solicitors come to dine,' she said slowly. 'I don't want to lose you, lass, don't think I want to get rid of you. But Mr Jordan seems decent enough and he lives out of Ripon ... somewhere near Kirkby, I believe.'

'Do you think that I'd have a chance?' Susan asked. 'He once said how young I looked to be a cook.'

'Aye, but he's always praised your dinners and he's told Maud he enjoyed them, too. If you can make a list of what you've done, I'll tell you what to say – I'll give you a character, as I said before. You're a good worker, Susan, and you've a cool head. It is important in a kitchen not to panic when things go wrong.' Mrs Thomson smiled wryly. 'I can manage fine when the food goes wrong, but I can't abide injuries and such. You don't panic, lass and that should matter more than your size.'

In the blotched bedroom mirror it was quite clear to see that Susan hadn't grown very much. The strenuous operation of the beer pumps had added nothing at all to the size of her bust. It would probably take years of bar work to do that. Even the grey eyes looked young, peering through the fringe. It just wasn't fair.

For the next few days Susan rehearsed in her mind what she might say to Mr Jordan. He was a middle-aged bachelor, said Mrs Thomson, and he lived outside Kirkby on a farm. Everyone at the Mermaid knew he was very fussy about his food; he always scrutinized the menu carefully and asked many questions. Such a man could be hard to please, but on the other hand, Mrs Thomson pointed out that there would only be a small number to cook for.

'It would be a holiday compared to the Mermaid. No wife or children, just a housemaid or two and perhaps a housekeeper. Dead easy.'

Surely there would be other people there at times? 'But it's a farm as well, and that means more work for the kitchen. There's haytime and harvest, for a start, with hired men coming in and having to be fed. Not that I mind, of course. It would be lovely to be back in the country, especially in spring.'

To get out of Ripon, into the sweet fresh air was beginning to seem like an impossible dream. To some, of course, it was a lovely old city with its chiming cathedral bells and narrow, ancient streets. There were handsome buildings round the square, from where the streets sloped down on every side. Two rivers cradled the town and five minutes' walk along the river paths took you out into the fields. But to a homesick country person, Ripon was a prison, a tumult of noise and smells and flickering gaslight, and for an assistant cook there was very little time to take the river walks.

Mrs Thomson was keeping to the point. 'So, you need to write a good letter in a fair hand, I know you can do it. Say what your experience of cooking has been. Don't mention the cleaning and bar work, you want to be a cook. It's important to make the position clear.' And, she seemed to be saying, don't forget the social distinction given to a cook, a trained specialist. 'Let him know that you can plan meals and give directions to a scullery maid. You've got to be able to take charge.'

Taking charge was a terrifying thought to Susan.

CHAPTER NINE

Rather breathless, Susan looked up at the imposing wrought-iron gates of Ringbeck Hall. Taking the carrier's cart from Ripon was easy, but the last few miles from Kirkby village had been hot and dusty on a sunny spring day. It was harder to walk a few miles now than in the days when she lived in the country and it would be good to get used to walking again.

When Susan approached him as he sat digesting a good dinner at the Mermaid, Mr Andrew Jordan had seemed surprised. The solicitor had looked over his glasses at her when she mentioned that she would like to apply for the job as his cook and put a letter into his hands. The letter had been dictated and signed by Mrs Thomson and it contained a long list of skills and attributes, all of which the cook said were true and honest. It was good to hear that she'd been a quick learner, been trained by Mrs Thomson, and had the benefit of basic training in the kitchen of Ellen Gill from a young age. Mr Jordan might know the Gills, and could be impressed. At least it was evidence that she could cope with country life. And by now, she could take responsibility for a banquet, Mrs Thomson had said at the end.

'But you look so young! Are you sure you can manage a kitchen on your own, with all the associated ordering, organizing, supervising and so on, that the position will entail?' He managed to make the work sound very complicated.

Susan was sad to leave Mrs Thomson, but she wanted to get

away from the inn. She was by now desperate to get back to country life, after her years in the town. True, Ripon had its advantages; she had been able to borrow books from the library to read on her day off, and she could see her brothers quite often. But when the soft spring breezes blew the scent of blossom through the streets, or when the heather moors blazed with purple in the late summer, Susan had thought of all that she was missing.

'I suppose there are no laws against a small cook,' Mr Jordan said, with a slight smile to show he was being humorous. 'We would be doing nothing illegal. However, I must say that most cooks are much larger and considerably older than you are. It is of course a position of some responsibility and carries with it a certain standing in the community, of which you are no doubt aware. The position of cook in my household requires that you will be able to procure good quality ingredients for the dishes at a reasonable cost, negotiate with my gardener as to the availability of vegetables and fruit when planning your menus, provide forward menus for a week at a time and supervise a scullery maid in her duties. I expect my cook to make notes of the cost of the food in order that I may keep track of household expenses, and of course to work closely with my housekeeper.' He paused. Was he trying to discourage her?

'Yes, Mr Jordan. I can manage all that.'

'Of course, it goes without saying that the cook should be able to cook competently, and I will expect a standard as high as that which Mrs Sanderson achieves at the Mermaid. As you are no doubt aware, I am very interested in good quality food.' Mr Jordan leaned back complacently.

'You've been kind enough to praise my dinners, several times,' she reminded the solicitor quietly. 'And Mrs Thomson, our cook, has given me plenty of responsibility.' Susan was sure she could do the job. One household would mean far fewer meals than the

Mermaid's dining-room provided, on any day of the week. But on the other hand, here she had Mrs Thomson behind her, to bully the grocer and charm the butcher ... perhaps Mr Jordan's house-keeper would be a support.

After his colleagues had gone home, Mr Jordan had pulled up a chair and made Susan sit down at the table with him. She had decided, looking across at him, that he wasn't so old after all. He wore stiff collars and his horn-rimmed glasses aged him. When she looked carefully, she noticed that he had brown hair and the dark eyes behind the glasses held a wary sort of expression. Mr Jordan would never stand out in a crowd, but he looked safe enough. Susan didn't want to end up with another employer like George, but she felt that her experiences at the Mermaid had taught her to spot those types of men very quickly. Some of the clients were worse than George, with no Maud to restrain them. She now knew a few tricks herself and had managed not to injure any of the men too badly with her hatpin. But it was tiring to be on the defensive all the time. There were too many lonely men at the Mermaid, passing the time they should have been spending with a family.

Mr Jordan was different from most of the other solicitors, his colleagues. He was also a farmer and lived on his farm for most of the time, riding into Ripon for business on a horse that was stabled at the Mermaid.

At the end of this interview, Susan had been asked to visit the hall. 'I would like to see you at my residence for a further inter-view, if you please.'

There was much last-minute good advice from Mrs Thomson about how to talk respectfully at the interview; young girls these days were sometimes too forward, the cook said with a sniff. On the other hand, she must act the part of a qualified cook and not be afraid to say what she could do.

There was also an examination conducted over the washing up, during which Susan had to answer questions about managing a kitchen. How would she plan the menus and do the ordering? This would be with the approval of the employer, of course. 'It's easier when they know what they want,' said Mrs Thomson wisely. 'But men often don't have much idea. You have to guide them, make suggestions and tell them what's in season.'

And now, with fifty pieces of good advice buzzing around in her head, the day of the visit to the hall had come. All too mindful of her youth and inexperience, Susan pulled her shoulders back and took a deep breath. She would have to convince Mr Jordan that she was old enough and good enough for the job, and strong enough to take heavy pans off the stove. Away from the familiar surroundings of the Mermaid, it was so easy to feel nervous.

The old stone house was beautiful, weathered by several centuries and partly covered in ivy. It looked peaceful enough on this sunny afternoon. There was the scent of spring blossoms as she passed the orchard, and the twittering of nesting birds. How good it would be to get back to the country! There would be drawbacks to every job, but it would be worth a lot to be back on the High Side, a part of the changing seasons.

The doorbell clanged importantly when she touched it and soon Susan was let in by a sour-faced woman in black, with a high, prominent bosom and an elevated nose. 'Wait here.' Perhaps she should have gone to the back door, the servants' entrance. The woman came back, still with her nose in the air, and motioned Susan to follow her. Through a panelled hall they went into a large, rather untidy office lined with bookshelves.

Jordan sat behind a mahogany desk and indicated a chair oppo-site. 'Please sit down.' He looked benign, but rather impersonal.

Why did she want the job? 'I love to cook. I really like working with Mrs Thomson and I'll be sorry to leave her. But I'd like to get back to the country, sir. And that's why I would like to work at Ringbeck Hall.'

Andrew Jordan looked at her carefully. 'And how did you get the position at the Mermaid? What did you tell Mrs Sanderson to influence her to take you on, some time ago, I gather? You would have been even younger and smaller than you are now.' He looked down at her critically.

She blushed. 'Well ... I said I could cure a ham and treat sheep's feet.' It was important to tell the truth. 'They took me on as a chambermaid, but I ended up in the kitchen. It's much more interesting.'

A faint smile flickered over Jordan's face. 'I asked Mrs Sanderson, of course, and she was quite resigned to your leaving. Girls often leave, she said. She had nothing bad to report about you and she said you worked well, but were rather shy and had little confidence. Now, you must understand that confidence will be required for this position. As I intimated to you previously, much responsibility attaches to the position of cook at the hall. You will be aware that this is a residence of some note and also a large farm, with seasonal requirements of a culinary nature. In other words, you will have to cook for the labourers at certain times of the year.' He steepled his hands and looked over the big desk at her. 'And why here, in particular? One would naturally expect a young woman to prefer a position in town, or at least in a village. Ringbeck is comparatively isolated.'

'I once lived in the area, and I love the edge of the moorland ... it feels as though I belong.'

'Where exactly did you live?' He might have been in court, examining a witness.

'Ashtree Cottage; not far from here, near the Larton Road end.'

Jordan looked uncomfortable. There was a moment's silence and then he said, 'Good gracious. I was not aware that you were Toby Wood's daughter. I had no idea, indeed I had not.'

Here it was coming back once more, the disgrace of having a

father in jail. No one at the Mermaid had connected her with the supposed criminal Toby Wood. But of course, Mr Jordan was a solicitor and would know such things. Oh, dear ... this was a bad start and it might be the end of it. The solicitor was looking shocked.

Papa was another reason why it was important to get back to Kirkby. He was due to come out of prison soon and he would look for his children at the cottage. She hadn't told him about working at an inn.

'You – knew my father?' Her voice sounded faint, even to herself.

'I think I ought to tell you that I defended Toby Wood at his trial,' said Jordan quietly. 'He was misguided, of course, but I always found him a very pleasant fellow, your father. Unfortunately we were doomed from the start, you understand. There was no possibility of exonerating him from the blame, although I did my best on technicalities. You may know the details, although I suppose you would have been quite young at the time. He may not have wanted his family to know the truth. And then his wife died ... most unfortunate.' He shook his head gravely. 'I knew there were children, but assumed they were being looked after.' The tone was indifferent.

This was devastating. 'You mean – he did it?' The Woods had always told each other that their father was innocent. 'No ... we don't know the details. But Papa said he was innocent.' Susan felt herself shivering.

Jordan put on a sad face. 'He was probably trying to protect you. I am afraid that unfortunately, he was guilty. It was too tempting, when the engraver showed him what they could do. They became very good forgers and were only found out when the paper supplier became suspicious. But,' and he changed his tone, 'that is behind him now, and Wood will have to start again. He has paid his due to society.'

This was shocking – how could she tell the boys? Toby's children had consoled themselves, all these years, with the thought that their father was locked up for a crime he didn't commit. It was unjust, but they could accept it. Guilt was another matter entirely. Susan felt faint; she was the daughter of a criminal!

No wonder the Gills had taken the children to church, and lectured them about lying, if they'd suspected this. The mythical Aunt Jane had been keen on manners and education, but the Gills had emphasized morals and the right way to live. Growing up, the Wood children had absorbed those values and this made Toby's guilt even harder to bear. But Martin hadn't condemned her father. 'It's not for me to judge,' he'd said.

Susan realized that Mr Jordan was talking to her. 'Have you any idea what he plans to do, when the period of incarceration is over?'

Susan hadn't. Toby had said he wouldn't write to them, he didn't want to drag them down. They'd heard from him every Christmas, that was all, a conventional letter with nothing about his future plans. She sat up straight, as instructed by Aunt Jane. 'Mr Jordan, are you willing to give me a job, when you know who my father is?' This was the stumbling block she'd always dreaded. How could they rise above the disgrace – now or in the future? It would be a cloud for the rest of their lives; the boys, too, would feel it. At the Mermaid, she'd been anonymous, just part of the staff. But in the country, people were curious about where you came from, who your parents were.

Looking straight at Jordan, Susan saw the man's calculating expression. He paused importantly and then said, 'I will set aside your parentage for the present and give you the opportunity to prove yourself honest and trustworthy. I need a cook rather urgently, and besides, it is probably my civic duty to support the children of criminals where I can, and where there is relatively little risk to society.'

Biting back her anger was difficult, worse even than keeping calm at the Mermaid. 'Thank you, Mr Jordan.' It was best to agree with the pompous little man and to put up with being patronized. It would take time to get over the shock of Papa's guilt ... if indeed it were true. It was hard to believe, but how could Mr Jordan be wrong?

Jordan was rambling on again. 'My dear mother died some months ago, a sad loss as you will understand. So now there is no one to play her piano and no lady of the house ... I should explain that I am not married, there is no mistress of the hall; the house-keeper performs that duty.' He paused again as if thinking and Susan waited. 'Well, Miss Wood, as I said I am willing to take the risk and employ you, for the time being. I sincerely hope that you will not betray my trust. It is always difficult for the children of criminals to be accepted and you will be no different. Life will not be easy for you, but I am willing to put aside the stigma attached to your father, provided that you remain honest while in my employment.'

I think you said all that before, Mr Jordan, Susan wanted to say. Children of criminals! Was it possible that he was mistaken? Papa had never seemed like a criminal; he had led a perfectly respectable life until he went to jail.

Mr Jordan gave a sigh. 'But let us get back to business. We mainly need a cook for the household, of course. I have not entertained a great deal since my mother passed away. But I am the host for weekly card parties, which is my form of social interaction with the neighbours. Once a week I require a light supper for the guests and I like to give them something different every week.'

'Very good, Mr Jordan.' It was hard to concentrate on the duties, after the shock he had just given her. Would her father want her to work for the man who had failed to keep him out of jail?

'However,' the solicitor went on, 'I give an occasional dinner party for a larger group, consisting of the better families in the district, people with some standing in the community. As it happens, I have to tell you that it will be necessary to give a dinner party soon, to persuade a group of local families to support one of my charities. No doubt you would be capable of providing dinner for about fifteen guests?'

This was frightening, but Susan sat up straighter. She would meet the challenge of the 'better families' when it came. 'Yes, sir.' When it came to the push, she had more confidence than Mrs Sanderson gave her credit for.

'And then, there are the Queen's Jubilee celebrations in June, the hall is to supply refreshments for the small farmers and labourers and so forth, so that the lower orders can be involved. That can be discussed at a later date. For the moment, let us go to the kitchen and meet the rest of my servants.'

The hall staff members were drinking tea in the kitchen. Susan looked round carefully, but there was no George type of person in sight. The sour woman who had let her in stood up deferentially, but Jordan motioned her to sit down.

Apart from Mrs Bain, as Jordan called her, there were two younger women at the table, and a young lad about Ben's age. He was Robbie and the girls were Daisy and Hannah. The women all wore curious, closed expressions. Only Robbie looked open and pleasant; he gave her a smile.

Apart from the strained atmosphere, the kitchen was better than she'd expected. The red tiled floor made it look homely, there was a magnificent coal cooking range and the big scrubbed table in the middle was just the right height. Pots of cheerful geraniums lined the windowsill.

'The last cook left rather suddenly,' remarked Mr Jordan into the silence. Susan nodded. 'And Mrs Bain has done her best to fill the gap, but she has too many other duties. Mrs Bain is the house-keeper, you will understand.' The woman smirked.

A tour of the main rooms followed. The rooms were large and well furnished, but there was a melancholy feeling about them. The dining-room was almost oppressive; the vast mahogany sideboard bristled with silver, but the room was muted by the dark red of the velvet curtains, and the heavy William Morris wallpaper. Perhaps the house needed children, young people, to bring the rooms to life. The old, highly polished furniture in the main rooms and the drawing-room with its grand piano was impressive. This house must have been in the Jordan family for generations.

Mr Jordan suggested a six-month contract, after which they could 'review the situation', as he put it, which was all very businesslike. The solicitor went back into his office, leaving Susan with the housekeeper. She was shown a room in the attic that had belonged to the previous cook. It was a typical servant's bedroom with a pine chest of drawers, a narrow iron bedstead and a marble-topped washstand. But the room was sunny and pleasant enough and from the open window she could see the rolling lines of the moor above Kirkby, the moor she had dreamed about since she'd left the cottage.

Susan leaned out of the window, breathing the pure moorland air. It was so good to be back! Then she realized that Mrs Bain was waiting for her with a hint of impatience. 'Young lasses like you don't stay long at Ringbeck.' The housekeeper spoke indifferently with her back to Susan, moving towards the door. 'They want to get back to town. There's not enough company here, no young men.' She turned and looked Susan up and down with a faint sneer, and the girl felt very conscious of her small size and rather shabby dress.

'I like to live in the country,' Susan said quietly. 'I think I'll enjoy working here.' Mr Jordan was likely to be a reasonable employer, if a little fussy and inclined to use a lot of words; and anything was better than George.

Mrs Bain laughed mirthlessly. 'Of course, the other reason they leave, like Cook did, is one that Sir wouldn't tell you about.' She smoothed her black dress, stuck out her bosom and looked away.

This might be some sort of test. 'And are you going to tell me what it is?' Susan looked the woman firmly in the eye. She was no longer a shy young girl, she was a cook, and able to stand up to people like this.

'Aye, but you might not like it. Ringbeck Hall is haunted, you see. It's a fact. Folks have seen her ... we think it's the late Mrs Jordan ... she walks about the house at night, looking for something, ever since she died.' The woman shuddered as she spoke. 'I'm leaving myself, as soon as I find a new place.' She rolled her black eyes expressively.

Susan shrugged, and they went downstairs. It seemed best not to show any emotion; this could be a practical joke, a silly idea to frighten the new cook. But why such hostility? It was disappointing to find no motherly, Mrs Thomson-like figure at the hall. The cook would be on her own here.

The idea of a ghost was not too frightening. Susan and the boys had walked the country lanes in the dark, living serenely in their isolated cottage. They had discussed ghosts and decided not to believe in them. It was quite simple and saved a lot of trouble. When John was little, in their first days at the cottage, he'd heard strange sounds at night that scared him. But there had always been a rational explanation and Susan had been careful to find it. The sound might be the bark of a fox, the hoot of an owl, or tree branches rubbing together in the wind. There might be spirits in the world, but the Wood children were not going to worry about them.

Once, Susan remembered, she'd heard John in the woodshed, collecting firewood on a wintry night. 'I know you think you're there, ghost.' John went on picking up the wood as he spoke. 'But we don't believe in you, so you'd better go away.' And yet ... Aunt Jane had almost seemed real to them, hasn't she? It had felt as though there was an elderly presence in their house.

After the interview was over, Susan intended to spend the night at their cottage and go back to Ripon with the carrier the next day. She would need to give notice at the Mermaid, for as long as it took them to find another girl. She was dreading her return to the cottage; she had only been back a few times since they left and not once during the past winter. The place would be cold and damp, the garden would be a wilderness, she knew. And – would there be ghosts, after all?

As she strode along in the spring dusk on the familiar road, Susan's mind was crowded with memories. There were lambs playing in the fields, but a cold breeze ruffled their coats. She went down the steep lane and there was the garden, spread out below.

Instead of a wilderness, it was neatly mowed. The vegetables had gone of course, but the grass in their place was short and the trees and bushes looked as though they had been pruned. Someone had put chicken wire over the herb garden and the sage and rosemary bushes were still there. She smiled at that and looked closely at the ground. Sheep had been here, keeping her garden tidy. Moorland sheep were always looking for the next bite, in spring.

Relieved, Susan felt for the key in its accustomed hiding place in the privy and opened the door. Here was another surprise; the house was cold, but it felt quite dry. Paper and sticks were laid ready on the hearth, there were logs in a basket. The floor was clean and the furniture had been recently dusted. Well, sheep can't do housework, Susan thought wryly. Who has been in here? She lit the fire, but not before she looked at the papers in the hearth. And there was an old envelope, addressed to Mr Martin Gill. As the fire flared up, she said to the flames, 'Thank you, Mr Gill.' A strange man – he couldn't come to see her, but he took good care of the cottage, knowing she would visit one day.

As dusk fell, Susan ate the bread and cheese she'd brought with her and felt the peace of the cottage seeping into her slowly, draining away the tension of the day. In the old house it was natural to remember the past; and how happy they had been for those years when they lived and worked there. Protected by the Gills, the Wood boys had gone to school and Susan herself had learned housecraft and much more, from Ellen Gill. They'd always be grateful. Without Martin and Ellen, Susan and her brothers would certainly have ended up in the workhouse. But now she realized just how much they owed to the couple; not just food, not even their independence. The Gills had given them peace of mind, and happiness.

Would there ever be peace of mind again, now that she knew her father was guilty? Susan looked into the fire and wondered whether they would ever be free from the past. Rosemary for remembrance … happy memories, but also the terrible shock of losing Mama, Papa going to jail. It was going to make life difficult for them all. How could they tell Martin Gill?

CHAPTER TEN

'Cook, I wish to discuss the dinner party for next week ... you will come into the office, please. Naturally, I would wish for as much home-produced food as possible and perhaps you can advise me as to what is in season this month.' Mr Jordan looked serious. This was the first real challenge; Susan smoothed her apron and sat on the edge of a chair.

The first few weeks at the hall had been uneventful, apart from the loneliness. The other servants were not friendly at all and to her surprise Susan missed the cheerful bustle of the Mermaid, although not the tobacco smoke and the pervading smell of beer.

'How many people, and what would you like to eat? The early lambs should be about ready, I think. There's not much fruit in the garden except gooseberries.'

Jordan provided paper and pencil and together they planned a menu for fifteen people. Julienne soup, fish and lamb; he would arrange for the farm manager to have a lamb killed. 'You will need to tell Robbie to clean the silver, and I will see Mrs Bain about turning out the dining-room. It is quite a while since we had dinner guests and I wish to make a good impression. And of course you will ensure that the food is of the best quality and absolutely fresh, served and arranged professionally, and hot ...' He went on for some time.

Mrs Bain, when told about the dinner party, was obviously unimpressed. 'I suppose Mr Jordan expects great things. Well,

I'm sure I hope he won't be sadly disappointed.' She looked as though she rather hoped he would. The corners of her mouth turned down as she sneered. 'Have you any experience of cooking for superior folk? Your public house food won't answer here, you know. They won't be happy to sit down to tripe and onions in our dining-room.' She looked round at the long dining table. Mrs Bain quite frequently mentioned that Cook had previously worked at the Mermaid, which she tried to describe as a low sort of place.

'Mr Jordan has agreed the menu. He has requested soup à la Julienne, as a matter of fact. I don't think it will be a problem.' So there, you horrible woman, and I can speak French, too. The soup will be fine, but the fish course – that will rely on Mr Jordan to remember to buy some good fresh fish and bring it home with him. Stale fish could ruin the meal. It was more difficult to plan menus in the country, but already she had discovered that the local produce was usually excellent. Mr Jordan expected a costing on everything, even the food from his garden, because he wanted to see that the gardener earned his wages.

'And I don't suppose you'll even know how to lay a table properly for dinner,' was the housekeeper's parting shot as she posed in the doorway, head back and bosom thrust out.

'Isn't that your job?' Cooks were in charge of the kitchen. There wasn't going to be much help from Mrs Bain, that was clear.

Mrs Bain spent any spare time she had in the housekeeper's room and so did the two maids, although the maids were kept busy. They all took their meals in the kitchen, disappearing as soon as the washing up was over. They said very little to the new cook, and so mealtimes were silent affairs.

Mrs Bain's day off was always Thursday, so that she could go to Ripon with the carrier to see her old mother, she said. The Kirkby carrier plodded down to Ripon every market day, driving a wagonette drawn by two horses, pulling the farmers' wives to market with their baskets of eggs and butter.

One Thursday after lunch, Susan invited the younger maid, Daisy, to come into the kitchen garden with her. She needed to talk to Mr Hart, the elderly gardener about the dinner party, and hoped to gather gooseberries. It was time, too, to get to know the younger girls.

Daisy pushed back her dark hair under the cap, twisted her hands and looked uncomfortable. 'Nay, Mrs Bain said I was to keep polishing and if I finish that I have to sew in her room. I'm not to talk to you.' She looked down at her shoes. 'I'm right sorry, Miss Wood.'

It was hard not to laugh. 'Poor Daisy! How old are you – fifteen? Well, you have to do as you're told, no doubt. But why are you not allowed to talk to me? When I was your age …' Heavens, how old I sound. 'I learned how to cook from talking to cooks and working with them. You could do the same thing, if you've a mind.'

Daisy looked frightened. 'Mrs Bain said that Hannah and me was to keep away from you, because you're a bad woman. But – we don't think you're bad.' The girl's hand went over her mouth and her face grew red. 'I shouldn't have said …'

A cold shiver went down Susan's back … 'Now, what can be bad about me?'

'Oh Miss Wood, I don't like to say … but Mrs Bain says as you was entertaining men at the Mermaid, like … selling yourself … and your Pa's a bad man, he's in prison!'

Just for a moment she felt faint, until the shock wore off a little. 'Now, Daisy, you are old enough to judge for yourself. Make your own mind up. If you'd like to come into the garden for a few minutes, I am sure nobody will object. It's a lovely day.' She ushered the embarrassed girl though the back door, giving her a wicker basket.

The maid trailed unwillingly behind Susan, but once in the sunshine she appeared to settle down. They walked on clean brick paths between the neat rows of vegetables, spoke to Mr Hart and were shown some spinach grown under glass to gather for the evening meal. Susan loved the kitchen garden and went there every day. The scent of herbs was somehow soothing, reminding her of her little cottage a few miles away where the bees would be busy in the apple blossom at that very moment.

Things seemed almost normal. When they got back to the kitchen the kettle was boiling for the afternoon cup of tea. Before the others came in Susan said gently, 'Daisy, I would like you to know that I was a cook at the Mermaid. Sometimes I played the piano for parties ... but nothing worse than that. Now, does that make you feel better?' It was better not to mention Father.

The young girl nodded and poured the tea. 'Sorry I said owt, but Mrs Bain's that strict, we'll lose our place, Hannah and me, if we don't do as she says.'

'Well, you can talk to me on Thursdays, why not?' This might sound underhand, but the young girls seemed to need some influence other than that of Mrs Bain. 'I'll think of jobs you can help me with on her day off. She can't very well refuse to let you help.'

Mrs Bain came back from Ripon looking pleased with herself and the maids seemed relieved. They were the first to suffer when she was not pleased, which happened often. It was even more of an effort to be pleasant to the housekeeper after what Daisy had told her, but Susan would bide her time. The evening meal in the kitchen was slightly less frigid than usual; the cold mutton and mashed potatoes were polished off with no adverse comment from Mrs Bain. Robbie in particular seemed to like the food Susan cooked, and always thanked her politely after a meal.

Hannah, the other maid, was older than Daisy and seemed quite sensible. As they cleared the table after Mrs Bain's departure for her room, Susan asked Hannah about her family and discovered that her mother ran the village shop in Kirkby. After a few minutes, Hannah talked quite freely; they seemed to be making progress. 'If Mrs Bain allows, you can both help me with the dinner party. Would you like that?'

Hannah grinned and said she would. 'Are we going to do ever so many courses, Miss Wood?'

They were. The guests, whether they realized it or not, would actually be paying for their dinner, by the donations to be extracted from them. Mr Jordan had selected for invitation the families most likely to contribute to his charity, which delivered coals in winter to old people in the parish, as well as other good works. He had decided that a good dinner was the best introduction to the subject of charity to the poor, provided that it didn't cost too much; he seemed to be very careful with his own money.

'Mr Jordan likes an old-fashioned bill of fare, so we'll have soup to start of course, then fish, then the main course of lamb. After that, I'm not sure whether he'll want another savoury course before the puddings, and dessert.'

Hannah looked amazed. 'How can folks eat so much? My ma used to be in service and she's told me about the grand dinners, but I can't see how they get it all down!'

Susan laughed. 'I used to think the same at first, at the Mermaid. But some of the dinners we provided lasted all evening. The guests had a rest between courses and sometimes there were speeches. They drank wine too, people such as the solicitors. Mr Jordan says that gives you an appetite.'

Puddings! There was a lot of work in puddings. Mr Jordan wanted plenty of choice, so they had agreed on gooseberry tart, cabinet pudding, blancmange and vanilla cream. If they wanted to learn, the maids would gain some useful experience. They would also need to be trained to wait at table in a professional way.

It felt good to slip between the cool linen sheets that night, and she tried not to think about the dinner party to come. Sleep came quickly. If only Mrs Bain could be more pleasant, life at the hall could be quite enjoyable.

There came a strange sound, just on the edge of Susan's hearing. She held her breath and listened ... It came again: a faint moaning, almost a wail. Someone must be in trouble.

The door opened without a sound and Susan's bare feet padded silently down the attic corridor. There was the cry again, coming it seemed from the next landing below, more ghostly than human.

No, it's not a ghost, Susan persuaded herself. I don't believe in ghosts, in spite of Mrs Bain's warning and I am not scared to go down the stairs. Susan drew her shawl closer and went down.

At the end of the panelled corridor there was a vague shape and a greenish light. The light appeared to pass slowly along, then it hovered outside one of the heavy oak doors. It was the door to Mrs Jordan's room. What was it that Bain had said? 'We think it's Mrs Jordan ...' The light moved across the door several times and then receded, growing fainter as it moved away with a last desolate wail in the distance, eerily supernatural.

Perhaps she should have run after the light, but Susan couldn't move and she felt a shiver run down her back.

The corridor was draughty. In this gloomy old house at dead of night, was it possible that spirits could walk? There were so many stories about ghosts ... some of them might be true. There was even supposed to be a ghost at the Mermaid; one of the maids told Mrs Thomson about seeing a ghostly shape by her bed. She'd left the inn soon afterwards. The other girls had grimly joked that it could have been George ... poor girl, if she'd been frightened like this.

How could familiar, ordinary candlelight be green? Was it truly a ghost? There must be a rational explanation, just as Susan had always told the boys. Unless ... unless she was wrong, and the people who said they'd seen or heard the supernatural were right.

Spiritualism was very popular after all and there was even a group of people in Ripon who believed that they communicated with the spirits of the dead through a medium who lived somewhere behind the cathedral. What if they were right? Susan went back to bed on cold feet and drew the bedclothes over her head.

The next morning Susan made the breakfast rolls as usual, saying nothing about the strange event of the night. She decided as she kneaded the dough that the less said the better. If it were a hoax, better to ignore it. If a ghost had really walked it would only alarm the maids to hear about it. When the bell rang, Susan took Mr Jordan's breakfast into the morning room to find him reading a book as usual, as he drank his coffee. She put the heavy plate of ham and eggs in front of him.

'Good morning, Cook.' It was her job to wait on him in the mornings, since the maids were busy making the beds and cleaning. He was always polite and this morning was no different. Mr Jordan didn't look like a man who had seen a ghost.

Susan was leaving the room when her employer called her back. 'Everything is in order for the dinner party on Saturday? Good, good. Then I have another task for the kitchen. A workers' midday dinner will be required, because I have arranged that the shearers will be here tomorrow. I have engaged a gang of men to shear the sheep and our temporary farm manager will supervise.' He looked at her over his coffee cup as he took a sip and Susan stood still. How many men would there be? 'I do not believe that you have met the workers on the farm. I suppose you would normally require more notice, but the shearing depends on fine weather and so we have to get them in when we can, of course. But you will no doubt understand. We were lucky to obtain the services of the shearers at such short notice.'

Susan nodded. 'I know about shearing. It's hungry work, they'll need plenty of food.'

'There will be about eight men in all and as you say, they will require a hearty midday meal, as well as morning and afternoon tea breaks. I can send the groom to the village for supplies, if you need anything extra, always bearing in mind the cost, of course.'

Of course. A little more notice for the kitchen would have been a good thing, but it was too late to worry about that. 'Yes, sir, we can manage, except for meat. If the Kirkby butcher has fresh beef, we can give them beef stew and carrots. I'll bake some more bread and plenty of scones. May I have the two maids to help me, please?' This was artful, but it would also help to ease the load.

Jordan looked relieved. 'The men need feeding well. Perhaps you could make them one of your excellent steamed puddings? That would be appreciated, I am sure and it will be inexpensive and filling. You may inform Mrs Bain that the girls are to help you. It will give them practice for the dinner party.' He turned his attention to the food.

Mrs Bain shrugged when Susan asked for the girls. 'As you like. Er – did you hear anything strange last night?' She looked keenly at the cook.

'I'm a heavy sleeper. Now, Mrs Bain, where do you think the shearers should eat? What do you usually arrange?' It was an effort to speak normally; the thought of that unearthly light was unnerving. But Mrs Bain must know something, or have heard something last night. It was an uncomfortable thought.

It seemed that the farm men hired for shearing and harvest ate off trestle tables, out of doors if the weather was warm, or more usually in the barn. Susan sent the maids out to put cloths on the tables the next morning, following a little later to see whether there were enough benches to sit on. There was a cool breeze coming down from the moor, too keen to allow an outdoor meal. The poor sheep would feel that breeze, once they lost their fleeces.

In the barn the shearers were already at work. Each man had a pair of large clipping shears in one hand and a fairly unwilling ewe held down by the other. There was the acrid smell of sheep in the air. The men had their jackets off, although the morning was cold. As the shears moved slowly and rhythmically the wool seemed to roll off the sheep's back, piling up on the grease-polished boards of the shearing floor like foam. The familiar farming sounds and smells took Susan back in time to when she was at Holly Bank, being shown how to wrap up the fleeces by Mr Gill. She remembered how his big, strong hands had moved so deftly, sorting the wool. But it was time to get back to the kitchen; an early start meant that the shearers would soon be ready for their mid-morning tea.

In the doorway of the barn Mr Jordan, tapping his riding crop imperiously against his boots, was talking to a man who must be the farm manager. 'We should be able to manage them all in one day,' the manager was saying. He had his back turned, but the deep voice was familiar. It was Martin Gill.

'Do you know our cook, Susan Wood?' Mr Jordan said with his usual rather fussy manner, as she walked past them. 'No doubt you will be aware that Miss Wood is arranging meals for the men. The tables are set up ready and it's expected that you will join them for dinner. Miss Wood, this is Mr Gill from Holly Bank. He is at present managing the farm for me.' He'd evidently forgotten his cook's employment history, but this was no time to remind him.

'Thank you, Mr Jordan. Good day, Miss Wood,' the deep voice said quietly. Martin didn't quite look at her. 'Well, I'd best get the next batch of sheep in. We've a lot to get through today.'

Martin Gill from Holly Bank – but somehow, it wasn't the same man. He seemed remote, indifferent. It was a pity he'd seen her out walking with William. But why should that affect anything? Perhaps it hadn't; Martin had told her it wasn't possible for them to be friends and she wouldn't embarrass him here by claiming acquaintance.

It would be good to be free, to put the past behind her, to make new friends and move on with life; but William wasn't the answer. They had said goodbye with no regrets when she left Ripon. He was town and she was country, and they'd never have been happy together.

After that moment, there was no time for thinking about Martin, or anything else except the job in hand. Hannah, the older maid, pushed her ginger hair under the cap, rolled up her sleeves and 'got stuck in', as she said, to peeling a mountain of potatoes. 'It's grand having all these folks about!' Young men was probably what she meant, but Hannah was a great help to Susan that day. At ten o'clock they served out big cups of scalding hot tea from an enormous teapot with the locally famous Fat Rascals that Ellen had taught Susan to make, rich scones consisting of lard and currants with some flour to hold them together. The younger shearers teased the maids and laughed, while Daisy and Hannah blushed and smiled.

Mrs Bain graciously decided to help with the trays and when Susan went out the housekeeper was deep in talk with the farm manager. Unusually for her, Mrs Bain was smiling and animated, looking up at Martin and she seemed to be posing in a tight dress that revealed her full figure. She saw Susan watching her and flashed a triumphant look over her shoulder. 'See you at dinner time, Mr Gill,' she said as he moved away.

All too soon for the aching backs, the mid-morning break was over. The shearers sighed, stretched and went back to bring in the next batch of sheep. By then it was time for the kitchen team to start cooking the dinner. They peeled and chopped and stirred and stewed. A huge pot of beef steak and onions had been simmering on the hob from early morning, gradually growing tender with time. After a couple of hours carrots and celery were added for flavour, just as they'd done at the Mermaid. Fortunately, Mrs Bain was too busy to help in the kitchen, but she reappeared when the meal was served and made sure that it was she who dished out the large platefuls of stew and mashed potato, graciously receiving the men's thanks.

Martin Gill looked rather uncomfortable as Mrs Bain sat down next to him and leaned forward confidentially revealing an expanse of bosom, to ask about the improvements he had made on the hall farm. 'I am so interested in sheep! I believe you are an expert sheep breeder, Mr Gill. Perhaps you can explain to me why the Masham is superior to the Swaledale?' It was hard for Susan not to giggle, standing nearby with the steamed puddings.

The housekeeper would be about the same age as Martin. And she too was single, the 'Mrs' was a courtesy title. Although she usually wore a sour expression, there was an earthy, female quality about Mrs Bain that might attract a man. Should he be warned that she was a spiteful, mean woman? A lonely man like Martin Gill could easily be taken in by a woman like this who had ambitions to be a farmer's wife.

Martin came into the kitchen as the maids were talking over the day. 'I just thought I'd thank you lasses for the food, it was very good and the lads were pleased. Best grub they've had for weeks, they said. They go to Potters tomorrow and that's always a good meat house, but they'll have a job to beat Ringbeck Hall.' At least he knew who had done all the work.

Martin looked round at Hannah and Daisy with a smile, then at Susan herself more gravely. Surely she could have a brief word with him? 'I'll just check that we brought all the dishes in.' Susan made for the door and Martin opened it for her.

They walked in silence to the barn, which was full of the smell of new wool wafting from the pile of fleeces. Susan picked up a jug while Martin moved as if to go. 'I am glad to see you doing well, Susan, with a good job. I'd best be going.' He looked down at her in the twilight and there was no emotion in his expression. 'You've got a young man too, I saw you with William Darley.

They're a good family ... if you like him, you'll do all right with
the Darleys.'

'Oh, he's not ...' How wrong he was, if he only knew.

Martin went on: 'I've taken the manager's job here for a while,
but you won't need to see much of me. The farm and the house
are quite separate.' He sounded remote. One of the hall farm
labourers came up to him and he seemed to turn away with relief.
'Yes, Jim, move the bullocks into the nine acre.'

Turning herself to go back to the kitchen Susan found Mrs
Bain standing behind a door, straining to hear what they said.
Why was she so interested?

The next morning at breakfast, Mrs Bain smiled complacently.
'I am to visit Holly Bank, to see Mr Gill's sheep. He is such an
interesting man! Did you know that he won a championship cup
at Kirkby show last year, for one of his rams? Mr Jordan is so
fortunate to have Mr Gill to manage the farm.' She looked
triumphantly at Susan, as if challenging her.

The woman had obviously known who Susan was, she had told
the maids about Papa, so she probably knew that she'd worked
for the Gills at Holly Bank. Mrs Bain must think that it would
annoy Susan to talk about Martin.

'I am sure you're right.' The best place to escape was the
garden; plants always had a soothing effect. Rosemary spikes lined
the paths, yielding up their fragrance, taking her back in memory
to happier days.

CHAPTER ELEVEN

'You've got to shine for a dinner party.' That was the rule. Susan got up at five o'clock on the morning of the hall party, when the first cuckoos began to call; it was important to make sure they could get through the work in time.

Mrs Bain had been called to the bedside of her sick mother the day before and was not available to help, but this was a relief, in a way. Mrs Bain might have contrived to hinder rather than help and without the housekeeper's disapproving frown, the young maids would probably work better. No doubt she would be back by evening, but by then everything would be ready.

Mrs Thomson had been most particular about dinner parties. 'You've got to shine for a dinner party.' The Mermaid cook had looked over the top of her glasses severely at her apprentice. 'If you give the family good meals all the year and then something goes wrong for a dinner party, that's the one they'll remember. They're on show, you see. Showing off a little bit to their friends, their nice house and beautiful silver. And of course they have to have an excellent cook, one that the neighbours envy.'

These thoughts were just a little alarming; for the first time at the hall, Susan's performance was to be measured not just by Mr Jordan, who was fussy enough, but by his beady-eyed neighbours. The card parties didn't count; they were informal and for them, Cook was only expected to provide light dishes such as anchovies on toast. The guests concentrated more on the play than the food and once or twice, Susan had suspected that the extreme tension meant they were playing for high stakes.

Right from the start, Mrs Bain had provided considerable practice in being surveyed by beady eyes. She was always watching Susan, always quick to pounce, but the cook had managed to stay one step in front of the housekeeper so far. If an egg broke in the pan or the toast was a little too dark, it never ended up on the housekeeper's plate. It was a sort of game, watched from the sidelines by the apprehensive maids.

'Don't try anything ambitious for a party, unless you've had plenty of practice at it.' That was another helpful hint. You could fill a book with Mrs Thomson's hints, quite apart from the recipes. Like Mrs Beeton, she had an opinion on everything to do with household management.

The party wouldn't be too ambitious. Susan was well qualified to be a Big House cook, with plenty of responsibility. Only recently she'd realized that her early schooling in Harrogate had given her the advantage of good English; nobody would guess from her speech that she came from the country, and she read and wrote well, thanks to 'Aunt Jane'. The struggle at the cottage before they met the Gills had developed a toughness that was usually hidden, but it meant that when needed she could stand up to men like George, and to the Violets and Mrs Bains of the world, thank goodness. Mrs Bain underestimated the new cook; she hadn't worked out that the rose, although small and insignificant, had thorns.

Responsibility for her young brothers had robbed Susan of some of her childhood, but it had made her careful; she was the one who locked the door and damped down the fire at night. A firm character was necessary in a cook, because as Susan was finding out, there was more to the job than cooking. With a larger staff, no doubt there would be much more to contend with.

As was the custom in the country, Mr Jordan had chosen a night close to the full moon for the dinner, so that his guests in their carriages or traps could find their way home across the moor or down to the village in safety. The weather was fine, the gravelled drive was newly raked and Mr Jordan went off for a tour of his estate that morning in a very good humour. A fussy employer in the kitchen was the last thing you wanted. He had been known to interfere at times, probably because he had no wife to keep an eye on things. 'Are you sure this lettuce is perfectly fresh, Miss Wood ...?' was one of his favourite questions and the maids agreed they would have given a lot for a method of keeping lettuce crisp once it came from the garden.

By mid afternoon, everything was as ready as it could be. You could only prepare so much in advance; the rest had to be cooked as it was wanted. The two maids were sent off for a rest, as they would be on their feet for the whole evening. Restless, Susan wandered into the dining-room, checking the table for the tenth time. Then she went to the drawing-room to look for fallen petals from the flower arrangement, finally sitting down at Mrs Jordan's piano. It would be so good to play some of the pieces that Mama had played. Here was Mrs Jordan's music in the piano stool, a link with the past. She'd evidently liked classical music.

It was time to go back into the kitchen and make a start. Soon afterwards, the maids came in and the routine for the evening began. When the first vehicles were heard rolling up the drive and into the stable yard, a shiver of fear went through the kitchen. Mr Jordan's groom would see to the horses; the master himself would greet the guests at the door and take them into the drawing-room for a glass of sherry. And then ... how soon would he wish for the soup to be served? They had arranged that he would ring the bell for each course, but the cook would have to guess when that would be.

'Oh Miss Wood, I'm that scared! What if I drop soup down the vicar's neck?' Daisy, fresh in starched white, looked a picture, but was spoiling the effect by jogging nervously from one foot to the other.

'Just do as I've told you. Take your time, think what you're doing. And check before we serve that no one has kicked up a rug or left anything in the way for you to fall over.' Susan had a vivid memory of falling in the Mermaid dining-room with a full tray of dinner plates, because a client had left his large umbrella in the way. When you carried a tray in front of you, it was not possible to see the floor. She had made Daisy and Hannah practise carrying trays into and out of the dining-room so that they knew the route.

Checking the dining table for the last time, Susan straightened a knife. She hurried back and there in the kitchen doorway was Mrs Bain, coming out with her nose in the air as usual. 'Should you not be attending to the meal?' the housekeeper asked coldly, sweeping upstairs in her long outdoor coat.

'I will send Hannah with a tray for your supper, Mrs Bain.' It was the wise response to an older woman, although Susan seethed at the creature's interference. Why was she here, when she was off duty? Concentrating again on the dinner, she took a last taste of the soup Julienne, a vegetable mixture flavoured with herbs … goodness, something was wrong. The soup was so salty that it would be impossible to serve; a big handful of salt must have been stirred into the pan. There were a few grains of salt glistening on the top of the stove. What on earth could be done?

'You must always have a contingency plan,' had been one of Mrs Thomson's sayings and now was the time that a plan was really needed. There were only a few minutes to go before the meal, but the soup was unfit to serve. Worse, it was a deliberate attempt to discredit the cook. She was certain that the hand adding the salt had been Mrs Bain's.

'Did either of you touch the soup?' Susan demanded when the

maids came in. But of course they would not take such liberties; they looked innocent, but very worried.

'No, Miss Wood, we never.'

'There's too much salt in it. We must work quickly. You will remember that we half cooked double quantities of the vegetables, to have soup ready for our meal tomorrow? Put some more wood on the stove, Daisy. Get some sorrel and chervil, the dried herbs, Hannah. We must heat up another pan of soup and thicken it, as quickly as we can. The bell will ring soon.'

Heart thumping, listening for the dining-room bell, Susan stirred the soup, which needed to stew gently and thicken naturally – but if she added just a little flour, it would be quicker. From the sounds in the drawing-room, the guests were enjoying their sherry; a constant buzz of conversation could be heard, even through the big oak door. Everything else seemed in order; potatoes were roasting and the joints of lamb were nicely browning. The fragrant scent of rosemary floated out into the kitchen.

Bain would surely not have had time to do anything else? What about the puddings in the pantry? The blancmange and vanilla cream were standing demurely on the shelf next to the gooseberry tart. Then there was the cabinet pudding, it was time to put it on to boil. There was so much to think of all at once, without Mrs Thomson's guiding hand. Susan opened the window to let some of the heat out of the kitchen, and mopped her face. The evening was warm and the hot stove had taken the temperature up to about eighty degrees, which increased everyone's agitation a little.

Should she send up the salty soup for Mrs Bain's supper? Going back to stirring the new batch Susan was tempted, but it would set the maids a bad example, since they knew of the salt. She would wait until the soup was served and then quickly prepare eggs on toast. What had she done to the woman to be so hated? It was a strange situation and she couldn't imagine what went on in the housekeeper's mind. Unless, of course, she wanted Susan to leave the hall, one way or another.

By the time the cord twitched and the bell rang in the kitchen, they were ready to send the soup to the dining-room, with warm bread rolls and a sigh of relief. Daisy was even more relieved when she got safely back to the kitchen to report that not a drop had been spilled.

Mr Jordan's loyal servants were on edge all the evening, imagining what else could go wrong; but each course proceeded as it should, with no further calamities. The lamb was tender, the vegetables were perfect and each tray reached the table in safety. Hannah and Daisy were proud of themselves.

Eventually the guests moved back into the drawing-room for coffee and Mr Jordan sent a message to tell Cook that they had enjoyed their meal. She was asked to step into the drawing-room to discuss the next great event – the jubilee celebrations at the end of June.

'Our dear Queen's diamond jubilee shall be celebrated in fitting style. My tenants will be invited to a party, with races for the children, and speeches …' A large man with a red face was holding forth on the hearthrug when Susan entered, which gave her time to compose herself. She'd always found it difficult at the Mermaid to meet the guests after their dinner, all hot and greasy as she was from the kitchen, and it was unpleasant to be the centre of attention. Motioned to sit by Mr Jordan, she found a chair at the back of the room. The solicitor seemed tired and anxious, not at all how a genial host should look after a good dinner.

'We really should rebuild the Greygarth monument to mark the occasion,' said another guest briskly. 'That will last longer than a children's party.'

Mr Jordan evidently decided to bring them to the point. 'Yes, yes. But at the moment I would like you to suggest a menu. You have all been kind enough to help my charity and to contribute to the cost of the bonfire feast. Please will you tell Cook just what food you think the people would enjoy and what you would like this kitchen to produce for the occasion?'

It was ten o'clock at night; Susan had been working since five in the morning and there was still much clearing up to do, but none of the well-fed guests seemed to consider Cook, or to ask her opinion. A children's party would remain in those children's memories for the rest of their lives, wouldn't it? On the other hand, an old stone monument would certainly last, but who would remember why it was there in fifty years from now?

The Queen was going to ride in her carriage through London on jubilee day and she was to send a message round the world on the telegraph. Round the world ... it was hard to believe, but it was true that messages could now be sent to distant parts of the empire in a few minutes, Susan thought, dreamy with fatigue.

After about half an hour the discussion had produced a predictable list: baked hams, sponge cakes, scones, buns ... typical high tea for the working classes. Why couldn't the guests' cooks take a hand? They were all presumably from big houses themselves, with far more servants than Ringbeck Hall. But it seemed that they would find it easier to throw in some money and let Jordan's cook produce the party food. It occurred to Susan that as her employer seemed to be very careful with money, he would rather overwork his cook than contribute to the feast financially. But surely he was not short of money? The hall had been in the Jordan family for generations and she had never heard of a poor solicitor; presumably they were paid whether they won a case or not.

Card tables were now brought out by Robbie, and the guests settled themselves for play. Susan went back to the kitchen, finding with relief that the maids had nearly finished the dishes from the first three courses. She herself washed the delicate wine glasses, not trusting the maids to do it. The card party went on, with occasional laughter and raised voices; the work in the kitchen continued, well past the servants' bedtime.

At last the moon rose over the edge of the moor just as it should, to light the departing guests, and seeing him in the entrance, Susan thought Mr Jordan looked glad to see them go. Eventually he 'retired to rest', as he put it, allowing Susan to clear the last of the meal, sweep the crumbs from the table and put out the lamps. A good housekeeper would have been there to help after a dinner party, but Mrs Bain did not appear.

It was midnight before all was in order and Susan could go to bed, but although she was very tired she was not sleepy. The fires had died down and the air coming through the open windows was chilly for early June. Closing the windows, she pulled on a grey shawl for warmth.

Susan wandered through the silent house and sat down as she had earlier, at the piano in the drawing-room. The moonlight streamed in, silvering the room, transforming familiar objects with shimmering light. If things had been different Susan might have lived in a house like this and owned a piano ... if Papa had not been convicted.

The piano keys were shadowy in the moonlight; slowly, Susan's hands reached out and she began to play. With the soft pedal and a light touch on the keys, surely no one could hear? Heavy carpets and hangings in the room deadened the sound. The light was not good enough to read music, but this was Mama's music, Beethoven. It was sometimes called the 'Moonlight Sonata'; perfect for this night. Very slowly, softly the rippling notes drifted round the room, the notes she knew by heart.

It was a very good piano, still perfectly tuned and with far more depth than the instrument at the Mermaid. A soft touch on the keys was enough ... this was the same piece she had played and heard as a child, but now her reaction was different. Now she detected a haunting sadness in the music, reaching out for some impossible dream. Perhaps it was not so strange that your response should change; you understood more of life as you grew older. Soothing to tired spirits, the notes dropped into the moonlit silence slowly, one by one.

A piercing scream broke the spell and the keys jangled in discord as Susan jumped up in fear. There at the door, pale and shaking with terror, was Mrs Bain. 'The music! Your music!' she whispered, and fell to the floor in a faint.

Susan threw off the grey shawl and bent over the housekeeper in alarm. After a few moments the woman stirred and looked up. 'Did you see her? Did you hear the piano? *It was Mrs Jordan*!' A convulsive shudder went through her and she clutched at Susan's hand.

If Mrs Bain had seen the ghost, she should not be disappointed. Susan pushed the shawl quickly behind a cushion; in her kitchen dress and apron, no one would take Cook for a ghost. She helped the woman to her feet. 'You've had a bad fright. Would you like a cup of tea?' she asked soothingly. Trembling, Mrs Bain nodded and they tottered into the kitchen.

Pulling the fire together, Susan put on the kettle and got out the cups, giving the housekeeper a little time to recover. Outwardly calm, she was laughing inside to think that she had been mistaken for the Ringbeck Hall ghost. Served the housekeeper right for being so hostile. She lit the lamp, dispelling the mysterious moonlight and bringing them and the kitchen back to the normal world.

They drank the tea in silence at first; it would be a pity to spoil the effect of the ghost by chattering. At last Mrs Bain put down her cup with a hand that still shook. 'I never, ever thought ... that I'd see such a thing! I couldn't believe my own eyes and ears, but there she was, deathly pale, white, in something like a shroud ... the piano sounded faint, from far away ... oh, deary me, I was so scared! Did you see her? Did you?' She sounded eager, wanting confirmation of the horror she had seen.

'Well ... there was something, I heard a sound, that was why I was there and found you on the floor. Mrs Jordan's ghost, is that what you saw? But you knew about the ghost, you told me about her.' Rational and composed, Susan looked at the woman gravely. Of course – her own fair hair free from the cap, with her pale, white-rose complexion must have looked ghostly in the moon-light.

'That was different.' But Mrs Bain didn't explain herself. 'This was just how she played, the highbrow stuff ... the same piece, even.' She shook her head. 'It's a judgement. I'll never get over it, never. I'll never dare to sleep at night, after this.'

It was time to help Mrs Bain up the stairs to her room and try to get some sleep before morning. Shutting her door, the woman turned the key in her lock. Could you lock out a ghost? It was an amusing thought. A final tour of the house to check that all the doors were locked, and the day's duties were finally over.

Instead of sleep, images came; events of the day flashed in Susan's inward eye. Why had Mrs Bain been so very scared? Why had she said 'it's a judgement'? Perhaps she was thinking of the trick with the salt, and wondering whether it had been seen by Mrs Jordan's ghost. Thinking back to the evening, they'd been lucky to get out of the soup predicament so lightly; the dinner had been a success in the end.

The next morning Susan rose rather wearily but on time, lit the fire and prepared the breakfast rolls. The sun was shining, the usual routine proceeded, with Mr Jordan coming down to break-fast looking tired and just as worried as he had the night before, in spite of a successful party.

Something was missing; the housekeeper had not come down to the kitchen.

'Mrs Bain must have slept in. Would you like to knock on her door, Hannah?' Susan suggested.

Hannah was soon back in the kitchen, her eyes wide. 'Mrs

Bain's not there! I knocked and there was no answer, so I peeped in – and she's gone!'

Susan finished her own breakfast before going upstairs to the housekeeper's bedroom. The bed had not been slept in; the cupboards and drawers were empty, the key was in the door. Mrs Bain's trunk stood in the middle of the room, locked. On it was a note addressed to Mr Jordan. The ghost had been too much for the woman; perhaps she should have been told that it was only Susan in a grey shawl.

Mr Jordan read the note and looked surprised. 'Mrs Bain has had to leave us without notice to care for her mother … dear, dear. I should have thought that she would have waited to tell me herself, but there it is. I will ask Wilson to take her trunk to Kirkby, to the carrier. I really feel that a responsible housekeeper should have given notice in a proper manner, after all, she had known of her mother's ill health for some time. But of course one has a sacred duty to one's mother.' He stopped, looking solemn. Susan nodded, but said nothing; the least said, the better.

'Now, as to the work of the household, I am sure that the rest of you can cope quite well, can you not? No doubt I will find a housekeeper to replace her, but it may take some time.' Jordan paused. 'I suppose the right thing would be to increase your wage slightly, Susan, to allow for the extra responsibility of your position.'

'Thank you, Mr Jordan.' Thank goodness that the dreadful woman had gone; already the hall felt fresher without her. It was well worth the extra work to get rid of her; it was possible that they would discover Mrs Bain did very little work herself. Now, what would the housekeeper have been organizing today? The laundry; better light the wash-house copper straight away, to get the water hot in time.

Susan had turned to face the door, her mind full of the work ahead, when her employer called her back. 'No doubt we are all rather tired after the events of yesterday. But last night I made a discovery that must be reported to the police at once and I have sent Wilson to call in Constable Brown from Kirkby. Some of my dear mother's jewellery is missing, Susan. Are you able to shed any light on this matter at all?'

CHAPTER TWELVE

Missing jewellery ... oh dear, there was going to be trouble. Stay calm, think carefully. With Papa in prison, his children could easily be suspected of crime. Was Mr Jordan looking at his cook over his glasses with suspicion?

'Do you not keep the valuables in a safe, Mr Jordan?' Susan knew he had a safe in the office because he opened it to pay the farm workers' wages.

'Well, of course some things were in the safe, but unfortunately not all. I was intending to show several items, necklaces and rings, to Mrs Bellerby last night, after dinner – one of my guests, you understand.' He looked rather sheepish, unlike his usual complacent self. 'She was – ah – interested in buying some of them. Some of the jewels were still in my mother's room ... which, as you know, has been left just as it was when she died a few months ago. The last necklaces and so on that she wore, as she left them.' Mr Jordan sighed. 'I have intended to sort out her things, but it was too painful, you understand. And time went by ... it is hard to realize that months have gone by since she passed away. I went to the room before dinner and found her jewellery box, which was locked, but almost empty. The most valuable items have gone.'

Now was the time to confront Mr Jordan, before things got any worse. 'I can understand that you may well suspect me, because of my father. All I can do is assure you that I did not

138

know of the jewellery, Mr Jordan. I have never been into Mrs Jordan's room. I have never stolen anything in my life. I hope you will believe me.' Stand up straight and look him in the eye, speak the truth and shame the Devil, as Ellen Gill used to say.

The solicitor looked away, not meeting her eyes. 'Well, Wood, I did not think it of you, although I must say that Mrs Bain warned me about you when you first came. I had formed the opinion that you are an honest woman, but of course temptation is a terrible thing. Women, especially the servant classes, can be tempted by necklaces and rings, or on the other hand, by the money they represent.'

'Mrs Bain. Would you mind telling me what she said, sir?' Mrs Bain had been responsible for cleaning Mrs Jordan's room. There were a few facts here that needed to be put together.

The solicitor passed a hand over his eyes. 'All this is so worrying. It was a mistake not to keep everything in the safe; I see that now, but there has never been anything of this kind at the Hall before. I ought to have known that times are changing, and not for the better. Yes ... Mrs Bain had heard that you were Toby Wood's daughter, as I knew, but further, that you had been dismissed from the Mermaid for stealing and immorality. I thought that this was not likely to be true, on the balance of probability as Mrs Sanderson spoke well of you. I told Mrs Bain so, although with the reservation that you did seem very keen to find another position.'

He obviously didn't believe that servants had human feelings. 'But, sir ...' Anger was rising as Susan looked at the pompous, self-satisfied face.

Mr Jordan ignored the interruption. 'It is possible Mrs Sanderson was not possessed of all the facts. I have observed that lapses of conduct sometimes occur in the Mermaid stables, in which you might conceivably have been involved. However, Mrs Bain had perhaps been misinformed by some malicious person. Therefore I advised her to say no more of the matter, to give you the benefit of the doubt. I determined that I would judge you as I found you, but of course this theft has put a different light on things.'

The malicious person was no doubt the housekeeper herself. How could anyone defend themselves against a liar? Perhaps the rest of her life would be like this, a constant battle to prove her innocence. The woman had also tried to alienate her from the maids with lies. To think that they suggested she might be up to something in the stables, presumably with George or his cronies! Susan felt sick.

'I am telling you now, so that you understand that all the servants will be questioned and also, in case you can remember having seen or heard anything suspicious. I also have to tell you that the drawing-room window was open; someone has been careless. A thief could easily have entered that way during the night. Who was responsible for locking up last night? I assume it was you, Wood.'

There was a knock on the door and the groom's voice said, 'PC Brown to see you, sir.'

I locked up, Susan thought to herself and I remember closing the window in the drawing-room because it was cold.

Turning to go, Jordan looked back. 'Of course, you must remember that Mrs Bain has been with our family for many years. She was my mother's trusted maid and it is unthinkable that she would do anything to harm the family. Mrs Bain had warned me some months ago that she may have to leave without notice to care for her mother ... eventually, I believe she will return to Ringbeck Hall.'

Preparing lunch was a relief after the interview with Jordan. Cooking itself was satisfying, but the patronizing way in which domestic servants were treated was very hard to swallow. Susan was beginning to dislike Mr Jordan.

PC Brown never hurried; he was too stout. It took all morning to interview the hall staff, which included the garden and farm workers as well. They were taken into Mr Jordan's office one by one. Martin Gill was impassive when he appeared, although he must have known that Susan's father might cause her trouble in a situation like this. He nodded a curt good day to her as he went out through the kitchen. At the end of the morning no one, it seemed, was any the wiser, but everyone was on edge.

When the kitchen staff were allowed to go about their duties, Susan made everyone a cup of tea. 'Let's get to work,' she said briskly as soon as the tea was drunk. 'We can start to make some of the cakes this week for the jubilee party, the ones that will keep. We all have extra work, since Mrs Bain has gone. Perhaps we can forget about sewing the linen for a while, but we must keep up the standard in the main rooms and see that Mr Jordan has everything he wants. Now, Daisy, I will put you in charge of the laundry. Do you think you can manage that?'

Daisy looked very nervous, so Susan said she would oversee the work for a while as Mrs Bain had done. The washing was done twice weekly at the hall, the day sometimes varying to take advantage of fine weather. Today was Friday and the day appointed for washing house linen and the servants' work clothes. 'The copper is boiling, I lit it before breakfast … collect up the laundry bags, Daisy, if you please, and don't forget to check the pockets.'

Beating butter and sugar together in a large bowl, it was hard to keep her mind on the job. The strange events of last night and this morning kept crowding back; it was clear that Mrs Bain was not the angel Mr Jordan thought she was, but did she steal the jewels? *Assume that she was the thief.* It would perhaps explain why she wanted to get rid of the new cook, somebody who might see something or ask awkward questions. She'd made several attempts: the gliding green ghost, the lies told to their employer and worst of all, the salt in the soup. But how had she hoped to get away with it?

As soon as the cakes were in the oven, Susan ran up again to the housekeeper's room. Perhaps there was a clue there to what might have happened. The cupboards and drawers were bare; all the woman's possessions were in the locked trunk. Running her eyes round the room, Susan noticed a small paraffin lamp on a shelf, the sort used as a bedside lamp. She took it down and laughed as she realized this was the ghostly light. The lamp had a green shade. The woman had obviously left it behind, having no further use for it.

The sun shone, the breeze blew and Daisy hung out the washing in the garden. Susan's first batch of jubilee cakes turned out well and the kitchen staff sat down to their midday dinner quite pleased with their morning's work in spite of the doom hanging over their heads. 'Nice and peaceful without Mrs B,' Robbie volunteered, then covered his mouth with his hand. 'Though I shouldn't say so.' It was true; those baleful black eyes had made them all uneasy at times.

Susan went into the wash house, where Daisy was putting away the mangle. 'I found an envelope in Mrs Bain's pocket,' the girl said. 'It's on the window ledge over there.'

Susan picked up the envelope, but just then the gardener came in with a question about the vegetables for dinner. 'I'll come down and look at them,' Susan decided, putting the envelope in her apron pocket.

As the jubilee celebration drew nearer, the pace of the work at the hall increased. Various parties had been planned across the moorland during the whole week, but theirs was on the actual jubilee date, 27 June. Midsummer's Day came and went without any particular rejoicing; the 24 June was not important this year – all eyes were on the jubilee. Portraits of the Queen and union flags appeared, speeches were polished and best of all, hams were baked ready for the feast. 'A knife and fork tea' had been promised, the best kind of feast you could have.

During the morning of the jubilee day, Martin Gill set up the trestle tables while the farm men brought up the last loads of heather from the moor to the hill where the bonfire would be lit. 'You have to look to see if there's any heather left, we have so much,' Robbie said happily. The tough, dry heather stalks would make a brilliant blaze.

Susan walked up the hill to check on the cutlery and crockery, which had travelled in hampers. Martin was supervising the chairs, clean and tidy in his good tweed jacket, with his fair hair shining in the sun. No wonder Mrs Bain fancied him; at least she wouldn't be there tonight, if her mother was ill.

Martin turned away, although he must have seen Susan. Whatever was wrong with the man? Perhaps this was another case of needing to meet trouble head on, getting to the bottom of the problem. Maybe he thought she would expect him to look after her, help her out. He'd had enough of the Woods, and probably he didn't want any more responsibility.

Martin had left her alone for years, hadn't he, although she'd been longing to see him again. It was natural enough, after four years of working for the Gills and seeing few other people, that she had felt terribly isolated when he didn't keep in touch. All that time at the Mermaid and she'd seen him only twice. They'd only met again now because coincidence had brought them both to work at the hall, and he was ignoring her presence. But why couldn't they be friends?

Catching up with him away from the others, Susan stood in front of Martin, barring his way. 'You can treat me just like any other person, you know. There's no need to worry about being responsible for the little Woods any more, Martin. They've all grown up and are managing quite well for themselves.' She was breathing quickly, she must calm down. 'I can see that you feel you did enough for us at the time, and you don't want to get involved again, but I can assure you we wouldn't want that, either.' She paused and bit her lip. Somehow, the speech had not come out as she meant. She'd sounded hostile, bitter and very childish.

The farm manager was obviously taken by surprise. 'This is the lass with the prickles, the little Yorkshire rose! What ails you, lass?' The blue eyes met hers, and she thought that deep down, he knew what she intended.

'That's the whole point, Martin. I am not the little lass who used to work for you and you really don't have to worry about me any more. But you might be civil and not try to avoid me!' Susan was getting more agitated as she spoke.

'Oh, Susan.' The deep voice sounded weary, dejected, although only a moment ago he had been giving orders briskly to the workers. Martin sighed and for a moment it seemed that he might say something friendly, but he turned away once more. 'Well, the past is over, as you say, and there is no bond between us now. I am surprised you feel so strongly about it.'

It was devastating. The whole conversation had gone wrong and in the end, Susan was cut off from the person she most cared about. If only she hadn't plunged in like that … if only she could forget about the man. He obviously wanted to forget about her.

Never mind Martin, there was quite enough to do. Susan was so busy organizing the food that she barely had time to change her dress before the hall staff were expected to serve the meal. The sun was sinking down behind the moor, the children's sports were finished and it would soon be time to light the bonfire on the little hill above the playing field.

About fifty people sat down to a hearty supper, with even enough for Susan and the maids to eat as well, although they held back for a while, just to be quite sure. Weary but satisfied, it was good to sit on a bench for a while, watching the sun set while the first flames of the fire leaped up against the skyline.

Susan heard a quiet cough behind her and turned to see a man looking at her intently; a man of middle height, with silvery hair and a face that was lined, but somehow serene. 'Is it – Papa?' It was her father, but she hardly recognized him. He had aged; seven years of prison had turned him into a much older man. Toby Wood slid down on to the bench beside her; there was nobody watching or listening because the bonfire was now the centre of attention. 'How long have you been here?'

'I've been at the cottage for a couple of days ... and I thought I might find you here. I saw the boys earlier, I could hardly believe how they've grown. Thank you for writing to tell me where to find you all, Susan. My, it's good to see you, lass! Of course, you have changed too – you're a young woman now, a bonny one. You've even grown a little.' Toby leaned over and kissed her swiftly on the cheek, then sighed. 'The worst part of it all was that I missed seeing you all grow up.' He thought a while. 'No, not the worst: the very worst was not being able to provide for my little family. How did you get on without me? I suppose Mrs Lawson was there as long as you needed her?'

This was not the time to tell her father of their struggles to survive. 'It's a long story ... I'd like to spend a little time at the cottage with you, perhaps next week if I can get away from the hall, although it will be difficult – the housekeeper has just left. Then we can talk, catch up a little, Papa. But as you've seen, we are all doing quite well.'

Martin Gill walked by with one of the men, checking for sparks from the fire. In a dry time it would be easy to set the whole moor alight, and the peat could burn underground for months until the rain came. He looked over at the bench where Susan and her father sat and then looked quickly away again. 'Martin!' Susan called after him, wanting to introduce him to her father, but there were several guns fired in salute at that moment and he passed on without hearing. Perhaps it was just as well. It was too late to take back what she'd said in the morning.

'I am sorry, my dear, but I can't stay long. I've been offered a small studio in York and plenty of work, but tomorrow is the day my friend is travelling back to York and I am to go with him. Once I'm established you can come to me there. How about that? And we can talk and talk …' Her father looked genuinely sorry.

It was hard to hide the disappointment, to turn to Toby with a smiling face. After all these years, he was going away again so soon! 'Of course, Papa. I've never been to York, it will be interesting and I can catch a train from Ripon station. I will ask for a few day's holiday from the hall.'

Toby frowned. 'I was hoping you might give up your work and come to live with me, Susan. Surely there will be no need for you to earn your own living, with me to provide for you? It is so demeaning to be a domestic servant. Your poor dear mother would have been horrified. It's bad enough that Ben is a tradesman … but for our little daughter to be a cook is not right, you know.'

This was a shock. No need to earn her living? In one way it was tempting, and no more than any father would have offered. It had been hard work to earn her independence, but she now understood how demeaning domestic service could be, working for a man like Andrew Jordan. Would it be a backward step to give up her position as the Cook? In a year or two she might find a job in a larger establishment than the hall, with greater challenges and a little more respect. 'Well, thank you, Papa. But I might be a burden to you; it will be hard to establish yourself where you are not known, and it might not be clear for some time how much work you'll find. In any case, John will need some help, if you are able to give it. York could be a good place for John – he'd like to train to be a printer. He could be old enough by next year, and …'

Toby looked doubtful and Susan wondered whether he'd prefer a useful daughter, a trained cook, in his house to a young son who might need expensive training. She would need to push John's case a little. He tried to interrupt with his own argument, but Susan persisted. 'And I really prefer the country, Papa. Ripon was too big for me, and York must be a far larger city. I want to work in the country, cooking in a country house. But surely you could spare a little time tonight? Why not come back to the hall with me?'

Toby Wood shook his head. 'I don't particularly want to see Andrew Jordan and it would not be polite to visit without his knowledge. But I can sit with you here for a while of course, until you have to leave.'

Susan thought a while and then took the plunge. 'Papa, are you going to try to find out the truth? What really happened when you were sent to prison? It would be so good to clear your name!'

Toby shook his head. 'I used to think so, but my time with Jacob has changed my outlook. He's a Quaker ... they visit folk in prison, you know. At first I was bitter and angry, but he taught me how to forgive and forget. I now have peace, but I don't want to go back to Harrogate, find my enemies, and perhaps start another court case. My conscience is clear – I can forget the past. And,' he continued with a smile, 'York would be a good place for a fresh start, for all of us. That's why I want you to come to me, my dear.'

Toby wanted to forget the past. Did it mean that he was guilty, but was trying to shield her from the knowledge? It was shameful to think like that about Papa, and yet, perhaps he's been led astray and now regretted it. The Woods needed to know the truth, however unpalatable it was.

Susan thought the party might end soon, but for some it was only just beginning. One of the men got out an accordion and soon couples were dancing on the short moor turf, bitten by sheep to smoothness for the occasion. Dancing on the moorland was a surprise; it was normally such a staid and sober community.

Susan looked on at the dancers and there she saw Martin Gill, dancing with the little maid Daisy. The next time she looked, he was giving Hannah a whirl. Those girls would not forget the jubilee feast, and Martin was making it more enjoyable for them. It was a pity his generous spirit didn't extend to the cook.

'Why do you not want to see Mr Jordan, Papa?' Perhaps he didn't want to be seen as the cook's father. Toby had his middle-class pride, probably more so after the prison years. Even worse, Jordan had failed to keep him out of jail.

Her father thought for a moment. 'I suppose I should tell you. It seemed to me that Jordan did not do all he could to help me as my solicitor, although he was very friendly, always telling me he was doing his best, saying he could do no more. It's just a feeling … I believe that an innocent man should not be convicted, if he's defended properly. If there is any justice in the world, that is.'

Papa was saying he was innocent. Oh, if it were really true, how happy she would be. 'Then perhaps I'd better tell you what Mr Jordan said to me.' Susan looked round, but there was nobody near enough to overhear them. 'He's always been very patronizing, but fair enough as an employer. He told me he'd defended you but that he could do little for you, because you were guilty. The temptation had been too much, he said, once the engraver showed you what could be done.'

By the light of the bonfire, Toby's face registered dismay. 'He told you that? The villain! My poor girl, you've been thinking that your father was a criminal!' He moved restlessly, then took Susan's hand. 'I worked with Taylor the engraver, but we had separate keys to the premises with the printing press. I hardly knew what other work he had. For me, he converted my drawings into plates for book illustrations and then printed them. I don't want my children to believe their father did wrong.'

They looked at each other. Was this convincing enough? He didn't actually deny the crime. Susan shook her head.

Toby shifted on the bench. 'I have spent seven long years worrying about you all,' he admitted. 'Let us now start again, in York, where my past is not known.'

Susan thought about her employer. 'I've not been long with Mr Jordan,' she whispered. 'He was shocked when he found out who I was. He probably only employed me because the cook had left suddenly, and he likes good food.' Should she tell him the rest? 'Last week he had some jewellery stolen that had belonged to his mother. I told him straight out that I didn't do it ... but I'm not sure that he believed me. The police haven't found it yet.'

Toby groaned. 'You'll feel very sensitive about honesty, I suppose. But Jordan of all people should know ... It's a terrible thing to destroy a family's good name. I shall have to forgive him I suppose, and take Jacob's advice to put it all behind me. But this makes it all harder, of course.' He thought for a while.

'Jacob Green helped me to keep my sanity, in prison. He was allowed in to talk to prisoners and see to their welfare. Jacob managed to report back about you and the boys, once or twice. He found out that they were going to school and you were working on a farm, and I assumed that Mrs Lawson was still there.'

'I hoped you would,' Susan smiled. The music changed to country dance tunes and set her feet tapping. 'I must admit we were not very kind to her ... and she hated the country. Things were a bit hard for a time, but we managed, and then Mr and Mrs Gill gave me a job and more or less looked after us. They took us to church and all that,' she finished rather lamely, having just seen Martin in the distance, talking to Mrs Bain. The former house-keeper must have come up with the group from Ripon, for the celebration. The mother couldn't be so ill, after all. She held out a hand and motioned to Martin and after a little hesitation he joined the dance with her. Mrs Bain had quite a good figure and danced well; her normally sour face was all smiles.

It would have been good for Martin and Toby to meet, but not now. Not with that sneering face looking on, full of curiosity about the criminal father. Mrs Bain must be quite interested in Martin – and why not? A man with a farm of his own, quite hand-some and of good character, would be a good catch – although she might not understand how hard the life could be, especially in winter. On his side, to marry a respectable housekeeper and settle down at Holly Bank would solve his problems ... except that she had a thoroughly unpleasant nature. Susan deliberately turned away from the dancers and back to her father again.

'And so,' Toby continued, still speaking softly, 'Jacob taught me not to hate, and hatred was eating me up inside. Eventually I felt sorry for whoever had got me into prison, rather than for myself. I began to lift up my head again and to help some of the other prisoners, where I could.'

'How could you do that?' It was hard to imagine prison life.

'Well ... I could do little at first. My sentence involved hard labour, but I wasn't used to it, being an artist. I was exhausted all the time. But as I gradually became used to the work, Jacob asked me to teach a young lad to read and he brought some books for us. That was hard work, too, but very rewarding. After a couple of years the lad could read and write quite well and he had a much better outlook on life. When he left prison, he was going to go straight.'

The hall servants were going back to tackle the washing up. It was time to go. It was sad to think that after waiting all these years to see his family, Toby Wood should go away so soon.

'Of course, Papa, I'll come to see you as soon as I can.' Susan kissed her father sadly and turned down the hill.

CHAPTER THIRTEEN

'There's always summat,' said Robbie happily, polishing the brass oil lamps in the scullery. 'We've just got over the jubilee and it'll soon be haytime. Do you know about haytime, Miss Wood? There's extra men come in, like they did for the shearing, only it lasts longer, and there's hell on if it rains.'

'Don't swear, Robbie,' said Susan automatically. 'Yes, I do know about haytime. I used to work on a farm.' Her thoughts went back as she kneaded the bread dough, to the hot July days at Holly Bank when she was Robbie's age. She recalled the fragrance of drying grass, spangled with wild flowers, turned over with long two-tined forks to make the sweet, fine upland hay. She heard again the jingle of the harness as the horses came up the field under clouds of flies, attracted by the acid smell of their sweat. Martin would take off his jacket and wipe his streaming face, while the sun burned down from a blue sky and somewhere a lark was always singing ...

Susan had loved the summer days of field work, relished the fresh scones and cold tea that Ellen brought out to the field in her big wicker basket. It must have rained sometimes, of course, but in Susan's memory the sun was always shining and they always wore straw hats.

'Fat rascals! We'll need plenty of those, and parkin, teacakes, and apple pie.' Susan mind turned to the reality of haytime, the extra food that would be needed. 'I wonder how many men they'll hire.'

'I wonder if there'll be any beer.' Robbie sounded wistful.

The men who worked for the Gills had told Susan much about the traditions of the hay harvest. In the old days, they said, a farmer would provide a barrel of beer for the men, but since the rise of the temperance movement the drink was cold tea. 'And we work the better for it,' they'd admitted. Martin had a glass of beer occasionally, as was permitted by the Church of England in moderation. Ellen had one glass of sherry at Christmas, but they both respected the Methodists who had 'signed the Pledge', a promise never to drink alcohol. Many of the local folk were Methodists, so there was no beer at Holly Bank for the harvest.

Working at the Mermaid with the smell of stale beer everywhere in the mornings had put her off drink completely, Susan had decided long ago. 'I shouldn't think there'll be beer, and in any case you don't want to get a taste for it,' she warned Robbie.

Since the night of the bonfire, Susan had been thinking hard about what she should do. There was a little money left from her wages at the Mermaid and although Mr Jordan had not paid her yet, she could afford to go away for a few weeks. It was an attractive idea; a visit to her father at York would give her a change of scene, and get her away from the hall and Martin Gill for a while, the new, cold Martin who did not want to know her. But it was impossible to walk out now, when there was no housekeeper. Without Susan there would only be Robbie and the two young maids, and haytime would cause extra work in the kitchen. Also, if she were to leave suddenly, somebody might wonder whether she had stolen the jewellery. It would be good to find out where it had gone, but there had been no news since the morning after the party.

Toby Wood sent Susan a cheerful letter from York. It sounded as though he'd fallen on his feet, with a small attic studio near the river Ouse on South Esplanade and a garden. 'You will love it, I am sure,' he wrote happily. He was able to pay his way by helping

the owner of the house and also by selling some of his old paintings that had been kept for him by a friend in Harrogate. He had
some commissions and had already sold several water colours of
York's quaint old alleyways, and he had some paid work as a
teacher, working with the Quakers. It seemed that he was
thinking of John's future too, planning for him to finish his
schooling at York.

Susan wrote back regretfully, telling her father that she would
visit as soon as she could get away – which might be after the corn
harvest.

Early July was wet and windy, but in the middle of the month
the weather cleared and farmers got ready to harvest the hay. One
morning when the maids were upstairs Martin came into the
kitchen, which was a surprise. Susan had only seen him in the
distance since jubilee night and they had ignored each other.

Taking off his cap, the farm manager gave her a straight look
with his blue eyes and a faint smile. 'I must talk to you about
feeding the labourers, Susan,' he said quietly. 'We start to cut the
hay soon.'

The last time they spoke, the words had been bitter. Susan took
the boiling kettle off the stove with a hand that shook slightly.
'Please sit down, Martin. I will make a cup of tea. Yes, we need to
know how many men there will be and at what times during the
day you would like them to be fed.' They needed to heal the
breach and a cup of tea was a good start.

The kitchen was quiet for a while, but as he took his cup
Martin looked at Susan again. 'You were right, lass, that day on
the hill and I should apologize for the way I spoke to you. It's just
that ... no matter.' He sighed and moved uneasily in his chair. 'I
hope we can forget about it. We have to work together, here at
the hall. We always did get on well, and we can be friends, right
enough. I wouldn't hurt you for the world, my dear, and I would
protect you if I could.' It was a long speech for a moorland

farmer, and the tone of voice in his last sentence held some of the warmth that had been missing of late.

Susan didn't trust her voice for a minute or two. She had a friend in the world, after all. Her heart singing, she drank her tea and made a list of the food that Martin suggested. After all the arrangements had been agreed he did not seem in a hurry to leave, so Susan risked a question. 'If you don't mind my asking, why did you come to work at the hall, Martin? Surely there's enough to do at Holly Bank?'

'You're right, of course, I've quite enough work. But Andrew Jordan asked me to try to pull the farm round and it was a bit of a challenge, it appealed to me. Hall farm has been losing money, going downhill, but that's not for everybody to know.' Susan cleared the tea things as Martin moved in his chair to face her. 'The land's in poor heart, lass. Hay and straw have been sold off to earn a bit of quick cash and there's been too much corn grown.'

It was not surprising that Martin had been chosen. While Susan was there, Holly Bank had become a model for other farmers to follow. Even in the worst of the depression when prices were poor, Martin had managed the farm to improve the land and the stock, while others had tried to take a quick profit. It was not clear quite what he did that was different, but he had a reputation as a good farmer.

'How much corn is too much?' She wanted to keep him talking, to keep him with her as long as she could; but she was also interested in his thinking.

'Well, as a rough guide, tenant farmers usually have a clause in the lease to say no more than one third of the land should be in corn, in any one year. That's good practice on the bottom land, of course. As you know we can't grow crops on the moor, it's just a sheep run. Ringbeck Hall has had nearly three quarters of the good land down to corn, oats and barley. That means less livestock. Of course it's his own land, he can do what he likes with it. But it's not good farming.'

Susan thought about this. 'If you don't have many cattle or sheep, I suppose you don't need to pay so many workers. Just casual help at harvest time.'

Martin smiled. 'That's what Jordan reckoned. But with less manure to spread on the land, you can't replace what you take out of it, and these new artificial fertilizers are not all they're cracked up to be. And then, too, you need to rotate crops – remember we did that when you were at Holly Bank? It's better not to grow corn on the same spot two years running. You get more pests and diseases, for one thing, and you exhaust the soil. So I reckon it's better to give the land a rest, put it back to grass and run cattle on it. I bought him a new Shorthorn bull the other day, to improve the stock.' He got to his feet, somewhat reluctantly. 'I'll do what I can while I'm here, but he's not forced to do as I say.... Well, it's been grand to talk to you, Susan, thanks for the tea. I must be off.'

'How long will you stay at the hall, Martin?' Surely he's not going to make a life's work out of someone else's problems, even if he's lonely.

'I've promised Jordan to stay here for the summer to sort a few things out, and then to plan the crops for next year. Of course, I spend the odd day at home when I need to. Once the hall hay is safely in, I'll think about cutting my own. But this winter, I'll be back at Holly Bank.' Martin gave her a strange, rueful look as he went to the door.

The talk with Martin seemed to pose more questions than it answered. Why would Mr Jordan be keen to sell off produce for cash? Martin hadn't mentioned the theft of jewels, but it was always at the back of Susan's mind; Jordan had told her that on the night he'd found them missing, he was going to offer them for sale to one of his dinner guests.

Of course, it was easy to lose money in farming. Ellen Gill had often said, 'It's a gamble, Susan. We gamble on the weather, the prices, crop and stock diseases ... and the competition from farmers lower down the dale.' It was a wonder any of the farmers survived, Susan used to think. But then, Mr Jordan had inherited his land; he wasn't borrowing money to pay for it.

Mr Andrew Jordan presented himself as a well-established country solicitor. Mrs Thomson had told her that he specialized in land transactions and property leases, which made Susan wonder whether Papa had picked the wrong man to defend him. Surely a criminal lawyer would have been a better choice? Was Jordan a good solicitor? If so, he should be earning a respectable living.

Mr Jordan looked prosperous; he had a fine house, good horses and a circle of friends with whom he played cards. No wife, but he didn't seem to be the marrying kind. Another thing: how did it all tie in with his perplexing defence of Papa? Was there money involved there, too? Jordan had told her that Papa was a criminal, which was a terrible thing to do if it were not true.

Today's talk with Martin had been the best they'd had since she left Holly Bank. Perhaps they would be able to have more conversations, so long as they kept to interesting topics like farming – and well away from feelings.

The Gills had been wonderful teachers, but it was clear as soon as she went to the Mermaid that Susan lacked practice in talking to folks. Working in the dining-room and playing the piano for parties had helped her to hold her own in conversation, but she didn't feel confident. What had she learned in Ripon? That people usually enjoyed talking about their own affairs. Rule Number One for future dealings with Martin would have to be: talk about the farm. She smiled when she thought about Mrs Bain on shearing day, trying to chat lightly to Martin about sheep.

Slowly, as the long days went by, the hay harvest was carried and stacked in the old stone barns in the farmyard. Martin went home to Holly Bank at night, but often not until it was nearly dark, so Susan tried to make sure that he had something to eat before he left. The short ride home was not much to worry about, but it must seem a long way when you were tired. The truce seemed to be holding and it was good to see more of the farm manager, and also more of the farm, as she came and went with the food.

'It's a good crop this year, you'll be able to feed more cattle over the winter,' Martin told Jordan one day when the owner had ridden out to view the progress of the work in the hayfield. Susan, delivering the afternoon tea, looked up to see a grimace cross Jordan's face.

'I'd like to sell some of it, Martin. Potter at Village Farm asked me particularly for a load or two,' he said. Mr Jordan seemed to like looking down on them from horseback, as if to emphasize his status.

'Well, that's as may be, but if you keep to the plan, Mr Jordan, you'll have a better farm.' Martin spoke firmly.

'Very well, have it your own way.' The solicitor sounded almost petulant. 'But you must allow me to sell some oats. You said yourself we should grow less.'

Susan went off with her empty baskets. Crossing the field, she could still hear Martin's deep voice, patiently explaining to Mr Jordan his plan for the improvement of Ringbeck Hall farm. She went through the farmyard just for the pleasure of sniffing the familiar farmyard smells, seeing the hens, geese and pigs scratching about. By the bull pen she admired the magnificent roan animal that Martin had chosen to improve the herd. It was so good to be back in the country again.

As the days began to shorten the sunlight took on a more golden tinge, the binders went in to cut the corn and once again, Susan was called on to feed the extra hands. One day a labourer offered to help her carry the heavy baskets and as they walked down the lane to the cornfield, he said he'd been one of the shearers, earlier in the year. 'John Hawkin, from Thorpe,' he introduced himself. With a sly grin he said, 'Best not let the boss see me helping you, he might not like it.'

'Which boss?' Who did the man mean?

'Well, Mr Gill, of course, him what's in charge. He's mighty particular about Miss Wood. One of the lads was saying how you're a nice looking young lady, nothing too disrespectful, mind, and that he wouldn't mind taking you for a walk down by the river, and the boss jumped down his throat. He was not to speak so of the young lady ... he was hopping mad. Since then we've been careful not to say owt about any lass at all, or mention that they have a nice figure.' The man laughed, obviously trying to embarrass her, but Susan had worked in a pub long enough to know how to deal with John Hawkin.

'Well, Mr Hawkin, how long will it be before this field is finished?' And if you get any nearer I will tread on your toe, you lout, she almost said.

'I don't know, I'm not the boss ... at shearing time I mind there was another lass at the hall, older than you. She seemed to fancy Mr Gill, we thought. So where is she now?' Susan shook her head.

They'd got to the field gate and John left her, while Susan took the baskets to the shade of a big oak tree. Soon the men were gathered round enjoying the Yorkshire teacakes, a sort of bread bun scattered with currants and spread with deep yellow butter. They washed down the food with cold tea.

All too soon for the men it was time to go out into the burning sun, and time for Susan to go back to the chores in the kitchen. Martin took the baskets from her, lighter now that the food had gone, but still a burden for her to carry. 'I'll walk back with you, Susan, I need to see the groom.'

Susan could imagine the sniggers of John Hawkin when he saw the boss and the cook walking across the field together; but what did it matter, after all?

They walked in silence for a while, until Martin looked down at her. 'Do you see much of young William Darley? I suppose he could ride out to see you here.'

It was good to have a chance to put the record straight. 'No, I never see William. I went for a walk with him in Ripon once or twice, that was all. He's looking for a good wife, so I told him not to waste his time with me.' Susan laughed. 'We'd never be able to agree – he's a townsman, wouldn't want to live in the country.'

Martin looked surprised. 'Well, I thought you might be suited. Was he very downhearted? It must have been a shock to him to be rejected, if he was fond of you, Susan.' He picked up a stick and swiped a thistle in the hedge.

'It didn't upset him, Martin. He didn't know me very well, there wasn't time to get attached, or anything like that. But it wasn't fair to continue the friendship, when I knew there was no chance of a happy ending. He'll make somebody a good husband I'm sure, but not me.' She looked up at the farmer as he held open a field gate for her. 'How are you getting on with Lizzie Bain?'

This time Martin smiled. 'You mean the housekeeper?'

'I thought you might make a match of it,' Susan went on, trying to work out the true situation. You'll be needing a good wife to help you run Holly Bank, and she's had years of house-keeping experience. And she is so very interested in sheep!'

Ignoring the sarcasm, Martin sighed. 'You're right, lass. I should find a wife and settle down, have some bairns of my own and somebody to keep me company ... my mother keeps telling me so. Maybe I will, before long.' They were back in the kitchen now, and Martin put the baskets on the big table. 'You're right, a good housekeeper is what I need.'

And how I hope it isn't to be Mrs Bain, Susan thought bitterly as she unpacked the basket. Better not say anything, though. The woman was unpleasant, but perhaps she'd be kinder with a husband and a home of her own.

CHAPTER FOURTEEN

'I can give you another week or two,' Martin said to his employer one pearly autumn morning as they met in the stable yard. 'Of course I can always come over from time to time, to keep an eye on progress. But I really must get back to Holly Bank, there's a lot of work waiting for me.' Sheep needed his attention; he had to draft ewes, check feet, trim tails and sort them all out before the winter.

Jordan looked round the tidy yard with a frown. 'It's a pity, you know, it really is vexing that you can't stay. You must realize the situation from my point of view. I urgently need a manager or even a foreman, to see to the daily routine. To organize the men's work and so on and so forth, as you well know, Martin.' Jordan mounted his horse. 'I must be off, I have important appointments in Ripon today. But – do you know of anyone I could trust? See whether you can find me a good man.' The solicitor rode out of the yard on his big bay, looking happy that he had delegated the problem to Gill and could go down to his office in Ripon with a clear mind to face the rest of his problems.

Martin looked after the departing horseman. It was clear that the sooner he could think of a replacement, the sooner he'd get back to his own farm. Mentally he went through the men he knew, searching for likely candidates. None of the hall labourers was capable of taking charge. But Bill McTaggart, a tough Scotsman who lived in Kirkby, might be suitable. There were three regular labourers to oversee, as well as casual workers and the foreman would also need to get down to work himself, as Martin had often done. Bill had a small farm of his own, but often worked for other farmers.

It would be good to get back to Holly Bank, but ... it would be lonely. At the hall there was company of a sort, and always Susan's quiet smile as she passed him in the yard. They'd had some good talks lately.

Martin looked round the stables, cowsheds and barns. There was the satisfaction of seeing some results from his hard work, although any land improvement would not be evident for a year or two. Here, his changes were visible. The stone buildings were clean and tidy, with properly hanging doors and clean, glazed windows. The cobbles of the yard were swept clean and free from manure, which was stored in a long midden far away from the buildings. Much of the manure had been spread on the land, once the corn was harvested. The farm animals themselves were sleek and well fed. 'It looks a sight better than when we arrived, doesn't it?' he remarked to young John Hawkin, who had stayed on at the farm after harvest and was now coming towards him, full of purpose.

John agreed. 'Aye, it were a fair mess before you took over.' He shuffled his feet. 'Mr Gill, was we going to move that there bull? He's been penned up for weeks and he's getting frisky. I think you said he could go with the cows this week.' And then I won't have to feed him in the pen, John seemed to be saying.

It was certainly time for the bull to run with the herd, so that calves would be born the following spring. 'Aye, he'll settle down once he's out of the pen. He was quiet enough when we brought him in.' Martin took down a bull pole with a clip on the end. 'I'll lead him out, John, if you open the gates, pasture gate first and then the pen.' There was a ring in the bull's nose and he could easily be led by the ring, with the aid of the pole.

Martin looked him over with satisfaction; a young Shorthorn bull, well grown, with thick, slightly curved horns and a dappled strawberry roan coat, shining with health. He'd been expensive, but he had a good pedigree and his calves would grow well.

The manager slipped the clip into the bull's ring and the animal began to dance and throw up his head. Normally the pull on the nose would calm him, but this bull had been cooped up for a long time, with no proper exercise and he was restless in the extreme.

Martin was sure he could handle him, but as John opened the gate, the worst happened. The nose ring was pulled out with a fierce toss of the massive head and Martin was suddenly left with no control. He rushed forward to try to shut the animal back in the pen, but the bull had seen the way to freedom and was not going back into his prison.

'Go on, lad, get back!' Martin spoke firmly and walked towards the bull, who was now agitated, in some pain and with a torn and bleeding nose. You had to be firm with cattle, show them who was boss.

This time, the bull would not be dominated. Determined to be free, it rushed at Martin and knocked him down, then turned its head and thrust the limp body out of the way with one horn, anxious to be off. A more vicious bull would have trampled him where he lay. It cantered down the lane to the cow pasture, bellowing as it went.

Martin felt a sharp crack as his head hit the cobbles and everything went black for a moment or two. A searing pain in his thigh brought him round; through a haze he could see John, anxiously peering at him. 'Are you right, Mr Gill? Did he hurt you?'

'Get Susan,' he said between clenched teeth, and blacked out again.

Susan was washing the breakfast dishes in the kitchen, wondering how soon she would be able to visit Papa, when young

John Hawkin came rushing into the kitchen. 'Miss Wood, bull's got Mr Gill! Come quick!'

Martin hurt … how badly? If Martin was killed … Quickly Susan put the kettle on the stove for hot water, snatched two clean towels and ran with John into the farmyard. She would see what was needed, first.

Martin was lying on the ground just outside the bull pen, ash grey and breathing heavily. His eyes were closed. 'I think it's his leg …' John quavered. 'But I daren't look, I can't stand the sight of blood.'

Carefully, Susan felt along the arms and legs; no bones broken, she thought, but there was blood oozing through his torn clothes on the right leg. 'Go fetch a blanket and a pillow,' she ordered John. In Martin's right-hand pocket she knew there would be a knife where he always kept it, so she used it to slit his breeches further where the bull had torn them, to expose the wound. It was a deep gash, bleeding profusely.

Martin's eyes were open and he was watching her. 'Susan.'

'Oh, Martin.' The cry escaped her and then she bit her lip. 'Your head?' She ran her fingers gently round the back of his head, where a lump was already forming.

'Just stop the bleeding, lass, and I'll be right in a minute.' Martin spoke thickly. She wrapped the towels tightly round the leg.

When John came back with a rug, they gently covered Martin where he lay and then Susan ran back to the house. She poured boiling water over several clean dusters made from old sheets, for a bandage. The wound might be dirty, it would need to be washed out first … what to use? Ellen had used southernwood, but all the kitchen could provide in an emergency was salt.

Shaking, Susan put a handful of salt into the boiled water. Then she took a jar of her precious comfrey ointment, and put everything into a basket with a bottle of drinking water and a basin.

Back in the yard, Martin asked for a drink of water and Susan was glad she'd thought of the bottle. Then came the hard part. 'Martin, this may hurt, but I've got to clean the wound.'

'Can't we fetch doctor?' asked John fearfully.

'Susan can do it,' whispered the patient.

'We can't wait for the doctor … we'll call him later. Just hand me a cloth and the basin of salt water, John. You needn't watch.' It took an effort to peel away the towel and expose the long gash made by the bull's horn. Of course, it had particles of dirt and straw in it. Carefully she washed it out with salt water, mopping away the blood as she worked. When it was clean she applied the healing comfrey ointment, then bound the leg firmly with the sterile cloths.

By the time she had finished, the other farm men had appeared, having shut the bull safely in the pasture. Together they made a seat with their hands to help a very shaky Martin into the hall, where they laid him down in a room on the ground floor.

The doctor was sent for, but he was attending a difficult birth and was not available. Martin gradually began to look more normal, the men went about their business and Susan made them both a strong cup of tea, with plenty of sugar in it. Ellen Gill had always said that sweet tea was good for shock.

The wound was clean, but it wouldn't stop bleeding. After an hour or two the bandages were soaked and Martin was still losing too much blood. How to stop it was the problem – hadn't Ellen talked about the number of times men cut themselves with scythes in the hayfield, and how she'd had to find something to stop the flow? Think … what had she used to stop bleeding? A cut on the finger could be wrapped with a plantain leaf, but this was deeper and more serious.

'How about shepherd's purse?' Martin looked at Susan.

Shepherd's purse, that was the thing, a straggly weed and very common. The herbalist at Kirkby had told Ellen Gill how good it was, for both internal and external bleeding and Ellen, poor woman, had taken it as a herbal tea, hoping to cure her lungs. It had not worked for Ellen, but it might be good for Martin and it wasn't a poison, so it couldn't harm him. There must be plenty of shepherd's purse on the farm? Yes, a wide border of the weed grew in the long, uncut grass at the edge of the nearest hayfield.

Martin had dropped into a light sleep as Susan set out to find the herb. What would Ellen have done? Probably this very thing. She cut a basketful of the rather stringy plant, which had small heart-shaped seed pods just beginning to form. Breathing fast, she ran back to the kitchen, where she boiled the whole plant in water for a few minutes to make a strong solution.

The weed had a strong smell, rather unpleasant, but in Susan's memory it took her back to the kitchen at Holly Bank, where shepherd's purse had been boiled up for a variety of uses. Martin had given it to calves at times and he'd once told her it belonged to the cabbage family.

'I don't know how this will feel, but no doubt you'll tell me,' Susan said lightly, and the patient's blue eyes opened wide as the infusion was applied to his wound. She wrapped up the gash in fresh bandages, watched anxiously and after a few minutes she was sure that the bleeding had stopped. Bending over Martin, she finished off the bandaging and felt again the nearness of him, familiar, as if the years without his presence had slipped away.

This would never do. Hadn't Martin gone off and left her at the Mermaid, all alone, with no friendly face? He'd got rid of her as quickly as possible, once Ellen died. True, they had worked together with varying success since she'd come to the hall, but that was of necessity. Martin had been trying to shake her off for years – and she must never forget it.

The patient moved slightly and then sat up with some diffi-culty. Susan found a pillow for his head. 'Thanks, lass, it's much easier now. Where'd I be without you?' The deep voice was low, still rather hoarse. 'Susan ...' He turned his head on to her shoulder. 'My dear.' The words came out on a long sigh of exhaustion.

'Martin ... please be more careful in future.' Susan managed to sound severe and professional. He was in pain, that was all.

The next day the patient was improving and the doctor said Susan had done a fine job. He even approved of comfrey ointment for healing, having seen it work on other patients. But there was a gulf between herself and Martin once again. The thorny side of Susan's nature had surfaced. She was afraid of getting too close to this man, who had a tendency to back off just when she needed support. It was easiest to be helpful but rather detached, impersonal, and the easy relationship of the last few weeks, the intimacy of the day before, was all but gone.

The farm manager stayed at the hall on doctor's orders for over a week. Susan found papers for him to read and as his leg healed, he was able to come into the kitchen. To lighten the rather gloomy atmosphere and to break the silence, Susan started to talk when they were alone about her father in York, and how important it was to her that his name should be cleared.

Susan soon had reason to worry once more about her own good name. Mr Jordan sent for her one day while Martin was still confined to the house. But instead of the usual slightly pompous expression, her employer looked very stern.

'Wood, I am very disappointed in you. My worst fears appear to be realized.'

What on earth had she done? 'Was the breakfast not right, Mr Jordan?'

'This has nothing to do with food. But I have to tell you that Robbie found an envelope on the floor and brought it to me ... and it seems to implicate you in the theft of my jewellery.' He held out an envelope, and Susan recognized it immediately. It had been found in Mrs Bain's apron pocket in the laundry, and

Susan had forgotten about it until now. 'I think you sold it, in Ripon.'

'I'd forgotten … but that was Mrs Bain's paper! It was in her pocket!'

Jordan shook his head. 'Please don't lie, Wood, it will make things worse.'

With shaking hands Susan pulled out the sheet of paper, which was a receipt from a Ripon jeweller. It itemized several pieces of jewellery, rubies and pearls, with the prices paid for them. Jordan pointed to the top of the receipt, where there was a scrawl in a different hand: 'S. Wood.'

'Can you deny it now?'

What a thing to say. 'Of course I can! I did not steal your things! Look, anyone can see that the jeweller who listed the pieces didn't write my name there, someone else did!'

Jordan peered at the sheet, and then shrugged. 'I admit it does seem rather odd. Perhaps we should reserve judgement … I will go to see the jeweller and ask him for more details and whether I can get my property back. Meanwhile, you are under notice and under suspicion. I will report this to PC Brown, of course.'

Turning, Susan marched out of the study with a burning face. She felt like leaving the hall and never coming back, but there were two reasons why she must stay. One was to establish her innocence and the other was Martin. He needed her to bandage the wound every day and she would stay until he was completely healed.

Susan was so upset when she took in his tea that Martin asked her what had happened, so she told him the story. Thank goodness he at least believed in her innocence. 'Now I know exactly how Papa feels,' she said quietly.

'You are more likely to be suspected, as in this case, when he is branded a criminal.' Martin looked gravely at Susan.

This was all too true. 'Mr Jordan told me that my father was a forger. Yet he must know … would it be possible to defend a man and believe him guilty, without knowing he was innocent?'

Martin moved as if to take her hand, but then withdrew. 'Susan, you can't be held responsible for what your father did. You may have to accept that he did – make a mistake, got involved in criminal dealings. He now regrets it and doesn't want his family to know about it … that is perhaps why he wants to go away, to start again. His children will have to lead their own lives. Don't worry too much.'

At least she could try to clear her own name. Susan decided on action. She took a day off and went down to Ripon with the carrier, to visit the jeweller in his ancient medieval shop with its timbered front. She asked to see the owner and a round-shouldered, elderly man came shuffling out of the workshop at the back of the shop.

'This is one of your receipts … with my name on it. Now, can you ever remember seeing me before?'

The man shook his head. 'What's this about, miss?'

'These items belong to my employer … can you tell me who brought them in?'

The jeweller looked alarmed. 'Nay, it's nowt to do with you! But …' He seemed to soften as he looked at Susan. 'I know the woman right well, as it happens, she's been disposing of her mother's things for some time. Dark, thirty or so, she is … but I can't see how …' He looked at the paper again. 'Are you S. Wood?'

'Yes,' said Susan grimly. 'That is the problem.'

The only thing to do was to tell PC Brown the story, and let him work it all out. The woman must be Mrs Bain. She'd been selling jewellery from the hall … and that was probably why she'd wanted to get rid of the new cook who might be too inquisitive.

By good luck, as she was walking through the market place Susan spotted the Slaters, Martin's neighbours who helped him out from time to time. She knew them from the farm name on the side of their trap. Motioning them to stop, she told them quickly about Martin's accident.

David Slater promised to do what he could to help with the urgent farm work. 'I'll have a talk to him first, about what he wants to do,' he said. Then he looked at Susan thoughtfully. 'Didn't you work there once – a long time ago? I remember a little lass with a fair fringe …'

'Yes, a long time ago.' I was a little fourteen-year-old, trying to look sixteen … and now I'm twenty-one and a grown woman, but some folks can only see the child, she thought bitterly. I should have grown big and fat since then.

'You'll know Martin well, then. To tell the truth, we're a mite worried about the lad, he's that dowly these days. Seems to have something on his mind. I told him to get wed and start a family, to cheer him up a bit.'

'I've thought the same thing,' Susan admitted. 'But you can't change Martin's mind, of course.' He has his own mysterious way of thinking.

Alice Slater leaned over the side of the trap. 'Would you like a ride home, lass? We can drop you at the hall, it's on our way.'

That evening, a strange thing happened. Mr Jordan came home from Ripon with a white face and informed the kitchen that he did not require dinner. Susan had planned a meal before she left for Ripon, but in the event she was home before Mr Jordan. Not require dinner? It was the first time that he'd ever done such a thing. What could be wrong?

The staff, including Martin, ate their own meal round the big kitchen table in a subdued frame of mind. 'P'raps he ate something at the Mermaid,' suggested Robbie helpfully. 'Upset his belly, like.' As they washed up, they heard Mr Jordan pacing up and down the hallway. Eventually he went into his office and shut the door.

Once the table was cleared, Martin got out some farm papers and was soon deep in calculations. It seemed rude to interrupt, although the scene in the jeweller's shop was still vivid. The maids and Robbie went off to bed, leaving silence in the kitchen.

'No more can be done tonight ... I'd better go to bed.' Martin was halfway to his feet when they heard a dull, muffled shot from somewhere in the house. Then silence. They looked at each other in dread.

'You stay here,' Martin ordered, limping off into the gloom of the big hall.

This was not the time to obey orders from Martin Gill. Susan caught up with him at the office door, following him into the room.

Andrew Jordan was slumped over his desk with his head on the blotter. His twelve bore shotgun, the one he often used to shoot rabbits, was on the floor beside him.

As they looked, horrified, the body twitched slightly.

CHAPTER FIFTEEN

Susan almost fainted, but she made an effort to stay upright, clutching the table for support. Then she heard a faint groan; Jordan was moving. Incredibly, his head was intact. They had heard the shot but whether the gun had gone off by accident or not, the solicitor had survived.

'Look, I don't think it touched him.' Martin bent over the chair.

Jordan looked up, weeping. 'I couldn't do it, Martin. I thought it was the easy way out ... please shoot me!' He covered his eyes with his hands.

Martin deliberately broke open the gun, took out the second cartridge and put the weapon back in its place in the cabinet. Then he turned to Jordan. 'Thank goodness you couldn't. Do you realize how messy it would have been?' He pointed to holes in the ceiling where the pellets had lodged. The solicitor shuddered.

Still weeping, Jordan asked for some brandy. Martin poured him a small amount from the decanter, then drew up a chair for Susan and sat down opposite. 'I think you'd better tell us about your trouble,' he said quietly. 'We may be able to help you.'

'Don't tell anyone! No one must know!' Jordan half rose and then fell back. 'I was going to ... end it all, and – I changed my mind at the last minute. So I'm not guilty of anything!' He seemed very excited. 'I shall say I was cleaning the gun.'

Susan sat down thankfully at the other side of the desk. 'No need to say anything, nobody will know. But Mr Jordan, you must have some very big problem. Won't you talk about it?'

Jordan looked at his cook, surprised. 'Tell my troubles to the servants? Why on earth do you suppose that I should?'

Martin smiled. 'We are fellow human beings, even so. It's nearly the twentieth century, Jordan, you needn't be old-fashioned about it. We're not your slaves, remember – I'm your farm adviser and you know Susan's background. It's business that's worrying you, is it?'

There was a deep sigh. 'Very well, Martin. I suppose you may as well know. Today I found out that I'm to be declared bankrupt. Everything must be sold – the farm, the hall, everything. You can sort out the details for me ... perhaps you would give the other servants notice tomorrow. I tried to get more time, to raise another loan ... but I failed.' Jordan flopped back in the chair. 'You can be in charge of selling the place.' He was heaping his problems on to the other man.

Susan looked at Martin. 'You know about these things. Can you help?'

'I've some experience of capital, debt and so on, having farmed in the depression and worked with my father as well. It might not be as bad as you think.' Martin spoke deliberately, still trying to calm the man down. 'Have you any idea what you're worth?'

Jordan shook his head and then winced. 'No. I've never thought of selling ... so I have no recent valuation. They just told me I'd have to sell all I possess, but of course they don't know, either.' He looked at Martin. 'I'm not thinking well ...'

'Once you are bankrupt that is the case, as you will know. But until then you might sell off part of the estate, pay what you owe or a part of it and survive, so long as you don't panic. I'd have thought you would know just what to do, from your training in law. If you have land, it's usually possible to survive.'

Jordan sat low in his chair, quite deflated; it was almost possible to feel sorry for him. 'You're right, Martin. I did panic, it was foolish of me.'

'If you're committed to farming, keep as much of the land as you can. Your antique furniture and old paintings will be worth a bit of money, you could sell the livestock and the crops ... and maybe live to farm another day. So it's not happened yet – the bankruptcy? If you keep your head, we may be able to avoid it.'

There was a glimmer of interest. 'Do you think so? I must admit that although I'm considered to be a fairly good lawyer, I am not good with money. People think that the two go together, but it's not always so. Perhaps I need good financial and estate management advice.'

Martin appeared to think for a few minutes. 'Well, maybe you could sell those few outlying fields near Kirkby, the ones that are detached from the rest of the estate. I'm sure we could find a buyer. That could be a short-term solution, then with care you could escape the disgrace and keep most of the place intact. I'll be pleased to help, maybe get advice in confidence from other quarters, but on one condition.' Martin looked briefly at Susan.

This was a chance Martin was giving her. 'You must tell the truth, Mr Jordan. Admit that I did not steal your jewellery. And tell the truth about Toby Wood. His disgrace is with him still – of course it affects my brothers and me.' It seemed hard to press him tonight, while he was still in shock, but it might be the only way to get their names cleared, once and for all.

Jordan recoiled. 'But that was the truth! It's all there in the record of the trial – Wood was found guilty, there was no doubt at all.'

'We mean the genuine truth.' Did she sound as grim as she felt?

Jordan threw up his hands and Martin seemed to feel sorry for him. 'Tomorrow, then. We must get some sleep. But tell me – how did a man like you get into this pickle?'

'Card play,' Andrew Jordan said at last. 'And then, I regret to say, gambling again to pay off debts, mainly cards, but also horses. Getting deeper and deeper ... it has been a nightmare. It's addictive, you know ... but I hope never to gamble again.'

The next morning Jordan stuck to his story of Toby's guilt, which was disappointing. But it seemed best to do what was possible to help the solicitor, such as organizing for the farm produce to be sold. They could work on him later, when there was more time. And so, very abruptly, Susan's career as the hall cook was ended, after only a few rather uneasy months.

Typically, Martin took on the job of finding places for the young people and it was soon arranged. Hannah was to go back to the Kirkby shop to help her mother, while Robbie was found a place as an assistant groom at Larton Manor, to his great delight. Daisy was given a wonderful letter of reference and taken home to Pateley, where her parents lived. None of the staff was paid any wages, but Martin said grimly that he would attend to it in time. 'When we get some cash coming in, I'll make sure he pays the wages. Can you make me a list of what's owing?' he asked Susan.

Before they left, Martin asked the three young people not to talk about Mr Jordan's debts, although it would be tempting. 'Least said, soonest mended,' he reminded them of a favourite moorland saying. 'He might be able to work his way out of it, if he keeps his head and there isn't too much gossip about him. And then you'll get paid.'

Martin said little, but he hoped that one day he would get more information out of the solicitor. 'Don't worry about me, lass. My leg's healing up grand, thanks to you. You should have been a nurse!'

On the last day at Ringbeck Hall, Susan and Martin helped Jordan pack up the ornaments and smaller items of furniture for sale. The younger servants had gone. When Jordan went to bed early, a strange silence settled on the house. Susan's trunk had been taken to the cottage, so she had very little packing to do.

'I suppose you'll be off to Holly Bank tonight,' she said to Martin when their work was finished, as she lit the lamp in the kitchen. It was a mild autumn night with no moon.

'I can manage to ride home now, but I'd better stay here tonight. Make us a cup of tea, lass, I want to talk to you.'

This was the last time they'd be here together in the kitchen, drinking tea at the table, the last evening she'd watch the familiar face in the lamplight. Mechanically Susan went through the ritual of warming the teapot, spooning in the tea and pouring on the boiling water from the huge kettle on the stove.

The farmer watched in silence until the tea was made. 'My, I don't know how you lift that heavy kettle, little thing that you are.' He shook his head. 'Boiling water's that dangerous ...' He was patronizing her again.

'I am a professional cook, Martin Gill, and quite capable of kitchen duties. Would you like to see my references?' Oh dear, that sounded prickly.

Martin laughed and the tension eased a little. 'Now come and sit down, drink your tea. Talk about a thorny Yorkshire rose! Ellen was right about you, you know.'

Susan turned her back on him and cut two slices of teacake. They ate and drank in silence, until at length Martin pushed his cup away. 'Now, Susan, I've something to say to you. Your life is going to be difficult, once again ... you've lost your place here at the hall, and I know you don't want to join your father in York. It's not a good prospect.'

Tired as she was, Susan felt somehow irritated that he assumed responsibility for her, as though she was still a little girl. 'I thought you'd know that by now I can get a job when I need one. It shouldn't be too hard ... some people think I'm quite good, as a matter of fact.'

'Now, lass, don't be prickly. What I want to say is, that maybe we should get married ... it would be a solution, perhaps. I've always thought that I was too old for you and maybe that's so, but we manage together very well and with you at Holly Bank, we could maybe make some money. And you wouldn't have to go off and look for another place. What do you think, Susan?' Martin looked over the table at her, but she could see no expression on his face because the lamp was behind him.

Martin was talking like an old farmer. He was suggesting marriage as a convenience for them both, no mention of love, nothing romantic at all. Anger was rising in Susan, a bitter anger that nearly choked her. This was the man who'd left her to sink or swim at the Mermaid when she really needed support, who had held her at arm's length all these years. She'd thought she loved him, but now, she suddenly realized she had grown out of the childish infatuation. That's all it was, she reminded herself.

'Well, perhaps you are too old for me,' she said bitterly. 'You're so detached, so elderly! This sounds like a business arrangement, hardly the way to think of marriage, at least in my view. Thank you, Martin, but I can manage quite well. Surely you can see that you don't have to look after the Woods all your life? Ellen said you were a good man and I know you are, but I don't want to be looked after as a duty. I don't want to be told what's right and what's not, and protected from the wicked world.' Susan was getting carried away by now; it was hard to stop as all the bitterness came out, all the resentment. Martin Gill had kept her waiting too long; her love for him had soured and she saw him now as a father figure.

'Hey, lass, don't get so upset!' Martin passed a weary hand over his face. He sat where he was, and for a fleeting moment Susan wished he would come over and take her in his arms. But the moment passed and she held on to her resolve.

'I am sorry if that was rude, but I am quite sure of what I want to do – to stand on my own feet … you and Ellen trained me well, I can earn my own living and I expect to do so. Thank you for helping us when we were little … but please don't worry about us any more.' Susan stood up and began to clear the table.

'Susan – maybe I didn't explain myself very well.' Martin looked tired and suddenly, rather old. 'I thought you'd understand …'

'I do, perfectly. You feel obliged to give me work, and because people might talk if we lived in the same house, you are offering marriage. You offer to make an honest woman of me, as they say, so that I can be the housekeeper at Holly Bank without any scandal. Well, it's kind of you, but no, thank you. I'm sure you will be able to find a good woman to suit you better than I would. And now, I must go to bed. Goodnight.'

Martin said nothing more and they parted in silence. When she got up in the morning, he had gone.

The day after Susan left, a grim and bitter Mr Gill had an appointment with Mr Jordan. He was furious with himself for talking to Susan as he had; why hadn't he told her the truth, that he loved her, had always loved her? The moorland reticence had come between them, not for the first time, and now it was probably too late to mend matters. He'd better stick to business.

Since the night of the 'accident' with the gun Martin had assumed the upper hand with the solicitor, not from any sense of power but because he felt that he knew better than Jordan what should be done. 'I've looked over the land and I reckon there's about seventy acres near Kirkby could be sold. I'll try to find a buyer.'

'Do hurry!' Jordan looked scared. 'I've only got a few weeks to find the money.'

After this Martin intended to carry out a quiet survey of who might like to buy the land and more importantly, who could afford it. His plan for Jordan was to sell land to get out of trouble,

and then to pay off the staff and smaller debts by selling the stock and crops. It was almost winter, the farm could wait for restocking until spring and if Jordan worked hard at his profession, he might earn enough to get him on his feet again. It was odd how the man relied on his farm manager to get him out of trouble; Martin supposed that the blind panic which had led him to think of suicide had prevented him from planning how to pay his debts.

Unfortunately for Jordan, the day after this interview Martin was called away urgently. 'My grandfather has died, I have to go over to Pateley,' he told Jordan before riding away.

It was still hard to climb into the saddle, but Martin was managing to get about in spite of his lame leg. He was sorry about the death, but it wasn't entirely unexpected; Grandfather had been in failing health for a few months now.

The surprise came after the funeral, as Martin was thinking about Holly Bank and getting back to work again. He discovered that Grandfather Jeremiah had left all his considerable fortune to his two grandsons, Martin's brother Billy and himself. Martin was richer by a few thousand pounds, out of the blue. 'It doesn't change anything,' he said stubbornly to his mother, who seemed to think that now he could marry a princess, if he wanted one. 'I never expected this – I thought that Father would get it.'

The money would take some getting used to. Martin had always been careful and by now Holly Bank was paid for, but there had never been much to spare. His farm was a little too small to yield a comfortable living, although heaven knew there was always plenty to do. But with more land, he could employ a labourer, which would make things much easier.

Before Martin left Pateley, he and his brother Billy had a talk about what they would do with the legacy. 'Remember the old joke?' asked Billy. 'Farmer comes into some money and says, "Well, I reckon I'll just farm until it's all gone." Farms soak up brass, my lad, you know as well as I do, and you can't see much improvement for it. Me, I think I'll buy railway shares!'

'Aye?' Martin smiled. 'A good idea, but I could do with a few more acres.'

A light rain fell as the farmer left Pateley the next day, riding with his head down against the wind, trying to make good time over the moor before the weather worsened. Gradually, as the horse trotted over the short moorland turf, Martin formed an idea. With Grandfather's money, he could step in and buy Jordan's land.

The thought was attractive from a farming point of view; the land was good and clear of stones, well fenced with hawthorn hedges, and next to Martin's boundary on the low side, in fact, it would give him more 'bottom land', fit for ploughing. He could even build a new house on the lower land, nearer to Kirkby, he thought as the stone walls of Holly Bank loomed out of the rain. He could build if he had the will to do it, of course, and a family to build it for. But he wouldn't think about that.

By the time that Martin saw Jordan again, he had a fully formed plan. This good fortune, the first he'd had for many years, was going to work in two ways.

'I will buy the land privately, no need for anyone else to know,' he told Jordan the next day. 'Your office can do the transfer of ownership, keep it all quiet. I will give you a fair deal, but there will be no haggling. You'll have to take my price.'

The solicitor nodded, already beginning to get back to his normal self. 'I'm very grateful to you, Martin, very grateful indeed. I hope you will be able to help me with the rest of it, the selling of stock and so forth. I will pay you of course, for all this time you have spent on my behalf, as soon as I have the money.' He leaned back in the office chair, looking pleased with himself.

'Yes, yes. But there are conditions. Solemn conditions, Andrew Jordan.'

'Such as?'

'I don't really need to buy more land just now, although I'll admit it will be useful. But this deal will only go through if you tell me what happened in the trial of Toby Wood.'

Jordan sighed. 'You are still harping on about that old story? It's nearly eight years ago, Martin – I can't be expected to remember every detail of every case I take to court! My dear fellow, you have no idea how much tedious detail—'

'Tell me!' Martin interrupted. 'It is extremely important to Toby and his family that he is known to be innocent, if that is the case. Tell me now, or the deal is off. And there's no time left to find another buyer.' Really, Grandfather would be proud of me, Martin thought. He liked to drive a hard bargain.

The cold rain beat against the windowpane and Andrew Jordan drummed his fingers on the table. There was a long silence in the room, until Jordan moved. 'Very well … Toby Wood was as guilty as hell, although he seems to have convinced himself otherwise. That is quite common, you know, in prisons. It is natural enough to justify oneself, and gradually to change the whole story so that one is innocent. This, I think, is what happened to Wood.' The ticking of the clock was loud in the silence. Jordan sighed.

'He had a key to the shed, the printing press and all the equipment used for forgery, because he was the artist. And I couldn't prove that the engraver was lying. He said, on oath, that they were both in it, with Wood in the lead. I know that Toby was involved … it needed a good brain to set up the jobs, and that was Toby's role. But I lost the case. I can't tell you anything more.'

'Have you got press cuttings of the trial?'

Jordan shuffled. 'Somewhere, there is a folder with cuttings of all the trials I've been involved in … but I don't know where.'

This was bad news. Susan would be wise to look after her own affairs and not to worry about her father; but it was hard to think that she might have inherited bad tendencies, poor lass. Martin was thankful that he and Ellen had stressed honesty above everything else when the Wood children were young.

Susan had said that her father wasn't willing to investigate the case; he wanted to put it all behind him, to forgive his enemies and live in peace, in a new environment. That was his best plan, especially if he were guilty.

Martin knew he must try to avoid thinking about Susan so much. He had been shocked to find that she wanted to get away from him and live her own life. All those years, he had kept away for her own sake – but he had thought, at the back of his mind, that she loved him, as he loved her. Maybe his approach had been wrong – but how could a moorland farmer express what he really felt? He still worried about her ... where would she go, how would she live? She might find work on a farm where she'd be taken advantage of, even abused.

CHAPTER SIXTEEN

Ashtree Cottage was to be sold. Susan would soon be without a home, without that sense of security, of belonging that she had fallen back upon even when she worked at the Mermaid. All security was gone and she felt alone as never before.

As the days grew shorter, she had wondered whether she should have agreed to go to her father in York, taken the easy option. But it had been so good to be back in her own home again. She had tidied the cottage garden, picked blackberries in the hazy sunshine and enjoyed the sense of freedom from being a hall servant, at Jordan's beck and call. One day soon she would have to look for a job ... before the cold winter set in.

A week of freedom passed quickly, and then the brief respite was over. Susan's world was shattered by a letter from Toby Wood, a loving letter from her parent that plunged her almost into despair. 'I am sure you will understand, my dear ...' There was much affection in the letter, but the news was dire. 'We all have to face the facts. There is no future for any of us on the moorland, but on the other hand, York is full of opportunities. I loved the cottage, it has fond memories for me, but we must move on.' There was no thought of whether his daughter was ready to move on. This was gentle coercion; her father was trying to force her to go to York. Did he really know Susan? It was obvious he thought she was a quiet, biddable little thing. Well, he might soon find out that she was a Yorkshire rose, and getting thornier as she grew older. That was a frightening thought, she would probably end up as a sharp-tongued old maid, but Susan would not be coerced.

Toby was going to sell the cottage as soon as he could, in order to buy a little house in York – if the money would stretch that far. Susan was to send their furniture to the sale rooms immediately, to sell for what it would fetch. 'Of course, if there is anything you really want to keep, you can bring it here when you come,' Toby wrote blithely. The auctioneers already had their instructions and he wanted to sell before the winter snow kept potential buyers away.

This was what Ben had suggested, some time ago. He would approve of the sale and John would be happy enough to go to York. Only old-fashioned Susan wanted to hang on to the past, to live in the old stone house with no modern comforts. Most younger women would prefer gas for lighting and cooking; even water closets were becoming common in the town. But they could never compensate for the loss of freedom, of dawns and sunsets spreading above the moor, the call of the curlew or the delight of the changing seasons.

For a young woman who wanted a future on the moorland, things looked grim. What about the books that had sustained the Woods as they were growing up, and the old rocking chair? Everything was to be taken from her – and she had no job. An undersized, out of work cook with no friends, that's what she was. There had never been time to make friends.

If she hadn't been desperate, Susan might never have talked to Hannah and her mother Bessie at the Kirkby shop. Both women were concerned, she could see, that Susan hadn't been found a place. As she bought flour and sugar with her dwindling savings, they tutted about the problems of earning a living.

Hannah looked at her mother and then at Susan. 'There is one place we heard tell of,' she began slowly. 'But it's a big job, Miss Wood ... I couldn't manage it, that's for sure. I'm not sure I should even mention it. If it brought you bad luck I'd feel ever so guilty.'

This sounded interesting. It couldn't be worse than the Mermaid, could it? 'Tell me about it, please,' Susan demanded.

Bessie nodded. 'It's not for the faint-hearted! There's a farmer over the moor yonder that's in need of help. Not just in the house, mind you – he really needs a shepherd, or at least some-body to help his man with the sheep. But it's rough up there, lass ... the house is right neglected. Not altogether the place for a person like you.' She looked down at Susan, evidently weighing up her lack of height and breadth.

For some reason her first interview at the Mermaid flashed through Susan's mind. *I can cure a ham and treat sheep's feet.* Maybe this time it would be the right answer. 'What sort of a man is he?' Susan had a vivid mental picture of a moorland George and she had no intention of being chased round any farmyard by a lecherous old sheep farmer.

The shopkeeper smiled. 'John Ashby is, well, at heart he's a kindly gentleman ... but he's, well, he's very old and a mite strange. The poor man lost his wife last year, and then he fares badly with the rheumatics. There's a man for the farm work, but the house is gone to rack and ruin and he doesn't eat properly. But there again,' and she glanced at Susan, 'there's plenty of money for wages, you'd be right enough there if you could stand the mess. There's a sight of work waiting for somebody, they say.'

If he had the rheumatics, he wouldn't be up to chasing females; this sounded interesting. 'Who says?'

The woman lowered her voice. 'Postman said as much. And doctor told me in confidence, like, to try to find some help for Mr Ashby – the old lad himself, he knows that summat should be done. If our Hannah was older ... but Hannah needs a year or two more in service with other folks, before she can tackle a job like this.'

'Where's the farm and how could I get there?' It was worth a look, Susan decided. She wouldn't promise to stay more than a few weeks and it might give her a little time to find another place. The cottage could be sold at any time, and then she would be homeless, and if that happened, York would certainly be her only option.

'Doctor said he would take you up there, if you were willing. He's off over that way tomorrow, he said. It's Blackthorn Farm – not that far, about four mile from Kirkby, you get to it down a lane off the moor road.' It became clear that Hannah had already suggested Susan to the doctor, knowing that she must be looking for work.

She did not want to ask Jordan for a character. If the farmer wanted a reference, somebody to speak for Susan, things would be difficult, because Mrs Thomson had retired to live with a sister in Hull. Heaven alone knew what George Sanderson would have to say about his ex-cook, so she wouldn't ask him. Most employers wanted to know your work history, especially in a case like this, where an honest woman was essential.

'You must be prepared to be very firm with him,' Dr Bishop said the next day.

Susan was perched in his stylish trap, travelling swiftly through the village on a hazy autumn day with a hint of chill in the air.

'Have you had farm housekeeping experience, can you be firm? You look very young to me.'

Not another one … another person to underestimate Susan Wood and her capabilities, just because she was small. Just as she had always done, Susan sat up very straight and spoke precisely. 'I have considerable experience of cooking and farm work … but what do you mean about being firm? I am determined, if that is required.' She put on a stern expression.

The doctor's careworn face relaxed into a smile as he looked over at her. 'My patient is at heart a kindly man, but he will need some managing. Old people often become very set in their ways. However, in this case his ways are not good for him and they will need to be changed.' He looked across at his passenger again. 'And of course, this may be difficult. Put yourself in his place, a man accustomed to being in charge, but now unable physically to do very much at all.'

As they swung off the moor road, Blackthorn Farm looked quite well kept. The farm road had no ruts, the hedges were trimmed and the farmyard was tidy. So far, so good. A small and skinny figure came out of the barn to meet them, but this was not Mr Ashby. 'This is Josiah ... thank you, Josiah,' and the doctor handed over the reins. The man grunted and led the horse off. 'He keeps the farm going,' Bishop explained as they went towards the house. 'He's a man of few words, as you can see.'

A torn and dirty curtain, flapping through an open window was the first sign that all was not well. The kitchen floor was hidden under piles of old newspapers and the table was littered with the remains of meals: mouldy bread, pieces of old cheese and chop bones. The smell was overpowering. Mr Ashby evidently needed some urgent help in the kitchen. It was hard to breathe ... or to make their way though the room, without falling over a piece of harness or an old scythe.

If anything, the parlour was worse. Several weeks' ashes surrounded the fireplace, where a smoky peat fire burned. The old man staggered to his feet as they came in, leaning heavily on a stick. He frowned at the doctor. 'What's this you've brought today? This ... woman? It's no good, Bishop, I'm not having a nurse. I'll go to the devil in my own way, thank you.' He sat down heavily and turned his back on them both.

The man was nearly invisible under a shaggy mane of white hair and a long beard. His black suit was green with age and his shirt was dirty. It was no good; Susan silently agreed with him. This was no place for Susan Wood.

'This is young Susan – she's not a nurse,' the doctor said comfortably, sitting down opposite his patient. 'She can help you to clean the place up, and cook a meal – that's all.' He looked at Susan. 'In fact, food might be the answer, you know.'

Food had certainly made a big difference in the days when the young Woods were almost starving; a good meal had changed their attitude to life. 'When did you last eat, Mr Ashby?' Susan asked in what she hoped was a firm voice. 'Have you had dinner yet?'

There was a growl and the man turned round. 'Dinner? Haven't had a good dinner since Lottie died. But I manage, I manage. Mind your own business, woman.'

'Well, I'll leave you here for tonight – I'll call back in the morning,' the doctor said relentlessly. He intended her to stay! 'Anything you want, just ask Josiah. He lives in the cottage down the lane.'

It was late afternoon and the autumn dusk would soon close in, shutting her into this terrible world. This was the biggest challenge she had met so far, but Susan Wood was not going to panic. It was only four miles to Kirkby and if necessary she could walk to the village, even back to her own cottage, if need be; it was a steadying thought.

Looking at her reluctant employer, Susan felt sorry for him. Who wouldn't be cross, having a stranger imposed on them in their own home? 'Well Mr Ashby, it's only for tonight, so we'll make the best of it, shall we? What would you like for supper?'

Mr Ashby seemed to struggle with his temper. After a pause he turned round and looked at Susan. 'Why don't you just go away? Damned women! All the same, interfering …' He spoke hoarsely as though unused to talking. 'Get out!' What could be seen of his face turned red with anger.

Susan turned and walked firmly out of the room. She would try to find some eatable food for him, just in case it improved his temper. There was a crash as something hit the door as she closed it. Mr Ashby was not in a good mood.

There was very little food in the house. What was the doctor thinking of, to leave her in this pickle? There was a pile of wood near the stove and Susan lit it, then put the kettle on to boil. A cup of tea would make a start. She found a large bag of flour but no yeast, so bread was out of the question; there were several pots of honey on a shelf. She would have to make what they had called at the cottage 'pan bread', flour and water mixed with a little baking soda and cooked in a frying pan. And she'd better find candles before it got dark.

Half an hour later, the new helper carried a tray into the parlour. Mr Ashby had lit the lamp; evidently it was part of his routine. 'Here's a cup of tea,' she said cheerfully, 'and some bread and honey. Do you keep bees, Mr Ashby?' Let's hope he doesn't throw anything else at me, she thought. There was a shattered vase on the floor behind the door; it would have knocked her out if the door hadn't closed in time.

The farmer staggered to his feet and grabbed the poker from the hearth. Waving it like a sword, he advanced on Susan. 'Go away! I told you, I don't want help!' he shouted.

Susan put down the tray on the table with shaking hands, but she stood her ground; she was between him and the door, safe enough. He was just like one of the drunks at the Mermaid: all threats and very little action. 'Please put the poker down immediately, Mr Ashby. And eat some bread and honey.' There was sugar in the tea; that might help. The old man stood in silence, looking at her. His expression could not be seen though the whiskers.

'Put the poker down and come to the table, or I will leave immediately!' Susan spoke even more firmly and she meant every word; enough was enough.

'Leave? Leave? You can't do that. Stay and talk to me.' Ashby collapsed heavily into a dining chair at the table, dropping the poker on the floor. Slowly he reached out and took a piece of bread and honey. He ate two pieces and then sat back. Susan waited. In a few minutes he belched and took another piece of bread. 'Yes, lass, I used to keep very fine bees. Heather honey's the best in the world ... do you come from the High Side, young – er – what's your name?'

Things were improving, but it would be best to tread warily. 'I'm Susan, Mr Ashby. Yes, my family has – had – a cottage not far from Kirkby. I worked as a cook in Ripon, but I like the country best.'

The farmer shook his head as thought trying to clear his memory. 'If you can cook, there should be some eggs in the barn ... the hens lay all over the place, these days. And I think there's a bit of ham left somewhere, unless that scoundrel Joss has pinched it. But don't touch anything. I can't abide an interfering woman.' He growled in his throat and frowned ferociously at her through the mane of hair.

Outside, the yard was deserted. After some trouble, Susan found a nest of eggs in the hay. She collected a dozen or so in her apron and was turning back to the house when Josiah appeared. 'What you doing, woman?' The tone was not friendly.

'I am collecting eggs for Mr Ashby's supper.' Susan met his stare with her own.

'I don't hold with wimmen coming here and interfering!' Josiah sounded rather like his employer. 'We manage. Boss is likely to kill you if you go too far, you know that? He's a violent man, these days. Gone funny in the head since missis died. You could just tip him over the edge ...' The man turned away. 'I'd leave right away, if I was you. While going's good. Then we won't have to bury you in the midden.' He laughed mirthlessly.

What did he expect her to do, burst into tears? This was not the place for polite conversation, so Susan told him what she thought. 'If you had any sense, you would try to help me. I'm not here to interfere, as you call it. I will try to make a decent meal for Mr Ashby and do a little cleaning, and I will leave when it suits me, thank you. I am not taking any threats from you.' Yes, she would leave in the morning, but this creature was not going to frighten her away. Even so, it was a chilly thought. Josiah had already planned that if she was murdered, they would dispose of the body! In fact she was entirely at the mercy of these two hostile men, far from any help. There were many dark tales of murder on the moorland; the young Woods had decided long ago not to believe any of them, but what if some of them were true?

Josiah seemed to approve of Susan's spirited answer. 'Bit of a fighter, are you, lass? Fancy that, and you so small and all. Well, I'll give you a few taties from the garden.' He picked up a bucket deliberately and went through a wooden gate into what turned out to be a large garden, laid out with orderly vegetable beds. Josiah at least was eating well ... why couldn't he make sure that Mr Ashby ate a good dinner?

'Never go in house yonder,' Josiah said as though following her thoughts. 'Boss ordered me out years ago and I never went back ... but farm's as tidy as I can make it and it turns a profit every year.' He dug up a handful of potatoes and added a carrot. 'He's a strange man, Mr Ashby. You mun be very careful.'

'Thank you, Josiah,' Susan said more graciously. 'I think that a good meal will improve his temper.'

Susan laid the table in the parlour, and after a struggle that included being sworn at and threatened half-heartedly with a knife, she persuaded Mr Ashby to sit at the table for his supper of ham, eggs and potato. It was getting dark and she hadn't yet worked out where she could sleep tonight – or whether in fact she should do the prudent thing and walk back to Kirkby. But first she would eat, too, to keep up her strength. It had been a long and exhausting day.

The old farmer ate his meal, went back to his seat by the fire and fell asleep. Susan guessed that he had not eaten so much for a long time. Taking a candle, she went up the broad oak staircase to a wide landing. Here were several doors, each with a tarnished brass handle. She stood for a while thinking and realized that she could hear the steady drip of rain from the roof. It was now a dark, wet night; she would have to stay at Blackthorn Farm for one night, at least.

Susan had noticed that the house faced west and she guessed that the master bedroom would be above the parlour, also on the west side of the house. That would probably be Mr Ashby's room, and she could imagine the rage if she as much as opened the door. This other door should open to a room on the south side, possibly rather warmer and drier than the rest. Taking a deep breath, Susan turned the doorknob, wondering what would be revealed in the leaping shadows cast by her candle. The door swung slowly open, the hinges creaking in protest.

CHAPTER SEVENTEEN

Susan let out her breath slowly. In contrast to the rest of the house, here in this bedroom there was order and calm, but it was almost as sinister as the confusion downstairs. A thick layer of dust coated the dressing table and spiders had festooned the corners with their webs; no one had disturbed the ghosts here for some years. Throwing back dust sheets from the big brass bed, she found it was covered with a patchwork quilt, lovingly sewn a generation ago by busy hands that were now at rest.

A huge oak wardrobe loomed at the foot of the bed; Susan tentatively opened its drawer and a faint scent wafted out to meet her. Here was clean household linen, neatly folded, fragrant with lavender. She took out sheets and pillow cases and made up the bed, thinking of poor Lottie, Mr Ashby's dead wife, who must have been a careful housekeeper. What sort of a life had she led out here on the edge of the moor? Had Mr Ashby been violent then, had she lived in fear – or were they happy together?

There was little she could do in the dark and so Susan climbed thankfully into the bed. She would get up at first light and try to clean up the kitchen before Dr Bishop arrived, but she would tell him that the job was too big for her. She would recommend that Mr Ashby should be persuaded to sell the farm and live in the village, with a decent couple to look after him. Such an arrangement would be safer for everyone, including Susan Wood, and it might give some honest folk an income.

It was a comfortable feather bed, warm and dry. Susan blew out the candle and thought about the moorland, as she'd always done last thing at night, especially during her time at the Mermaid. There it was outside the window, the high ridge of bracken and heather above the house. She pictured Blackthorn Farm in relation to Kirkby, and to her little cottage, not so far away. Suddenly, it came to her that Martin Gill was not very far away, either. He took a different road out of Kirkby and the farm gates were miles apart, but across country Martin's farm and Ashby's would probably meet on a boundary, right on the edge of the common grazing. Working with Martin's sheep, hadn't she once or twice looked over the wall and been told that the land belonged to John Ashby? Gradually, a memory came back to her from years ago of meeting this farmer, perhaps once or twice, when they were gathering sheep. He'd been old even then, but straighter – it must have been about five years ago at least – and his silver hair had been neatly cut. Mr Ashby had been well spoken and civil in those days, a kindly man. Odd that she'd forgotten him until now, although nobody would have recognized the wild-haired old man who lived here now; you could hardly see his face at all.

As Susan drifted off to sleep, a snipe called in the night, the familiar country sound. In spite of the dreadful mess downstairs and its dangerous occupant, she felt oddly at home here. That night she dreamed of the cottage and the old life at Holly Bank.

The rain cleared during the night and Susan woke to a bright autumn morning, with spider's webs sparkling like diamonds, their dewdrops caught by the sun. The first priority was to clean out the kitchen; she tied up all the old newspapers and put them outside, then scrubbed the floor, the kitchen table and all the chairs. The floor, once it could be seen, turned out to be of cheerful red tiles. With a bright fire burning, the kitchen was a different place already. The walls badly needed whitewash, but there would be no time for that before the doctor came to fetch her.

Breakfast would have to be eggs again, so Susan made some more pan bread, toasted it and piled scrambled eggs on the toast. She was about to take the breakfast tray into the parlour when the tapping of a stick was heard and Mr Ashby came into the kitchen. The helper held her breath. What would be his weapon of choice today? What on earth would he say? She got ready to move quickly, should the need arise.

The old man leaned on his stick and looked round the kitchen in silence for a long time. Then he sat down suddenly at the table. 'The place looks more like it used to do,' he observed. 'What's for breakfast, lass?'

Hoping for the mellow mood to continue, Susan poured them both a cup of tea and put the breakfast tray in front of Mr Ashby. 'More food? I suppose I'd better eat it, if you say so.' He seemed to have forgotten that he had asked about breakfast.

Susan and her temporary employer ate together at the kitchen table, and to keep him off the subject of changes, she asked him about the size of the farm and the stock it carried. Mr Ashby still knew exactly what was going on and all about the recent farm prices, and he seemed pleased to talk about his farm. But then with a sudden change of mood, he looked at Susan sternly. 'Who can I ask to give you a character, young woman? I shouldn't take on a housekeeper without asking about her manners and morals, should I?'

'Well, Mr Ashby, I'm afraid I can't stay, so I won't be your housekeeper.'

'But who can tell me?' The old man was becoming agitated now. 'I must check up on you, you know.'

To keep him happy, Susan thought for a moment. 'There's Martin Gill, I worked for them – until Mrs Gill died. You could ask him, if you must. But I'm leaving today, so it won't matter.'

Mr Ashby poured himself another cup of tea with a shaky hand. 'Today? Today? Just when I was enjoying a good talk? You'd better stay, young woman – what did you say your name was? There's a lot of work to do here ... and I saw myself in the mirror this morning. A sad sight! You'll have to cut my hair and shave my beard for me, before Dr Bishop gets here.'

The change in the farmer since yesterday was amazing; Susan decided that she would recommend ham and eggs for all cases of bad temper in the future. However, agitation was not far from the surface, and she was aware of the fragility of his mind. But to cut his hair – and he was so dirty! It was exactly what the poor man needed, to make him feel more normal and she could see that it was her duty to do as much for him as he would allow.

More bravely than she felt, she looked across the table. 'Have you a good pair of scissors, Mr Ashby? And had it not better wait until you have taken your bath?' Speak firmly and he might think it's his wife talking.

The man groaned. 'You sound just like Lottie! Light the copper in the wash house for some hot water – there's a big zinc bath in there. The Lord knows how long it is since – but yes, Miss ... what's your name? I will take a bath and try to find some clean clothes. But first, I am going to write a letter and ask you to deliver it.'

'How far? I can't stay long ...' Susan began, but the farmer interrupted, in a surprisingly strong voice.

'Nonsense, woman. Now, I will write a letter and you can walk over the fields – it's not far – to see Martin Gill. He will reply and you will bring the answer back to me. Your character, miss. I'll not have my hair cut by a woman with no character.'

Mr Ashby scribbled his letter and Susan, having lit the fire for the bath, put on her coat for the walk across to Holly Bank, a walk she would rather not take. As she crossed the yard, she heard Mr

Ashby talking to Josiah. 'I want a couple of chickens killed and dressed for tonight,' he ordered. 'With vegetables to suit ... I know you have them, you scoundrel. I'm going to keep an eye on you!' The shepherd was speechless, and no wonder. His boss had changed overnight.

Holly Bank was surprisingly close to Mr Ashby's farm, but there was no track between the two and Susan found herself scrambling over walls and climbing fences. All too soon she was walking up the back field and there was Martin, coming out of the stable with a bridle over his arm. This was going to be difficult.

'Good heavens, Susan Wood! The last person I expected to see. Where did you drop from?' Martin was obviously astonished to see her. He looked quite healthy and the last trace of a limp was gone. It was only two weeks since they'd left Ringbeck Hall, but to Susan it seemed a very long time – the start of the rest of her life, free from the shadow of Martin Gill. And yet here she was, visiting him.

'I am sorry to trouble you, Martin, but I've come over from Blackthorn Farm. To humour Mr Ashby, that's the only reason. He's sent you a letter and I am to take back an answer.'

Martin looked shocked. 'Ashby! Surely you're not working for that maniac? He's completely mad, they tell me. Since Mrs Ashby died, nobody can do a thing with him.' He put down the bridle on a cart. 'They'd no bairns, nobody to help in their old age and that's made it worse, of course. It's no place for a woman.'

'Did anybody try?' Susan wondered whether his neighbours had given him any support; usually moorlanders were good when you needed help, but in this case ...

'Yes, I did,' Martin said with a flash of the blue eyes. We weren't particularly friendly, as you'll remember – they were chapel and we were church, though why that should matter I don't know – Lottie was always polite, but that was all, and old John seemed to be rather shy. But all the same, I visited when she

died – and he chased me off with a shotgun, so I didn't go again.'
He looked carefully at Susan. 'That is no place for a lass like you!
Surely you're not going to work for him? I – Susan, I won't allow
it!' He was nearly as agitated as Mr Ashby.

Until that moment Susan was quite sure that she'd be going
back to Kirkby with the doctor, later in the day. But Martin was
so adamant that she made up her mind. Who was he to forbid her
do anything?

'Yes, Martin, this morning he asked me to stay, so I will – at
least until I've put the house to rights. There's a lot of work to
do, so please read your letter and let me get back to it.' Susan
glared at him.

Martin groaned. 'I've said the wrong thing again! Please, take
a bit of advice from me and get out of that place. It's not safe for
you, Susan, and if anything happened to you ...' he choked off
the words. 'I do think a lot about you, you know.'

Oh Martin, here we go again ... but I am not going to let him
affect me. Susan stood in silence and Martin opened his envelope.
'The old villain wants a character reference for you!'

Susan smiled sweetly. 'I suppose you are willing to give me
one? You don't seem to think that I'm up to the job!'

Martin walked over to a bench and took out a stub of pencil
from his pocket. 'I will give you a character, lass, but I hate the
thought of you working at Blackthorn.' He wrote quickly,
jabbing at the paper with his pencil, and handed back the letter.
'I'll come over there in a day or two. Just to see how things are!'

'Please don't worry about me, Martin.' Susan walked briskly
off without a backward look. It was odd, but the thought that
Martin knew where she was seemed to make her feel a little safer;
no doubt it was the lingering effect of her childhood.

Halfway back to Ashby's farm, Susan was assailed by temptation. What had Martin replied to the letter? She wanted to know,
and after all, the envelope was not sealed. There would be no

harm done if she took a look, surely?

On the boundary between the farms there was a spreading oak tree, now glorious in autumn colours. Susan stopped under the tree and slowly took out the letter from her pocket. She looked at it, and just as slowly, put it back again without reading it. It would be a betrayal of trust to look at a letter from one man to another. How could she face Mr Ashby, if she knew what Martin had said?

Back at the farm Mr Ashby, clean at last, was waiting for her. When he read the note he chuckled and put it aside. 'It seems that you can be trusted. Now, what about my hair? Doctor will be here soon and we must make a good impression.' He still spoke rather hoarsely, but the words seemed to come more easily.

Dr Bishop must have impressed him, Susan was thinking. Out in the garden under the pale autumn sun, Mr Ashby, sitting meekly on a chair with a towel round his shoulders, was divested of his long hair and most of the beard. Susan had cut her brothers' hair when they lived at the cottage, she was quite confident and she made the old man look presentable. He was all for shaving, but Susan suggested he kept a short beard. The thought of those shaky hands with a cut-throat razor was terrifying.

Dr Bishop was amazed and pleased, as Susan knew he would be, when he called in that afternoon. 'What a treasure you have found! Look after her well,' he warned Ashby. Privately he said to Susan, 'My theory was that good food would help him ... and company, of course, he's been alone too long. It seems that I was right. But he's unpredictable and you should watch out, young Susan. One never quite knows what he will do.'

'Well, doctor, I won't stay here for ever. Once the place is cleaned up, and if Mr Ashby settles down, he'll have no trouble in finding a housekeeper.'

The next few weeks passed in a flurry of activity, because Susan knew that once the winter set in, thorough cleaning would be impossible. Martin Gill came over one day and found her up to the elbows in hot soapy water. Mr Ashby was civil to him and offered a cup of tea; it was strange to see Martin sitting in the garden, talking about sheep to the man who had once threatened him with a gun.

'I can see he's better than he was, but take care, lass,' he warned as he left. 'Come for me if you have any problems.'

All the curtains in the house were washed and mended, the carpets taken up and beaten out on the washing line. The scullery, kitchen and pantry were whitewashed and the papered walls of the parlour rubbed down with slices of stale bread. The furniture was polished, the brasses cleaned and the windows made to sparkle. 'It feels cold,' the old farmer complained once, looking round at the shining, polished surfaces. But on the whole he was placid and Susan made sure that he ate extremely well; she asked Josiah to bring food from the village, and found that Mr Ashby was partial to roast beef.

Even Josiah, the farm man, seemed to be thawing a little. One day he met Susan in the yard and asked her whether she could handle sheep. 'I've got to gather moor flock tomorrow and it's a job for two at least,' he explained.

'I'll be pleased to help you, Josiah. I used to work with the sheep ... at Mr Gill's.'

'Eh, you were that little lass at Holly Bank! Well, I never. It's a small world.' Josiah looked amazed. 'But I tell you what, now. You can call me Joss. And I'll call you Susan. How about that?'

It was good to be working outdoors in the crisp autumn air and the sheep gathering went very well, except that they had to work with Mr Gill, because his sheep had the adjoining tract of moor. He, apparently, was in a grim mood and very little was said as they drafted the ewes into two pens, one for Holly Bank and the other for Blackthorn.

'Is he treating you right?' Martin barked at Susan as they

completed the work.

Susan considered. 'Thank you, I am quite safe. He has his own ideas, of course, but he's not violent.' She looked over at the next pen, where Martin stood, his face creased with tension. 'Please don't worry about me, I have had to learn to look after myself. What do you think it was like for a little country lass at the Mermaid?'

It was as though she had hit him. Martin winced. 'I always worried about leaving you there, Susan ... was it very bad?'

He deserved to be punished, just a little. 'Bad enough. That George Sanderson is a dangerous man. I think from what I've seen here that Mr Ashby is a gentleman, but just a little unpredictable. So, don't worry.' Susan suddenly felt guilty for causing Martin such anguish. 'I don't blame you for leaving me at the Mermaid, not at all. I needed the job, and I learned to cook there. But it would have helped if you'd kept in touch, just come to see me. You went to see the boys quite often, and they were grateful. But you left me alone.'

'What else could I do? They would have talked about you, Susan, made your life a misery. Maud Sanderson suspected me of seducing you, as it was.'

'I know. She asked me whether I was pregnant ... because you wanted rid of me in such a hurry.' Martin had, after all, been acting wisely; life would have been impossible at the Mermaid if he'd showed interest in the new chambermaid.

Martin sighed. 'Poor lass! That was just why I left you alone. They would have branded you a hussy, otherwise.'

It was time to be brisk, and Joss was waiting, politely just out of earshot. 'We'd better take the sheep back now, to get home before dark. Goodbye, Martin.'

'Take care, Susan.' There seemed to be a wistful note in his voice.

CHAPTER EIGHTEEN

The winter went by comfortably enough at Blackthorn Farm. There was plenty of wood for good fires, Mr Ashby was reasonably calm and Susan settled down to a pleasant, if rather dull, routine. Her brothers came to stay at Christmas. 'This is a grand spot, Susie,' said Ben. 'Much better than our old cottage!' But his sister still mourned the fact that the cottage was gone, sold to some landowner who was letting it to a farm labourer and his family.

Deep snow in January cut off Blackthorn from the rest of the world. Susan made the best of her time, mending linen and reading some of the old classics she found in a bookcase. Mr Ashby seemed rather frail, but quite alert, and he said he was looking forward to the spring. Susan had some long talks with him, sitting by a good fire and roasting chestnuts. He told her tales of the High Side in his younger days, and the adventures he had when he went off droving cattle, sometimes far into the Midlands. 'I've had a grand life,' he said one day. 'Only pity was, we had no bairns. My Lottie and me left it a bit late to get wed … make sure you get wed while you're young, Susan.'

The housekeeper laughed at him. 'But what would you say if I told you I was leaving to get married?' He looked alarmed and so she said quickly, 'I've nobody in mind and not likely to, so don't worry.'

Mr Ashby looked at her thoughtfully. 'I'm not sure about that.

I'd ask you myself, lass, if I were younger. You'll make some lad a grand wife, and you won't be short of choice!'

Well, that was a good character reference, but she could hardly ask him to write it down. Susan sighed and went back to her knitting. She had taken up knitting to provide Mr Ashby with new socks, although it made her feel as old as Aunt Jane. Soon, she would be in a rocking chair with a shawl round her shoulders.

One day in April they were having breakfast when Mr Ashby announced that he wanted to visit Harrogate. 'It's a long drive, but we can set out early – Josiah will drive the trap. Would you like to come with us, young Susan? I've business to do at the solicitor's, and you could have an hour or two to yourself.'

Before they left, the farmer opened his desk and gave Susan twenty pounds. 'Your wages,' he said. 'Just so that you won't go looking for another place.'

What riches – she would order some new dresses from the woman at Kirkby. Susan felt light of heart. Money was not really important, but in this case, it was a sign of appreciation and it felt good to be appreciated.

With a sense of freedom, Susan walked by herself through Harrogate on a pleasant, mild spring day. Harrogate looked different, but then Susan hadn't seen the town since she was fourteen. A new statue of the Queen stood outside the station and some of the buildings looked unfamiliar, but the ungainly bath chairs were still about, in which the infirm and elderly were pushed up and down the wide streets in the intervals between taking the waters. In the old days when Toby was a Harrogate artist, the spa had been a good place at which to meet the rich and fashionable and a good source of commissions. But how could anyone swallow water with such a nauseous smell? You could still catch a whiff of sulphur in Harrogate; it was in the air.

The parkland of the Stray was just as green and inviting as ever, and the Woods' old house was easy to find. It was strange to look at it from the outside, almost as a ghost from the past, through the wrought-iron gates into the garden where they had played long ago. On the grass was a slim young woman, laughing as she pushed a small child on a swing. That had been their swing ... and if Toby hadn't gone to prison, the girl might have been Susan herself. But as Martin would say, 'It can never be.' Good luck, strange girl in the garden. May your life be easier than mine.

The old house was a point from which to take bearings. Mr Taylor the engraver had lived a short distance away ... here was the shed, firmly padlocked as always, that had housed the printing press her father had sometimes used. And here was Mr Taylor's house, prim, double fronted and facing the Stray. What did he know about Toby's conviction? Mr Taylor had gone to prison too, but for a shorter time. On an impulse, Susan decided to try to see him, to try to get to the bottom of the story. It was her duty, as the eldest child, since her father was not here to do it himself. She was braver now and more independent.

The doorbell echo sounded hollow as though the house was empty and the front blinds were half down, like heavily lidded eyes. At length a woman in rustling black opened the door.

'May I see Mr Taylor, please?'

'No, he's not taking any more commissions. Good day.' The door was closing again.

'Are you Mrs Taylor? I am Susan Wood ... and it's important that I see him, if only for a short time.'

'Susan Wood – you're Toby Wood's daughter? Well, you'd better come in.' The woman's face was expressionless. 'Roger's very ill, you see. But lately he's been talking a lot about Toby Wood, seems to have something on his mind.' She led the way down a passage. 'Now, Roger, here's a visitor. It's Toby Wood's daughter.'

They were in a stuffy back room where Mr Taylor was hunched in an armchair before the fire, with a blanket round his knees. The man's face was shocking, yellow and drawn with heavy shadows under the sunken eyes. He looked nothing like the Mr Taylor who'd worked with Papa years before.

'Eh, lass, I never thought to see you again,' he wheezed. 'But I'm right glad you came. I'd never have known you – the little lass is a young lady, now.' A fit of coughing stopped him for a few minutes and his wife went out to fetch his medicine.

A skinny claw reached out and grabbed Susan's wrist. 'Quick, while she's gone … Gertie doesn't know what happened, I kept it all from her. I want you to tell Toby I'm sorry. That's all, he'll understand.'

'You mean about his prison sentence? But my father won't understand – he doesn't want to tell me anything about it.' It seemed cruel to press him, but it was important. 'Please tell me how my father came to be convicted. You must know – you were both doing the forgery, were you?'

The cracked lips drew back in a thin smile. 'It was a good racket for a while. But Toby knew nowt about it – he was dragged in to cover up for Jordan.' He coughed again. 'You'll not know Jordan – he was a solicitor and I drew up lovely legal documents with his help, all sorts, wonderful quality and perfect signatures and seals, though I say it myself. He knew all the legal stuff, the big words and he had plenty of customers that wanted to change the words in their own favour….' More panting. 'But then we were caught – and they knew I wasn't alone. Someone else had to be involved and it was easy to pin it on Wood, he used the premises and he knew all the nobs.' Taylor paused to cough again and Susan sat still.

'Toby was an artist with an interest in calligraphy and printing and all that, and he'd had a good education. So the accusation stuck. I – I admit I was scared of Jordan, he was a solicitor with a lot of friends. So Toby copped it, without realizing, poor lad. We were right up against it … Jordan defended us, and that made it easy.' The voice was a low whisper now, and it was hard to hear him.

'Of course, Jordan was clever enough not to use the papers himself, or to deal with the lawyers and folks that bought them – some of them wanted to change wills and that. He organized it all and I sent them, but mainly through the post, not face to face. I blamed Toby for selling them and I pleaded guilty to a minor part of it. I've felt bad about it ever since. Just tell him ... I'm sorry.'

The story stopped abruptly as Mrs Taylor came back. 'There, Roger, drink this. You've sent a message to Toby with the young lady? That's good, you can rest now.'

So Andrew Jordan was the real villain. 'Thank you, Mr Taylor. My father's in York, he has put it all behind him.' And now I've got at the truth, what can I do about it?

The man was racked with coughing, but the claw came out again and grasped her hand, while the rolling eyes seemed to be trying to tell her something. It was time to go; perhaps she could come back another day, maybe on the way back to York. But Mrs Taylor whispered as she opened the front door, 'Poor Roger. Of course he was wrongfully convicted of the crime, they both were, and he wondered whether Toby had survived the prison. But he hasn't got long to go now. He's suffered that much, it will be a happy release.'

This was the man who, with Andrew Jordan, had brought ruin on the Wood family. But what could you say to a man who was staring death in the face? 'I am sorry to hear it, Mrs Taylor. Goodbye.'

Thank goodness, Toby Wood was innocent. In spite of his reluctance to find out the truth, his willingness to forget the past, he was not guilty and his children were free from the shadow of criminal actions, of bad blood. Susan almost danced back to where she was to meet the Blackthorn trap.

*

'Please, Mr Ashby, may I have a day off?' Susan had waited a week after the trip to Harrogate, but she could wait no longer. She had to visit Ringbeck Hall, just once more, and confront Andrew Jordan for the satisfaction of telling the pompous little man that she knew the truth. Her huge relief at the knowledge of her father's innocence made her feel guilty; she should never had doubted him, and she owed it to him to see Jordan.

'I suppose so,' muttered John Ashby. 'Although I'll fare badly without thee, lass.' His head drooped theatrically. 'Fade away, I will, that's for sure.' They were now on such good terms that they could share a joke together.

'Thank you, kind sir. I'll be home for supper ... I will go tomorrow, if Josiah is going down to Kirkby.'

The next morning brought a light drizzle and the clouds hung low over the moor. Josiah dropped her in the village, promising to pick her up at the butter cross on his way back from Ripon market. Susan pulled back her shoulders and took the lane to the hall. Would Jordan be at home? In the months since she left, he had probably sorted out his money problems and regained his fussy complacency.

The hall was very quiet, with no sound but the distant bleating of sheep. The gravel of the drive was sprouting weeds and the effect was untidy, uncared for. Susan gave the bell a sharp tug and it clanged loudly, but no one came to the door. The rain began to fall more heavily; perhaps she should have stayed at home. She pulled it again and then just as she was turning away, there was a movement inside.

The big door swung partly open to reveal Mrs Bain. 'It's you. What are you doing here?' The tone was cold, but the woman looked rather warm for a chilly day. The housekeeper's dress was tighter than ever, the neckline was lower and the bosom even more evident. Some of her buttons were undone and she looked rather flushed and dishevelled. Rather, in fact, like a woman who'd had an encounter with George Sanderson, but for one thing.

'I'd like to see Mr Jordan, please, Mrs Bain.' Might as well be polite.

The nose went up in the air as usual and the housekeeper looked down it at the small person on the doorstep. 'It's Mrs Jordan, if you don't mind!' She spoke loudly and deliberately, watching to see the effect.

Mrs Jordan. Heavens, Jordan must have married her! How could he do such a thing? 'You mean, you've married Mr Jordan?' It was hard to believe.

The new Mrs Jordan puffed out her chest a little more. 'Andrew and I were married last week. And may I ask your business with him?'

'Well, I am owed my wages, I think he will remember.' That was to avoid saying why she was there.

'I don't think he can see you today, he's …' the woman began, but a voice behind her called and Jordan himself came out.

'Wood … I suppose you'd better come in. We mustn't let anyone say that the servants were turned off without their wages.' Jordan led the way to his office past empty rooms, stripped of their furniture and heavy hangings. 'As you can see, most things have gone. But I feel the worst is over. We will refurnish soon.'

'Of course it is, Andrew. With me in charge, everything will soon be right again!' His new wife spoke with great confidence. Did she know what had really happened?

The office was hot and stuffy, with a large fire in the grate. Jordan looked at his safe. 'I can give you a few shillings, that's all. But I realize it must be difficult for a servant, with no income of any kind whatsoever and no prospects. Have you found another place yet? Perhaps it is my duty to tell you that the jewellery has been restored, and no charges will be laid against you because of insufficient evidence. It is very difficult to determine the truth and so I have decided to drop the matter. But of course in the circumstances you can hardly expect me to give you a character.'

'Getting at the truth is certainly difficult where you are concerned, Mr Jordan.' Rage made it difficult to speak, pure rage at the man's superior tone, his complete indifference. How had she ever put up with working here? 'I have come to ask you about my father's trial, once and for all and I demand an answer. The jewellery was nothing to do with me, and you know it.'

In the background there was a snigger from Mrs Jordan. The solicitor now sat down in his big chair, with the new wife standing behind him. She began to fondle him and Susan felt embarrassed; it reminded her of George and Violet and some of the grubby goings-on at the Mermaid. 'Not now, Lizzie,' Jordan muttered, pushing her away. He looked shocked, swallowing several times as though thinking fast.

'I have been to see Roger Taylor and he told me how you ruined my father.' No point in beating about the bush. 'You were the criminal and you blamed Toby Wood, while you pretended to defend him. And now that we know, what will you do about it?' This was dangerous ground; Susan was the only one who knew, she hadn't been able to tell anyone as yet.

Jordan sighed and looked at the ceiling as though the subject bored him. 'Susan, Taylor is deranged – you would see how ill he is. He has delusions, of course. You should not believe him. No one else will, I can assure you.'

'But I do believe him, he's at death's door and he wanted to tell me the truth.' The man had been convincing. 'I am going to tell my father and he will probably take you to court.'

Jordan shrugged. 'Nothing can be proved. I would deny every-thing. My standing as a respected solicitor is rather better than yours, as a disgruntled ex-employee, suspected of theft. Nobody would believe you and indeed, why should they? And in any case, Taylor will be dead in a few weeks, I have heard. You have absolutely no case.'

'Darling, give her the money and let's get rid of her,' his wife cooed, running her fingers through his hair.

She'd been wrong to come here; nothing would come of it but the satisfaction of letting him know that she knew. Susan stood up. 'I won't take your money, Mr Jordan. Good day.'

Leaving her husband with another squeeze, Mrs Jordan opened the door and ushered Susan out. 'Don't worry, Andrew will do exactly as I say,' she boasted. 'And I'll tell him to give you such a bad character that you'll never get a job round here again. News like that travels fast.'

Susan stopped in the empty hall and looked up the stairs. 'That's where the green ghost walked … why did you try to frighten me? What was the point?'

The woman laughed. 'I might as well tell you, I suppose. You're so stupid you would never guess. I've been Andrew's mistress for years, shared his bed, but we kept it quiet because of his mother – old Mrs Jordan would never have approved. Then she died and just as I was getting him to the point where he'd marry me, after a lot of hard work, you arrived.'

'Why should that have worried you?' It was hard to see the connection.

'A young fresh lass – he might just fall for you, I thought, even though you're skinny and pale. He might go for you instead, and you might have learned a few tricks with men at the Mermaid. A lot of lasses do.' Mrs Jordan looked knowing. 'It struck me that you took the job with marrying Mr Jordan in mind, else why would you come here, to the back of beyond? There had to be a reason. Nobody would live on the moor from choice.'

'You thought I might compete for Andrew Jordan? Far from it,

I promise you. I never really liked him and now I can't stand the sight of the man.' Susan shuddered.

The housekeeper laughed, a hard, grating sound. 'So I tried to frighten you and then later I pinched the jewels – he still thinks you might have done that. And I even made up to that boring farmer just to make you jealous, so you'd get on with him instead. You do fancy that Gill, don't you?' The bosom heaved with laughter. 'But I needn't have bothered, I got my own way in the end.' The sound of rain on the windows was loud, insistent in the silence that followed.

Susan smiled in her turn. 'But old Mrs Jordan got her own back, didn't she? What about the ghost you saw? She'll maybe haunt you for the rest of your life, Mrs Jordan!'

Mrs Jordan looked away. 'I admit you took me in at first. But when I told Andrew, he said it must have been the cook. He knew you played the piano. He came to fetch me and brought me back to the hall, he'd been missing his bit of fun.' The voice took on a harder note. 'But I'd advise you, Wood, to keep quiet and not to go accusing Andrew of anything. Because you'd have me to deal with as well as him, and I would make things very unpleasant for you. Very unpleasant indeed.'

'Meanwhile, I'm quite sure that you'll make things very unpleasant for Andrew, whatever he does. He's got just what he deserves!' With that, Susan escaped into the rain and ran down the drive as fast as she could, to put the hall behind her.

For the first mile on the way home it felt good to think of the happy couple and how well they deserved each other. With a wife like that, Jordan was punished for everything he'd done to the Wood family. It was even good to feel the clean, soft country rain on her face. But as her clothes gradually became soaked and the clouds settled ever lower into a fog, a sort of melancholy came down with them. The hall was depressing and the selfish people in it were not pleasant to think about. The rain trickled down the back of Susan's neck – why had she not brought an umbrella? The road was deserted except for an old ewe, chewing dead grass with a pained expression. She'd almost forgotten what the moor could be like in bad weather.

There were two hours spare before she needed to be in Kirkby for her ride back to Blackthorn Farm; just time to call in at Ashtree Cottage, their former home. At her knock, the door swung open and there on the step was a young woman with a baby on her hip.

'Oh, I am sorry to disturb you … We used to live here, you see …' Susan trailed off, feeling rather foolish. But the girl smiled and beckoned her inside.

'You'll be Miss Wood, then! I'm Maggie Jackson, and this is our Peter.' She swung the baby on to her other hip. 'A big lump to carry, he is. We've been ever so grateful for your things. That lovely patchwork quilt, and the beds and rugs … it's made life easier for us, I can tell you. I want to thank you very much, and so will my Joe, when he comes home from work.'

'Your husband? Where does he work?'

The woman shook her head. 'It's hard to find work up here … he's with Mr Gill for a few weeks just now, but after that, we're not sure.'

Susan knew just how living with uncertainty felt. 'When we lived here, folks said we'd be better off in the town.' Looking round, it was good to see the house so clean and neat, and their old furniture lovingly polished. Suddenly, she felt more cheerful; life would go on in the little cottage, even though the Woods had grown up and moved away.

'Come when you like, we'll be pleased to see you,' the girl said as Susan left.

It was dusk when the Blackthorn trap clattered into the farm-yard and Susan was glad to get down; the place was beginning to feel like home. Josiah looked worried as he led the horse into the stable. 'There's no lamp lit, and that's a strange thing,' he said with a jerk of the thumb towards the farmhouse. 'You'd best go in quick and see if Boss is right.'

Mr Ashby was not right. He was lying on the floor, very still.

CHAPTER NINETEEN

Susan's heart was beating as she kneeled beside the farmer. His hand felt cold ... and then she saw that he was looking at her. 'Thought you were never coming back.' It was a hoarse croak.

'What happened, Mr Ashby? Can't you get up?' She helped him into a sitting position. He'd fallen, and the stick he relied on had spun out of reach.

'Nay, I was rigged like an old ewe.' There was the ghost of a chuckle. 'Gave you a fright, didn't I?' He grunted as Susan managed to haul him to his feet. 'No more days off for you, my girl. You're needed right here.'

Susan looked stern. 'I think you played a trick on me, Mr Ashby. Now go and wash your hands and I will make the supper.' But she could see as he shuffled off that John Ashby had not been tricking her; he was stiff and sore.

'It's the very devil to be getting old! But you'll see, young Susan – it will happen to you, one day.'

All too soon, no doubt. Breathing deeply, Susan gave herself a minute or two to get over the shock and then spread the table-cloth and got out the supper things. The fire was nearly out and the house was cold. It looked as though Mr Ashby was right; he should not be left alone.

In the following weeks, as the world outside warmed into a green spring, Susan watched the old man's decline. She learned a new lesson in those weeks: fortitude. 'Old age can't be mended,' he told her. 'It mun be endured.' And endure it he did, with patience and humour, so unlike the irascible, dirty monster she had first encountered at Blackthorn Farm. Now Susan could see what sort of a man he had really been, and could be sure that Lottie had been treated kindly, and with respect. Ashby sometimes called Susan by his late wife's name, Lottie, when he was tired.

When Mr Ashby took his afternoon nap, Susan escaped into the fresh air. It was the only free time she had now, but it was good to work with the sheep and she helped Joss with his shepherding. One sunny day, a lamb had strayed across the boundary on to Martin's land and just as she was retrieving it, the owner appeared. 'Trespassing again!' he called, but he seemed pleased to see her. 'How's the old boy?'

'Mr Ashby is ... well, he's frail, I'm afraid. I can only leave him when he's asleep, these days.' Susan looked up at Martin and thought how strong and vital he was, compared with John Ashby.

'That's a tie for you, isn't it? I'll come over again soon, maybe tomorrow.'

Ashby was pleased to hear that Martin was to call. 'I want to see the lad,' he muttered. But the next day, the farmer was too weak to get out of bed. He called out until Susan heard him and came in, wondering what she might find. She made him comfortable and then gave him a cup of tea. It was another challenge, but she had experience of nursing, although her small size would make it difficult to lift the patient.

'I think we'd better call the doctor, Mr Ashby. And perhaps you'd better not have a visitor – Martin can come over another day.' Susan tried to hide her anxiety as she plumped up the pillows. After a lot of persuasion, she had finally been allowed to clean the farmer's bedroom and to make sure that his sheets were changed. The room was spotless, smelling of polish and quite ready for visitors, but she felt that he needed to sleep.

'Nay, let him come up,' Ashby insisted and so, half an hour later, Martin was allowed upstairs. Susan was about to leave when her employer called her back. 'Stay and talk to us, lass – fetch another chair.'

Martin brought in a chair for her and she sat at the foot of the bed. 'Have you called the doctor?' Martin asked. 'Well, I won't stay long.' He shook hands gently with the old farmer. 'You're in good hands here, Mr Ashby. Young Susan looked after me right well until my leg mended.'

Ashby nodded. 'A grand lass, I'm very lucky. And so will you be. You're going to wed her, I take it?' There was an embarrassed silence; Susan looked at the floor and Martin flushed a little. 'Well, Martin? Have you asked her? I want to see her settled, before I go.' Ashby moved restlessly in the bed.

'You're not going anywhere ... doctor will have you right in a day or two,' Susan said quickly, wanting to change the subject.

Martin looked straight at Susan. 'She turned me down, as a matter of fact. I wasn't – I suppose I wasn't romantic enough ... it's hard for an old moorland farmer to find the right words.' He sighed. 'And then of course, I am too old for her, Mr Ashby. That was probably the real reason. You have to face the facts. Ten years is a big gap, I always come back to that.'

Susan gasped and then shut her mouth tight, in case something prickly came out. How like a man!

Ashby motioned to Susan. 'Fetch me my wallet, will you? In that drawer yonder.' He turned faded brown eyes to the younger man. 'I've got your character here, that note you sent for Susan. Shall I show it to her?' Without waiting, he passed the paper over and Susan took it gingerly.

'Dear Martin, I need a character for Susan Wood. Can she be trusted? Yours truly, John Ashby.' The message was short and to the point.

Underneath, Martin had written in large capitals. She remembered seeing him write them quickly, with no hesitation, that day she went over to Holly Bank. 'I LOVE THIS WOMAN AND WOULD TRUST HER WITH MY LIFE. IF YOU HARM HER I WILL KILL YOU. M. GILL.'

After a long time, Susan lifted her head and looked at Martin and she saw that his eyes were shining with love. 'It is true, Susan,' he said quietly. 'I would have killed him, if he had harmed you. Shall we start again?'

They both looked at Ashby, but he had lost interest in them; the patient was asleep, or pretending to sleep. Martin moved over to Susan and knelt down beside her chair. 'I love you, my dearest, and I always will. If you love me, please say you will marry me. All my arguments have failed, and I can't forget you, so ... So we might as well get wed?' It sounded rather like the first proposal and Susan laughed. For five seconds he waited and then Susan took his face in her hands and kissed him.

'I do love you, Martin Gill. In spite of your great age and my prickly nature! Yes, I will marry you, when I can. Mr Ashby needs me, just now.' She felt almost choked with happiness. Why had she wasted so much time with her hostility? Martin gave a huge sigh and wrapped his arms round her tightly; she would never feel unsafe again.

Ashby moved and looked over at them. His voice was a mere whisper. 'Well, if you two have finished over there, maybe an old man can have a cup of tea. Don't know what's wrong with young people these days. When I wed Lottie ... I knew just how to go about it.' He lay back, exhausted.

Martin stood up and laughed, a carefree sound. 'Maybe you should give me some good advice, Mr Ashby.'

When the doctor arrived, Martin and Susan went down to the kitchen. It felt like a dream; she was going to marry Martin and live with him, she would have a home and a man of her own, and even friends … it meant being part of the moorland community, instead of being an outsider. But best of all, she would be able to care for Martin and she knew he needed her, as much as she needed him.

The doctor wheeled into the yard and without wasting time, bounded up the stairs. 'I know the way,' he said over his shoulder.

As she went through the motions of tea-making, Susan remembered their last night at Ringbeck Hall, when she had been so furious at Martin's apparent lack of warmth. 'I'm sorry I was so – hasty, before.'

'You didn't give me a chance,' Martin said ruefully. 'I was working towards telling you how I really feel, have always felt. Couldn't you guess how upset I was, when I came to see you at the Mermaid? Didn't you realize that I was deliberately standing aside, to give you the freedom to choose your own way in life? If I'd just grabbed you when you were eighteen, you would have never known what the rest of the world had to offer. You might have resented me in time – in fact, you did resent my concern, when I heard you were working here. Didn't you?'

Susan nodded, reluctantly. 'I shall have to be more understanding, more patient.'

'And less on the defensive,' Martin finished for her. 'You won't need to fight the world now, you know. You'll never have the need to fight me again!' He laughed again, the new laugh. 'And for my part – there's been fault on both sides – I'll try to be more open with you, lass. I've probably been on my own too long. Just think, you're saving me from getting like John Ashby in my old age.'

Dr Bishop came in and accepted a cup of strong tea. He sat at the table, looking quite at home, and glanced over at Susan. 'I can hardly believe the difference you have made here, young woman. You've organized the household and tamed Mr Ashby – he's a different man.'

'How do you find him, doctor?'

Bishop said gently, 'He hasn't got long to go. He's just naturally winding down, you see – and at nearly ninety, it's not
surprising. Keep him comfortable, that's all you can do, and hold
his hand.'

It was hard not to cry at this verdict. After all these months
with Mr Ashby, she'd become fond of him, and he of her, she
thought. 'I'll hold his hand,' Susan promised.

It was good to have Martin's backing, during the weeks that
followed. He visited Blackthorn often, sometimes sitting with Mr
Ashby to give Susan a break. The old man slipped away gradually
as the doctor had said he would, seemingly with little regret. 'My
time's come,' he said, with just a tinge of sadness.

One day Martin brought a ring for Susan's finger, the first she
had ever owned, a lovely emerald that fitted perfectly. 'I suppose
I need to ask permission from your father,' he said. 'That means
a trip to York.'

'I could write to him and ask him to come here,' Susan
suggested firmly. 'He can see the boys as well, and I want to
explain about Roger Taylor – I haven't told him, yet. It somehow
didn't seem very important to him and I feel guilty, now, that I
needed proof of his innocence, that it was so important to me. I
should have taken his word.'

'From what you've told me, he had no idea of what happened.'
Martin had been told of the visit to Taylor and the last trip to
Ringbeck Hall. He too had been relieved at the thought of
Toby's innocence, and rejoiced at the picture of Jordan being
dominated by Lizzie Bain.

The letter was written and then Toby was forgotten for a while,
as Susan faced the loss of Mr Ashby. One afternoon, with the early
roses peeping through the window, she held his hand and talked
quietly to him as usual; when she came back an hour later, he was

gone peacefully into his last sleep. There was the funeral to arrange and people to be notified, food to prepare and the vicar to organize.

A handful of mourners followed John Ashby to his grave in Kirkby churchyard; older folk who remembered the man he had been. Poor Josiah was there, distraught and uncomfortable in a starched collar, touchingly dependent on Susan for comfort. 'What's to become of us?' he wailed. 'I've been at Blackthorn thirty years, man and boy – what now?'

Martin was with Susan and it was just as well, because she was shocked when Andrew Jordan and his wife, in ostentatious mourning, turned up at the last minute. They strutted down the aisle together and took the front pew, where they proceeded to sing and pray loudly, for the benefit of all. Susan, sitting in the back row, found herself asking for the grace to forgive them. What were they doing here, polluting John Ashby's funeral? She looked at Martin and he raised his eyebrows; he didn't know, either. He slipped his hand into hers and it was so reassuring, so warm and loving, that Jordan seemed not to matter so much.

The vicar had said there would be no eulogy, but Mr Jordan was determined to fill the breach. At the appropriate time he stood and faced the congregation. 'My dear Uncle John will be sadly missed by all who loved him ...' Susan wondered why all who loved him had not visited when he was alive and lonely. They had all neglected him, partly due to his strange behaviour, no doubt. But if Susan had been able to help him in the end, why couldn't his relatives? 'Uncle John' had never mentioned Andrew Jordan.

After the service and the burial, the mourners were invited to the Mechanic's Institute for the feast prepared by Susan, since the farm was thought to be too far out of the village to hold it there. The Jordans naturally came in with the rest. After glaring at Susan they both ignored her, although Jordan sidled up to Martin. He spoke loudly and with his usual fussy manner. 'Very sad occasion, Gill, very sad, of course, poor Uncle John gone to his long rest. Although possibly it was a mercy, if I may say so. I hear that he was sadly out of his wits, and of course he was never happy after Aunt Lottie died. You may not be aware that the deceased's wife was my mother's second cousin, twice removed. But of course, you were not bred in Kirkby, you could not be expected to know these things.' He smirked. 'I expect to hear from his solicitors soon ... as there were no children, of course, and as far as I am aware, there are no nearer relatives than myself.'

Martin changed the subject with no apology. 'You should get your shepherd to mind the sheep in the Long Garth, they've got foot rot. Most of your ewes are grazing on their knees.' He walked deliberately away. Later he said to Susan in the kitchen, 'It looks as though Jordan could inherit Blackthorn.'

'Goodness!' That was why he had come to the funeral, no doubt. 'Let's hope he keeps poor Josiah on, otherwise he'll have nowhere to live.' She looked through the serving hatch to where the Jordans were holding forth, with mourners thanking them for the lavish food, the feast that Susan had worked so hard to prepare.

Susan had given no thought to what would become of the farm; she knew that usually in such cases, some relative was found, even if they were now in Canada or New Zealand. But to have Jordan as the heir, coming into John Ashby's house, would be hard to take as a dutiful housekeeper.

It was when she was tidying up after the funeral that Susan received a letter from Harrogate. Ashby's solicitor was coming to visit, no doubt to formally dismiss the servants and take possession of Blackthorn, to hand over to the heir. Martin had gone to Pateley on family business and so Susan received Mr Jenkins alone in Mr Ashby's parlour, missing the old man very much. There was an empty chair by the fire, a space in the house and Susan still half expected him to come staggering through the door.

'Miss Wood, I am delighted to meet you. Mr Ashby spoke very warmly of you when we last met.'

No, he's not being patronizing, don't be prickly. 'Thank you … no doubt you will want to go through Mr Ashby's papers, check his affairs. Please let me know if there is anything I can do to help.' Susan stood at the door with her hand on the knob. 'His business papers will be in the desk, I expect.' She turned to go; this was none of her affair.

Jenkins looked surprised. 'I expected you to go through it all with me, Miss Wood.'

What did he mean? 'I think that Mr Jordan will want to do that, he wouldn't want me to know anything about it.'

'Jordan? Well, I'm sure he'd love to be here, but he wasn't invited.' The solicitor sniffed. 'He was in my office the day after Mr Ashby died, of course.'

'Of course. And now, if you'll excuse me … there is one thing I would like to ask. Could Josiah, the shepherd, be kept on at the farm? He lives in the cottage – and he's looked after the place very well for Mr Ashby.'

'Well, of course, if that is your wish, let the man stay. But now, Miss Wood, let us discuss what is to be done. Will you wish to sell, or not?'

Susan gazed at the man, aghast. 'Sell? Would I wish? But Mr Jordan will decide all that, he's …'

'I do beg your pardon!' Jenkins interrupted in some excitement. 'I thought you would know … Mr Ashby left Blackthorn Farm to you, everything here is yours!' His smile was one of pure delight. 'Mr Jordan was not pleased, naturally …'

Susan's head was spinning. 'Naturally. But – what did he say? Will he not contest the will?' Mr Ashby must have arranged all this, the day they took a trip to Harrogate.

'He was all for contesting it, until I put him right. Jordan had a document, a watertight will, dated ten years ago, leaving Blackthorn to him. But of course, only this spring Mr Ashby had me draw up his will, and it was witnessed and so forth by my staff. Jordan had no case; people can leave their property where they wish if they do it legally, and of course, the last will supersedes any previous ones.'

Ten years ago ... that will could have been one that was doctored by Taylor, a forgery like those that put Toby Wood in prison. It might have succeeded, if dear Mr Ashby had not decided back in April to make a will himself.

Feeling unreal, Susan sat down at the table. 'Mr Ashby never said a word ... and then Mr Jordan came to the funeral, and said he was the heir. Well! This is a shock.' What would Martin say?

During that afternoon, Susan discovered that the farm had no debts and considerable assets; John Ashby had been a good farmer and Josiah had carried on with the methods he had laid down. By the time the solicitor left, she was tired of papers and business. As dusk fell Martin clattered into the yard, coming straight back to her from Pateley. 'I'll take a bite to eat, before going home,' he said, giving her a hug.

'Martin, I have something to tell you.' How should she start? 'Andrew Jordan is not to inherit the farm, after all.'

Martin laughed. 'That's a relief, he would have been hard to deal with. Well, who's the lucky loved one, who does get Blackthorn? Some other neglectful relation, I suppose.'

'You won't believe this – I am now the owner of this farm!'

Martin took her in his arms and for a while there was jubilation. 'Little Susan Wood, landowner! Nobody deserves it more than you do! So now, what will you do with the farm? Should you like to throw our farms together to make a bigger holding? We could employ men, maybe Josiah and that Joe who lives in your cottage ...'

Susan said a little sadly, 'Well, it won't be mine for long, will it?

When I marry you, Martin, it will be your farm, then.'

'Are you looking for excuses to back out of marrying me, my lass? Well, I won't let you. And you are behind the times. You should have asked that Mr Jenkins. The law was changed when you were a little girl, Susan. A married woman is now entitled to own property, after marriage, in her own name. So – Blackthorn will always be yours, my love. What we do with it will be your decision.'

Over supper, Martin looked across at Susan in the lamplight. 'I am so glad you agreed to marry me before you became an heiress. If it had happened now, you would accuse me of being after the land.'

'No, Martin, you have never put your own interests first. But it might have been even harder for us to get together … I will have to lose the prickles, I know.'

'Dear little Yorkshire Rose!'